WARTORN
RESURRECTION

ROBERT ASPRIN

and

ERIC DEL CARLO

ACE BOOKS, NEW YORK

THE BERKLEY PUBLISHING GROUP
Published by the Penguin Group
Penguin Group (USA) Inc.
375 Hudson Street, New York, New York 10014, USA
Penguin Group (Canada), 10 Alcorn Avenue, Toronto, Ontario M4V 3B2, Canada
(a division of Pearson Penguin Canada Inc.)
Penguin Books Ltd., 80 Strand, London WC2R 0RL, England
Penguin Group Ireland, 25 St. Stephen's Green, Dublin 2, Ireland (a division of Penguin Books Ltd.)
Penguin Group (Australia), 250 Camberwell Road, Camberwell, Victoria 3124, Australia
(a division of Pearson Australia Group Pty. Ltd.)
Penguin Books India Pvt. Ltd., 11 Community Centre, Panchsheel Park, New Delhi—110 017, India
Penguin Group (NZ), Cnr. Airborne and Rosedale Roads, Albany, Auckland 1310, New Zealand
(a division of Pearson New Zealand Ltd.)
Penguin Books (South Africa) (Pty.) Ltd., 24 Sturdee Avenue, Rosebank, Johannesburg 2196,
South Africa

Penguin Books Ltd., Registered Offices: 80 Strand, London WC2R 0RL, England

This is a work of fiction. Names, characters, places, and incidents either are the product of the author's imagination or are used fictitiously, and any resemblance to actual persons, living or dead, business establishments, events, or locales is entirely coincidental.

WARTORN: RESURRECTION

An Ace Book / published by arrangement with Bill Fawcett & Associates

PRINTING HISTORY
Ace mass market edition / January 2005

Copyright © 2005 by Bill Fawcett & Associates.
Cover art by Duane O. Myers.
Cover design by Judith Lagerman.
Interior text design by Kristin del Rosario.

ISBN: 0-441-01235-3

ACE
Ace Books are published by The Berkley Publishing Group,
a division of Penguin Group (USA) Inc.,
375 Hudson Street, New York, New York 10014.
ACE and the "A" design
are trademarks belonging to Penguin Group (USA) Inc.

PRINTED IN THE UNITED STATES OF AMERICA

10 9 8 7 6 5 4 3 2 1

BRYCK
(1)

AT LAST HE rode to a halt. The hot living scent of the lathered mount permeated the rough traveler's clothes Bryck wore. He uncoiled from the saddle, climbing off, and stretched his softening middle-yeared body. The late evening was mild, with a hint of sultriness to the air. Above, stars and a crescent of moon stamped the sky. There were clouds, probably harboring late summer rain, to the distant north.

Bryck was sore to his bones. He was keenly aware of his every muscle and sinew, because each part of himself seemed to ache individually. Three days and two nights he had driven the fast borrowed steed, sleeping only during the darkest watches—and then only on a less than luxurious bedroll. It was all so very primitive, so brutally *physical*. Not at all the sort of activity in which he routinely engaged. Yet, this unaccustomed discomfort was pleasing. It was tangible evidence of the righteousness of his actions and of his personal sacrifice in undertaking this venture.

He surveyed the courtyard of the Chancellery to which the city guards had directed him. The building was a mean affair of grey stone—squat, functional, and unassuming, save for the high vaulted doors he now faced. The peaked panels were of glossy wood and etched with ornate images depicting the history of the city-state of Sook. It was not an awe-inspiring chronicle. Neither was Sook itself, which from what he'd seen was much less cosmopolitan than Bryck's home city of U'delph. He had wended its streets to this court, passing ramshackle structures and shabbier citizens.

Still, he had made this arduous journey to seek military aid from these people, so it wouldn't do to flaunt his disdain. And regardless, the humbleness of these surroundings only added to the marvelously crude reality of this adventure. Doubtlessly he had accumulated a wealth of creative material for his next several theatricals.

A lad with wispy red stubble outlining his jawbone detached from the courtyard's shadows and took the reins of Bryck's grey mount. The boy gurgled the unintelligible sounds of someone born deaf and waved toward the doors of the Chancellery. *Oh the pomp, oh the circumstance,* Bryck thought wryly. He hid his smile and watched his horse being led off to the stables, admiring the raw stamina of the creature. Its hooves clomped on the stones of the yard.

A pair of city guards bracketed the vaulted doors. They watched dispassionately as Bryck finished stretching the worst of the kinks from his body. Their uniforms were of blue and scarlet, the colors faded to similar states of drabness. Each leaned on a spear. Bryck wiped away the last trace of his droll smile and approached. This was serious business, after all.

"I was told I'd find an audience here."

The female half of the tiny guard contingent asked, "You the *grink* from U'delph?"

Not even trying to decipher that rustic *grink,* Bryck said simply, "I am."

They drew open the doors for him. He stepped through, unable to entirely suppress another small smile. Going unrecognized was most unfamiliar. In his home city-state, his face was well known, his reputation as a satirical playwright even more so—to say nothing of his social standing as a noble, with lands, capital, and all the respect and prestige that his status presupposed.

Here, however, he was merely a rider from a neighboring city, seeking an audience with the local authorities. U'delph required military assistance . . . required it desperately. The Felk wizards and their army were on the move. That was common knowledge. Now, however, those forces were closing toward U'delph. Scouts had assured that the city-state had six days of safety left to it. Before then, support from some other city must be secured. U'delph's standing army wasn't much to speak of, a few companies of undertrained recruits under the command of a handful of aging, experienced military leaders. They needed more and better numbers.

Volunteers had been needed to ride out to petition for aid. Too many of U'delph's concerned citizenry had turned out to offer their services. Dice had been thrown to decide who would take the fastest mounts.

Bryck wanted to do his share. Noble or not, celebrated dramatist notwithstanding, he wanted to help. He felt strongly about the matter. He felt, perhaps, magnanimous that he would risk a ride through open country to save his people. There was something heroic about it all.

He looked about the empty vestibule. Another set of doors stood at the far end. He crossed the dull tiles toward it.

He had cheated. He had used that trick of simple wizardry that aided him now and then in his gambling pastime. No one had ever trained him in magic; it came instinctively. Such minor talents were fairly common among noble bloodlines in the major cities.

He had influenced the roll of the dice. And had been selected to ride. And bade a farewell to his wife and children and friends. And rode off valiantly toward nearby Sook.

It might well be that he wasn't the most qualified of U'delph's citizens to have made this journey. He had, he admitted to himself, gotten lost on the way and used up much of a day reorienting himself after losing his bearings in a thick patch of woods. But he'd gotten back on course soon enough.

Bryck missed his wife, Aaysue, terribly, and his children—Bron, Cerk, Ganet, little Gremmest—and the comforts of his villa and lifestyle. But no matter. What he was doing was proper, honorable. And if his entreaty for military assistance met with success here in Sook, he might well prove himself to be the savior of U'delph.

Beyond the far doors of the vestibule, a corridor led deeper into the Chancellery. There were more guards here, their uniforms in no better repair than those he'd already seen. They eyed him warily. Receiving no verbal instructions, Bryck strode past them down the corridor, carrying himself with a lofty gait that was not quite a swagger. He smelled of the road. A steaming perfumed bath would erase these odors, but for the present, he was content to reek of his rough travels.

He couldn't recall the last time he had exerted himself so. He was nearing the end of his fourth tenwinter, moderately fit for a man his age. He was of average height, sagging a bit around the middle, owing to the luxuries of his class and the sedentary life of a playwright, which he'd been leading these past many years. His thick dark hair was streaked mildly with grey. His face, etched and somewhat full, often lit readily with merriment.

These were grim times. With the Felk army mobilized and backed by powerful wizardry, the historically precarious stability of the entire Isthmus was threatened. No one knew what the Felks' ultimate goal was—expansion of their territory, full conquest? Individual city-states lay

ahead of the Felk forces like so many children's stacking
blocks, waiting only to be tumbled.

Grim times, indeed. Not the sort of period in which one
would expect a satirical playwright to thrive. But so it was.
Perhaps it was Bryck's audiences' need to lose themselves
in his comic—and frankly silly—works that accounted
for the durability of his fame. Bryck's name was synony-
mous with humor. People always needed to laugh. They
perhaps needed that release now more than ever.

Bryck, of course, was aware of the perilous state of
things. The pall of the Felk hung over the land. Yet, the
threat had seemed remote, detached from the familiar daily
business of living . . . had seemed so until now, that was,
when the invaders were suddenly closing toward U'delph,
toward home, toward everything he held dear.

He didn't fault himself for his attitude. It was human
nature. Certainly he felt proper sorrow for Windal and—
what was that other conquered state?—Callah, yes . . . but
Bryck knew a menace only became truly real when it was
directed at oneself.

He reached the end of the corridor, finding yet another
set of doors and one lone stocky guard. In addition to the
standard blue and scarlet costume, this one wore a gold
scarf twisted in a complicated knot. *A royal retainer,*
thought Bryck, being careful not to smile this time as he
met the man's rather stony gaze.

"I've come from U'delph for an audience," he said.

The guardsman's eyes softened at that. Some not quite
identifiable emotion crept onto his plump features. He
dipped his thick chin and opened the doors, and Bryck entered the chancellery's main chamber.

Once more the dearth of stately trappings tickled his innate sense of the ironic. The room was a simple square, the
walls bare but for Sook's blue and scarlet standard, which
hung behind a large table. Around this table sat a collection
of what Bryck assumed to be Sook's ministry. They were
men and women with the harried look of bureaucrats,

rather than the reserved air of nobility. Some eight of these figures were in agitated conference as he approached. Parchments were scattered across the long table, being passed hand to hand and flourished, as one minister or another tried to drive home some point in the free-for-all debate.

Bryck couldn't pick a leader out of the bunch. Not one of these people, each wearing a scarlet mantle and the chains of office, appeared above any other, either in demeanor or in the deference the others would offer a superior. Their squabble continued as he came to a halt, no one showing any awareness of his presence.

He tried to unravel the topic of deliberation, but it was hopeless. The matter had evidently digressed into niggling particulars of the central issue, and what was left was a jumble of mere argument. He studied the scene a moment. By the madness of the gods, Bryck thought, he could create a fine political farce from these characters, merely by emphasizing their petulance and making the subject of their debate something absurdly trivial. Yes, perhaps they would be wrangling over the ponderous question of the true color of the sun, since at dawn and dusk it was red, during the day yellow, and grey when the weather was inclement. Yes . . .

He shook this off just as a smooth-headed minister raised his face and asked, "Yes?"

This didn't slow the surrounding quarrel, as papers continued to fly and voices rose.

For the fourth time since his encounter with the city guards at Sook's limits, Bryck said, "I've come for an audience. I am from U'delph."

These words brought everything to a standstill. The seven remaining faces turned his way, expressions ranging from anticipation to something like curious pity.

Well, thought Bryck nonplussed, he had their attention at least. Making a bid for a greater impression, he added,

"My name is Bryck," purposely leaving off his title. He calmly searched the attentive faces for reaction.

Oddly, the normal magic of his name's invocation didn't seem to be working. Odd, since his repute as a playwright was widely known, far beyond the confines of U'delph. His theatricals were regularly exported and staged by traveling troupes in cities as distant as Q'ang and even Petgrad. It wasn't vanity to presume that at least *one* of these squabbling ministers should know who he was and be duly awed.

He waited through the lengthening silence and the strange stares. Something evidently was amiss. It might be, he realized, that they didn't believe his claim. These men and women wouldn't know his face, only his name; and here he stood in his coarse traveler's apparel, unshaven, smelling quite like the horse he'd been riding. He nearly chuckled.

Before he could, another of the ministers—an elderly woman with unhealthy, milky eyes—said, "If you wish asylum, we will grant it." Her tone was almost reverential, and she carried only a trace of the bucolic Sook accent.

Bryck's brows drew together slightly. "Why . . . no." He didn't know with what name to address this body and so did not, avoiding any potential breach of etiquette. Who knew what behavior this ministry of yokels expected from a petitioner? Bryck, however, was a noble and knew the ways of stately protocol.

"What, then?" asked the minister with the hairless skull.

Bryck gathered a breath. "I bring a formal appeal from the city of U'delph. I—"

"From U'delph?" asked a third one among the mantled figures. He was a spindly male, the youngest at the table. He gazed at Bryck with patent incomprehension.

Bryck suppressed an impatient sigh. Had he not made it clear where he came from? "Yes. U'delph. Your neighboring city. We ask your support, humbly and respectfully. We are in a time of urgent need, as you may—"

"U'delph?" echoed the crone with the poor eyes. They were now all peering at him as though he babbled nonsense.

Bryck blinked at the group, thoroughly bewildered.

"How can you bring an appeal from U'delph?" asked the first minister.

"I assure you I have been authorized to do so by my city's ruling council," he countered, wondering if this was the source of this body's baffling response to his petition. It was true he carried no official documents substantiating his right to make the appeal. Evidently that had been an oversight—and one he might have to pay for in the form of this wasted journey. Three days and two nights on the jouncing back of that steed, all the hardships of his excursion, all his intrepid efforts . . . for nothing.

A hot blossom of indignant anger opened in his chest. How *dare* these boors! Didn't they know who he was, what sacrifices he had made?

Checking his ire before it bloomed fully, he tried another tack. "The military situation is grave. The Felk are nearing the borders of my city. We do not have sufficient numbers to hope to oppose them. We ask, I promise, with the deepest esteem for this good state of Sook, for aid in countering this threat. The armies of the Felk, as you must know, are formidable. It is no great stretch to imagine that once they have finished with my people, they may turn toward yours."

There, Bryck thought with some satisfaction. Make it personal for them. Let them see that their own throats are exposed.

Again the response wasn't what he expected. The bald minister—perhaps the leader after all—said, "We're very aware of the menace of the Felk, make no mistake. Our scouts are desperately monitoring their movements." He waved a fistful of papers, scrawled with text and slapdash maps. "We are presently trying to see to our own defenses."

Ah, that was it, Bryck finally decided. They can spare no troops. Too concerned about their own safety. It was an attitude that, once more, he couldn't rightly fault.

Still, it was disappointing, if not outright irritating. His journey here had been worthless. Drawing himself stiffly erect, he dipped into an exaggeratedly courtly bow, ready to deliver a mocking apology on behalf of the unworthy people of U'delph who had sent him, a lowly rider, to unfairly disturb this august ministry in its momentous defensive preparations.

Before he could deliver this speech, however, the chief minister said, "Rest assured, we have nothing but sympathy for your tragedy. Our offer of asylum is sincere."

"My thanks," Bryck pronounced. "But I must decline your generous proposal. Your fair state of Sook is too overwhelming in its grandeur to quarter one so common as myself." Yes, he was laying it on a bit thick, but there was no insult so fine as one couched in immaculate tact. "And so I make my farewell."

"To go where?" asked the spindly, apparently dimwitted lad.

Bryck nearly ignored him, but instead fixed the youngster with a dark gaze and said, "Home."

"To U'delph?" he asked, eyes widening with undisguised astonishment.

Perhaps the boy was a mascot, rather than a true minister, Bryck judged. Ah, bugger them all anyway. He turned from the table.

"You've no home to return to," came quietly from behind. "Don't you know that?"

Bryck halted before he reached the chamber door. He turned the words over in his mind, looking for whatever sense was to be made of them. It was drivel, he concluded. These ministers were idiots, the whole lot. Yet he found himself turning back toward the table.

It was the milky-eyed woman who'd spoken. Her pruned face was twisted into a look of profound commiseration. The others were staring with similar expressions. Despite the mild evening air, Bryck felt a cool fingertip tracing his backbone.

Without conscious will he found himself asking, "What do you mean?"

Silence once more; and now he recognized the tenor of the wordless pause. They were afraid to speak, as one will reflexively hesitate before imparting dire news to the individual it will most affect.

The chief minister folded his hands atop a scattering of paper, set his eyes to the table, then lifted them a moment later. His gaze was solemn.

"U'delph is no more."

Bryck did not react, outwardly or inwardly. *Nonsense,* was all he thought, the single word clanging through his head.

"Our scouts have informed us that the Felk overran the city last night."

Nonsense. Nonsense.

"It . . . has not been captured. It has been laid waste to. Likely as an example, so that other city-states will not put up resistance."

Nonsense.

"You have our sincerest sympathies."

Bryck made as if to speak, but no words came. His journey here had been a waste indeed. Three days and two nights, only to find this pack of moronic provincials playing at government. He had been quite correct, then, earlier when he imagined this group as players in a political farce. What could their scouts know that U'delph's did not? His city, he'd been told as he set out, had six days of safety left. It simply wasn't possible that the Felk armies had advanced so rapidly. It was . . . nonsense.

He swallowed whatever pointless words he'd meant to utter, turned once more, and left the chamber.

Outside, in the courtyard, he called for his grey mount. It was eventually retrieved by the deaf lad with the wispy red beard. Evening had become night by the time Bryck rode out past Sook's limits, ignoring everyone and everything as he kicked the horse into a faster and faster stride. Its powerful hooves were soon tearing up patches of sod, as Bryck made for home.

DARDAS
(1)

ONE NEVER REALLY appreciated being alive until one had been dead . . . at least once.

It was not the first time this thought had run through Dardas's mind, and would probably not be the last, but he found it inescapable as he stood outside his command pavilion staring out over the ant-like activity of the Felk army bivouac. To all outward appearances, he was observing the efficiency of his officers and their troops as they prepared for evening mess.

Well, on one level, he was, though he had seen it all thousands of times before. Armies didn't change much over the centuries, except for the uniforms and the effectiveness of the weapons. He could monitor the movement and mood of the troops without really focusing on them, his attention only drawn to any abnormality or break in the rhythm. What he was really doing was enjoying the sunset.

The fiery colors of the dying day were accented by the gathering clouds. They had bivouacked just south of U'delph, or what had been U'delph and was now a jumble of smoldering rubble. In fact, the smoke added to the spectacular colors of the sunset.

Strange how he had ceased to notice such trivialities when he was alive before. Now that the gods of fate had given him another chance at life, he had every intention of savoring every moment of it.

That fate, it seemed, had taken the form of Matokin, a powerful Felk magician with a vision for conquest who needed a general to run his army for him. Dardas still did not truly understand just how Matokin had gathered his consciousness from beyond the void and deposited it in a host body. Neither did he have any clear recollection of the time while he was dead.

He was, in fact, astounded to learn after having been revived that more than two hundred and fifty years had passed since he had last been an active participant in life. Still, he had adjusted to the incredible fact. He had a soldier's grim constancy and could adapt himself to *anything*. He was alive again now and planned to exploit the opportunity for as long as possible.

What was most troubling to him right now was this mage. Matokin had brought him back to life. Matokin, in a sense, owned his life. Dardas was unaccustomed to any status other than that of supreme and uncontested leader.

He had had little use for mages in his prior life, in fact had only minimal dealings with them. They were few and far between, throwbacks to an age before the Northern and Southern Continents had collapsed into disarray.

In Dardas's day magicians mostly conducted themselves as healers. He had never really understood them, nor cared enough to educate himself as to the mechanics and limitations of their skills. Such creatures were often shunned. But that, he acknowledged, had been a long time ago, and even quite some physical distance away. This was the Isthmus, which lay between the two great continents. Once, it had been nothing but a trade route. Times, evidently, had changed.

In contrast to that of his old military career, the force he was commanding now seemed to be crawling with mages, like parasites on a feral dog. In addition to healers, there were also communication mages and transportation mages. These were daunting, he had to admit. Being able to move troops and supplies instantaneously over great distances was, frankly, the ultimate weapon of this Felk army.

And now they had at last used that weapon, in their latest conquest. U'delph had, almost literally, never seen them coming . . . or even if that city's scouts had seen their approach, they could do nothing against an army that was so suddenly and overwhelmingly upon them.

It was a war of magic. But it was still *war,* Dardas told himself. And war was his craft.

Inquiries as to where all these magicians had come from were swept aside with vague references to the Academy, a school in the northern city of Felk that Matokin had founded to train those with magic potential for positions in his force.

What was even worse was that Dardas now had to adapt to having a magician as an immediate superior. Matokin was not only a rising major power figure in these lands of the Isthmus, but one who literally held Dardas's continued life in his hands. Dardas's resurrection, he'd been told, would have to be periodically maintained by rejuvenation spells. Clearly this was a situation he would have to deal with eventually.

"Lord Weisel?"

Dardas was suddenly aware that his aide was trying to get his attention. Had been trying, in fact, for some time now. It was one of the annoying sidelights, he'd learned, of living in a host body. Getting used to being hailed by another name.

He fixed the aide with a flinty glare.

"I'll say this to you once," he said. "We are in the field, not in court. You will address me by my rank, not my title."

"Yes, Lord . . . General."

"Now, what is it?"

"I was just wondering, sir, if you would be dining alone or with your officers tonight?"

Dardas suppressed his annoyance at having his reverie interrupted for such a trivial matter. The junior officer was barely in his twenties and standing duty as aide for the first time tonight, so he couldn't be expected to be familiar with the general's routines or proper protocol.

"I'll dine alone tonight," he said. "In my pavilion, I think."

"I'll see to it at once, sir," the aide responded and hurried away, obviously eager to get out from under his commander's scrutiny.

In spite of himself, Dardas was amused by the youth's discomfort. Among others, he had implemented the policy that officers from various units were to rotate through the position of his personal aide. Partly this was being done so he could familiarize himself with the officers under his command. More important, however, was that it allowed him to dismiss those favored officers who would normally have held the post permanently. They would be the ones most likely to notice the changes in the "Lord Weisel" they had known for years.

Even now, after only three campaigns, Dardas was overhearing murmured comments, most of them expressing pleasant surprise as to how effective a battle leader the previously discounted Lord Weisel was proving to be. Apparently there had been no small measure of protest and concern when Matokin had named Lord Weisel as the commander of the army.

It seemed Weisel, who affected pretenses of military aptitude, was traditionally indecisive and easily confused. The critics were pleased to admit the error of their misgivings, however, as the army was now functioning with superb efficiency.

Weisel was one of the few Felk lords who was *not* also

a mage. Matokin had otherwise surrounded himself with wizards.

Dardas himself took little pride in his successes to date, however. The campaigns had been simplicity itself, child's play to one of his expertise and experience. In his former life, he had driven an army nearly across the width of the Northern Continent and, evidently, into historical legend. He had outmaneuvered, outdesigned, and crushed his enemies. Those had been *real* campaigns. He had also waged them without the help of magicians.

He was unaware of exactly how Matokin had originally gained control of the city-state of Felk. He had not been summoned back to life until the mage had settled on his grand plan, which was to unite all the city-states of the Isthmus under his rule.

At that point, Matokin had evidently realized that he needed someone with more military knowledge than was available to him to organize and lead the army, and had settled on Dardas as the most likely candidate. Dardas the Conqueror. Dardas the Invincible. Dardas the Fox. Dardas the Butcher. In his day, depending on who spoke, his name was said in awe, respect, fear, or loathing, but none would contest his devastating effectiveness in the field.

Of course, if Matokin had researched Dardas a bit more closely than simply reviewing his legendary string of victories, he might have thought twice about his choice.

The first campaign in this current war had been to overthrow Felk's neighboring state of Callah. There was no great challenge there for Dardas, as there had been no open hostilities between the two city-states beyond border dispute skirmishes for many tenwinters. Callah was totally unprepared for an attack of the magnitude that Dardas had leveled at it, and fell in less than a quarter-lune.

The second campaign, against Windal, was even easier. Windal had failed to see the forces of Felk as a threat, assuming that the battle between Felk and Callah had been nothing but a personal dispute between the city-states' respective leaders. As such, they neglected to make any decent preparations, and when confronted by Dardas's army, now swollen by the assimilation of the surviving Callahan troops, they fell within a matter of days.

An even battle when one side was unprepared, and another when his forces outnumbered his opponents by nearly two to one. Nothing noteworthy there. Certainly nothing requiring a general of Dardas's unique talents. Any competent field commander could have managed as well. Of course, it was just as well that Matokin hadn't realized that, or Dardas likely would not be enjoying his second chance at life.

Of course, things should get a bit more interesting now, particularly with the annihilation of U'delph. The Isthmus's remaining city-states stretching to the south would no longer assume their own safety was guaranteed or that their usual defenses would suffice, since they were likely adequate only to repel skirmish-like onslaughts. Dardas was curious to see what his future enemies would come up with to try to halt him.

No, armies didn't change much, and so it didn't ultimately matter that he was leading these Felk, and not his own people. It didn't matter that this was the Isthmus, not Northland, though how puny a strip of land this was by comparison. Had he lived long enough in his last life, he probably would have gotten around to conquering this land, once the disposition of the Northern Continent was firmly settled. Or he would have left the Isthmus for his heir, except that he had never produced one. Instead, he had died, and his army had unraveled. Northland had since reverted to a kind of general barbarism, so he was told.

Dardas's death had been natural. A fatal wrench to his heart that had made him bedridden, then released him into the void only a few days later. He recalled the experience, and it was a very strange thing to recall one's own death.

"Your dinner is ready now, General."

It was the aide again. His composure regained, he was

standing by the open flap of Dardas's pavilion. He was a clean-cut looking young man with delicate features. Probably, like most of the junior officers, the second son of a noble Felk family, whose father had bought his commission to keep him out from underfoot while the elder son was trained to run the family for the next generation.

Dardas nodded at him and entered the pavilion, only to stop short when he caught sight of his small dining table.

"What's that?" he said, his voice edged with accusation.

Taken aback, the aide blinked in confusion.

"It's your dinner, sir," he said. "Roast chicken and rabbit with wild onions and carrots. The cooks prepared it special for you."

The general stared at him.

"I assume that the fare for the troops is significantly less grand?" he said levelly.

"Well . . . of course," the aide said. "I mean, some of them may have foraged something, but the food that's issued them—"

"Take it away," Dardas ordered, interrupting. "I want you to go to the nearest squad circle and bring me back a portion of whatever it is they're having. What's more, be sure the portion is no larger than that of any other soldier being served."

"Yes, sir!"

Do you have something against decent food?

It was the familiar, somewhat whiny voice of Lord Weisel intruding on the general's thoughts. One thing Dardas did have to admit to having difficulty with was adapting to the presence of a second mind in his head.

You wouldn't understand.

I understand that it's my body you're abusing.

And a decent body it was, too. Dardas appreciated the new vessel for his consciousness. Despite it being more than four tenwinters old, it was both fit and healthy . . . even reasonably attractive, not that it mattered. If only it hadn't come with the previous occupant still in residence.

Remember, I was summoned because I know more about running an army than you do.

But, as my advisor, you're supposed to be teaching me. How can I learn if you don't explain why you do things?

It seemed that Lord Weisel had consented to this arrangement on the basis that he would be second in power only to Matokin himself. Supposedly, Dardas's presence in Lord Weisel's body was to be as an advisor, helping to fill in the immense gaps in the noble's military knowledge.

It was unclear to Dardas if Matokin was genuinely unaware of the strength of the general's personality, or if he had intended all along that Dardas would be the dominant mind, but either way, the results were the same. Now *he* controlled the body as well as the army, and Lord Weisel was reduced to a sulking presence in the mental shadows.

Dardas had little respect for Lord Weisel, a not surprising view for a professional soldier and ruler to have of a pampered nobleman. Still, he felt it behooved him to maintain at least a pretense of courtesy. The man was, literally, his host. If nothing else, Lord Weisel was still his main source of information regarding this new land and age, so though it was annoying, it was in Dardas's best interest to humor Weisel's requests for instruction.

Very well. Consider what you said about my abusing your body.

What of it?

The same food you see as abusing your body is the main sustenance for your troops.

I don't understand.

Let me put it differently. Knowing the condition of your troops is of primary importance when planning your strategies. You have to know how far you can tax them and what their morale is like. One of the surest ways to know that is to make a point of eating the same rations they are getting. If you find the food intolerable, then probably so do they. It's a simple, but effective, test.

There was a moment's pause.

I didn't know that. Weisel's voice was suddenly heavy and tired. *It seems there is much I don't know about the military.*

Having made his point, Dardas was inclined to be magnanimous. *Cheer up, Lord. Matokin, for all his magical secrets, knows even less about the military than you do.*

Perhaps you can explain something else to me, then.

If it doesn't take too long.

Well, I was wondering about the attack on U'delph.

Dardas was suddenly wary. *What about it?*

I know I don't know a lot about military procedure, but why did you deliberately order that massacre? Level the town, no prisoners, burn or destroy anything we can't take with us. Was that really necessary?

Dardas had his answer ready. In fact, he welcomed the opportunity to rehearse the speech before formally explaining things to Matokin.

It's simply a matter of long-term planning. While we're under orders to unite all the city-states under Felk rule, I don't relish the idea of fighting and taking casualties for every victory. Our assault on U'delph may seem brutal, but it will serve as an example for any other city-states that consider resisting us. They will be more inclined to surrender peacefully and be assimilated rather than fight. Also, U'delph was an opportunity to demonstrate our ability to move through the portals those mages opened for us. That is an inestimable military advantage ... and one I would like to have rumored about throughout the Isthmus, which was why I ordered a few of those citizens spared so they could propagandize for us, so to speak. I want the remaining cities to fear us, and what could be more frightening than an army that strikes out of nowhere and destroys utterly?

There was a longer pause before he received a reaction to this.

Again, I have to yield to your experience. There are subtleties involved here that I have never even considered.

There are indeed. Now, if there are no other pressing questions, I must turn my mind to other immediate matters.

Of course. Sorry to have bothered you.

Dardas managed to conceal his smugness until he was sure Weisel had withdrawn to the isolated recesses of his mind.

His aide returned, rather contritely, with his meal. The rations looked edible, and the portion was of decent size.

Dardas contemplated the portals he and his army had passed through. The magic was called Far Movement. How strange it had been to follow his troops through those narrow magical portals. They had passed through ... through ... well, some *other* place, and had arrived on the outskirts of U'delph, finding the city-state woefully unprepared for their arrival.

Magic and war. War and magic. Did he still feel there was something unclean about mixing the two? Perhaps. But he was a warrior and a leader of warriors, and if those mages could provide him such a weapon, he would godsdamned well use it.

Matokin did indeed know even less about the military than did Weisel, and Dardas was counting heavily on that fact. It made them both relatively easy to fool. Of course, that task was made easier because they were both operating on an erroneous assumption. They both thought Dardas was fighting this war to win it.

While Dardas was thoroughly enjoying his second chance at life, he had no intention of living it at the whim of a magician. He had been resurrected, but magic that he didn't understand was necessary to sustain him in this new life. Somehow, he had to find a way to wrest control of his continued existence away from Matokin.

In the meantime, he had to see to it that the magician did not become too successful and powerful. The surest way to achieve that was to sabotage his campaign to unite the city-states. Fortunately, Matokin had placed him in the ideal position to do just that.

The destruction of U'delph was sure to send a message to the Isthmus's remaining city-states, one they would have to act on: Join forces against the Felk, or perish.

Dardas smiled to himself and started in on his dinner.

AQUINT
(1)

AS AQUINT'S MIND forced itself into consciousness, the first thing he realized was that he was lying under a bush. That momentarily puzzled him, even as he automatically noted and accepted that his normal slow morning thinking was being further hindered by having to fight its way through the remnants of a haze of alcohol. He had gone through the process far too often not to recognize the symptoms: the dry mouth and the too full bladder, not to mention the dull ache behind his eyes that made his vision alternately fuzzy and jarring. All those sensations were familiar. But what was he doing under a bush?

He closed his eyes again and tried to force his whirling thoughts into focus. There had been a party . . . not a party, a celebration. There were soldiers . . . he was a soldier now. That was right. In the Felk army. Sometimes he forgot. Sometimes he drank to forget. But last night there had been a party . . . a celebration after a successful battle. U'delph!

Like a bright, unwelcome ray of light, the name smote

his struggling mind. U'delph! He had been drinking to forget. Now he remembered.

They had moved on U'delph through the portals that the magicians opened up right out of the air. Rumors had been circulating through the ranks about the powers of the army's mages, but this amazing ability had been kept from the troops until the last moment.

Aquint, like many others, had been frankly terrified to step single file through the narrow opening. The portals were like gaps in reality. Hah! That was *exactly* what they were. They led into some other realm of existence, a strange, uneasy, milky place, where everything was unfamiliar. But apparently when one crossed a short distance in this other domain, it corresponded to a vast distance in this world.

Thus they had completed the final several days' marching toward U'delph in a matter of mere moments.

Now they were camped just south of the place, and U'delph was no more.

Aquint forced the memories away to deal with more pressing matters, like emptying his bladder. He considered rolling onto his side and relieving himself where he lay, but decided against it. While he was no great advocate of cleanliness, uniforms smelled bad enough when you lived in them without adding urine to the bouquet. With a sigh that was almost a groan, he gathered his legs under him and pushed himself to his feet. He was by no means old, but he certainly wasn't a youth anymore, either.

The bush was actually a small clump of scrub that covered him to his waist as he stood. That gave him an illusion of privacy as he relieved himself, not that it mattered. There was little room for modesty in an army, and the soldiers—men and women—were used to performing their natural functions in full sight of each other. After a while, one simply didn't notice.

As he finished, Cat rose from where he had been sitting

on the ground just outside the bushes and moved to his side. The boy's presence was no surprise to Aquint. Cat was always around.

"I figured you'd be needing this when you came to," Cat said, thrusting a large earthen mug of water into Aquint's hand.

Aquint drained it greedily, then held it out for Cat to refill from his waterskin, which the boy did. Aquint drank another half mug before pausing and heaving a sigh of relief.

"Thank you, lad. That helps."

Cat topped off the mug again, then restoppered the waterskin and sank smoothly back into his seated position. Aquint joined him, though he groaned slightly as he sat.

"Tell me, my young friend," he said as he ran a hand through his unkempt hair, "did we have a good time last night?"

Cat favored him with a level stare before his gaze returned to its normal pattern of scanning the immediate environs.

"I think you had enough fun for both of us."

The boy always had a proprietary, vaguely disapproving attitude toward the older man. Rather than being offended, Aquint found it amusing.

"That's right. You don't drink, do you?"

"I'm a thief," Cat said, bluntly. "A thief has to keep his wits about him more than a businessman . . . or a soldier."

It was an old conversation/argument between them. Stretching all the way back to the day they had first met.

Aquint had been running his freight-hauling business in Callah, with an unadvertised side in smuggling and black marketeering, back in those not long ago days before the Felk had come and captured the city. A patrol of city constables had come into his warehouse in pursuit of a cutpurse who had eluded them in the crowds outside. Aquint had sworn to them that there was no one on the premises other than himself and an alley cat he kept around to chase vermin, blandly ignoring the quick glimpse he had caught of a young sinewy boy slipping through his door just ahead of the patrol. After the constables had moved on, Aquint had expected the lad to vanish back into the city streets and alleys. Instead, the boy had remained and become his inseparable shadow. When asked for a name, he had simply shrugged and said, "I'm your cat . . . just like you told the patrol." And Cat he had been ever since.

When Aquint went into the army, Cat had followed, though he was never actually officially enlisted. Whether the other soldiers thought of him as Aquint's son or bed partner, they kept their opinions to themselves, simply ignoring the boy as they did the other camp followers who traveled with the army in their southward sweep. That army had come out of the Isthmus's northernmost city-state, Felk. It had moved south, capturing Aquint's home of Callah, then the neighboring city of Windal . . . then farther on, to U'delph.

"For once, I'll have to agree with you, Cat," Aquint said, darkly, sipping at the water while he stared straight ahead. "It doesn't take much in the way of wits for a soldier to do what we did yesterday. In fact, the fewer wits, the better."

"Don't start again," Cat hissed, looking at him sternly. "You said more than enough last night. They don't like critical talk in this army."

"I'm sorry, but it makes me sick," Aquint insisted. "That wasn't a battle. By the madness of the gods, it was butchery."

"It's the job of the generals to make decisions and issue orders," Cat said.

"That pitiful garrison folded in a matter of two watches. After that, we could have accepted their surrender and claimed the city-state. There was no reason to go to the extremes that we did."

"It's the job of a soldier to follow those orders," Cat

said. "That's how an army is run. If every soldier tried to make their own decisions and plans, it wouldn't just be ineffectual, it would be chaos."

"Are you saying you approve of what was done?" Aquint asked.

"I'm saying that my approval doesn't matter . . . and neither does yours. Even if you had been consulted about the battle plan—"

"Which I wasn't."

"—which you weren't, you would have been overruled. You couldn't change it then, and you certainly can't change it now that it's over. All your complaints and criticisms can do now is put you in jeopardy if you insist on voicing them."

Aquint drew a deep breath and blew it out. The lad was articulate for a thief who'd haunted Callah's streets and alleys.

"All right," Aquint said. "You've made your point. I'll try to keep my mouth shut."

"It may be a little late now," Cat said. "You mouthed off last night enough to get arrested for treason. I only hope you satisfied Sonya."

"Sonya?"

Cat favored him with another prolonged stare.

"The little corporal from Third Squad," he said. "The one with the muscles and the bad teeth. She was your companion there under the bushes last night."

Aquint winced as the vague memory struggled to surface in his still befuddled mind.

"Bugger. I must have been really drunk," he said. "I've been dodging that one for weeks now."

"Count yourself as lucky." Cat shrugged. "If she hadn't been so eager to get into your pants, she could have reported you for what you were saying."

"Well, I'll try to watch it in the future," Aquint said. "Bedding Sonya is too high a price to pay for the privilege of shooting off my mouth."

"I'd hold any plans for the future for a while, if I were you," Cat said softly.

Frowning, Aquint followed the youth's gaze.

There were three of them. A lieutenant and two guards. They were at the squad campfire speaking to his sergeant. As he watched, the sergeant looked around, then pointed directly to where he and Cat were sitting.

As the trio approached, Aquint briefly considered running, but discarded the notion. He was in the middle of an army encampment. There was no place to run to. Instead, he rose to his feet and saluted as the group came to a halt in front of him.

"Is your name Aquint?" the officer said.

"Yes, sir."

"You will come with me. Now."

With that the lieutenant turned on his heel and strode off, leaving Aquint little choice but to follow behind. As he did, he noticed the two guards were now positioned on either side and behind him. Cat had faded from sight as the contingent had approached, but Aquint had little doubt that he was watching from somewhere else.

Aquint wondered for a moment what would happen to Cat if he, Aquint, were imprisoned or executed, but shrugged it off, turning his mind instead to his own predicament.

Actually, he wasn't all that worried. This was far from the first time in his life that he had been hauled in front of the authorities, and so far his wit and glibness of tongue had saved him from any serious consequences. If this was about his comments of the previous evening, he would simply claim to have been drunk and to have no recollection of having said anything that could be taken as treasonable. If cross-examined, he would have no difficulty claiming support and loyalty to the army and its policies. Except . . .

Aquint blinked as a sudden realization struck him. Except that a part of him wanted to be punished. Maybe that was why he had allowed himself to voice his criticisms in front of so many people last night. What was more, it wasn't just the guilt of having participated in the destruction of U'delph.

He had made a suggestion, an observation, really. A forced quick march, leaving the supply wagons behind, would allow them to attack U'delph days earlier than if they stuck to the tradition of moving the army in its entirety as they had been doing since Callah, he had said. Hit them fast, before they had a chance to consolidate their defenses, and the city-state could be taken with the least possible losses on both sides.

A mere watch after he'd made this comment the army had halted and the various unit commanders had announced that the portals would be used to transport the troops the remainder of the distance to U'delph.

It was, in effect, a variation on his own plan. He couldn't help but wonder, in some irrational corner of his mind, if his suggestion had been passed up the line. What he had envisioned came to pass, except . . . he hadn't known the decision had already been made to make an example of U'delph.

Instead of a simple surrender, virtually every one of its inhabitants—man, woman, and child—had been put to the sword without mercy, and the city itself razed to the ground. Only a very small group was spared, survivors that were deliberately allowed to flee southward, to spread news of the might and terror of the Felk army and its wizards.

It was a startling revelation that he was taking the blame for that on himself. Now that he was aware of his deeper feelings, however, Aquint set his mind to quickly correcting them. Subconsciously seeking punishment was one thing. When one's life and limb were actually about to be put on the line, however, it was time to focus on self-preservation.

The lieutenant paused at the entrance to a large command pavilion.

"Wait here," he said, and disappeared inside.

Aquint ran his fingers through his hair again and tried to dust the twigs and blades of grass from his uniform. It looked as if his case was to be reviewed by the company commander, and trying to put on a presentable front couldn't hurt. Perhaps he could get off with a reprimand and a warning.

The lieutenant reappeared, holding the tent flap open and beckoning Aquint to enter. As he did, the lieutenant pointed to a spot at the center of the tent, then left, letting the tent flap close behind him.

Aquint moved to the indicated point and stood, forcing down an impulse to fidget. Looking exceptionally nervous or overly innocent would only label him as guilty even before the conversation began. Instead, he worked on appearing patient and curious.

The commander was seated behind a low table, scribbling on one of several pieces of vellum scattered across the table's surface. He did not look up or otherwise acknowledge Aquint's presence.

The only other person in the tent was a thin, pale woman in dark robes who sat in the tent's corner. Wizard, Aquint thought. He didn't often see them up close like this. It was incredible to think that this creature and her fellows had opened those portals, that any beings could have such power. It was rumored that they could also communicate directly with the city-state of Felk through magical means and often relayed orders from Matokin himself.

People, in Aquint's experience, generally feared magic. It was an ancient practice. But the Felk had embraced the art apparently, absorbing it into their own army, a tactic that had never been used in the history of the Isthmus. These wizards—wherever they were coming from—were formidable.

Aquint did his best to ignore the one in the corner. Looking at her only reminded him of how frightened he'd been to step through that portal.

"You are Aquint?" the commander said at last, looking up from his writing.

"Yes, sir."

"The same Aquint who came up with the idea for the quick march?"

Caught off guard by this line of questioning, Aquint hesitated a beat before answering.

"Yes, sir."

"Could you explain to me how that idea occurred to you?"

Aquint decided there was nothing to be lost by telling the truth.

"Well, sir," he said, "before I joined the army, I ran a small hauling and freight business in Callah. We charged different rates, depending on the size of the load and the urgency of the delivery. It just seemed to me that if I had run things the way the army has been moving troops, I would be out of business."

"How so?"

"Everything would have to be delivered at the same time, and by definition, that time would be dictated by the heaviest, hardest to move item." Aquint continued to resist the urge to fidget.

"Go on," the commander said.

"It occurred to me that if we expedited certain units of the army like I used to expedite certain cargos, those units could move farther and faster than the army as a whole."

"Interesting," the commander said. "A good business, was it?"

Was. He had the tense right, Aquint thought with wry bitterness. "Actually, the army commandeered most of my stock and wagons, so I didn't have much of a business left," he said. "I didn't have anything in the way of other marketable skills, so I, uh, enlisted."

The truth was of course that he had been conscripted as well. Few able-bodied individuals in Callah had escaped being impressed into the army. Luckily, no one had discovered the false-bottomed wagons and mislabeled shipments that marked him as a smuggler as much as a legitimate businessman.

"My point," the commander was saying, "is that you're new to the army, not a career man. That's good. One of the problems the army has is clinging to old procedures because they've always worked before."

Aquint had no ready response. Was he being complimented?

"Your idea was a good one," the commander said. "As it happened, we had . . . other means of quickening the speed at which we could move."

Aquint noticed the officer give an involuntary, uneasy glance to the magician in the corner. So, thought Aquint, even this army's higher-ups hadn't enjoyed stepping through those portals.

"Anyway," the commander continued, "this is a new means of transportation. I don't know how often General Weisel will want to make use of it, or even how reliable it is." Another look toward the corner, this one mildly defiant. "But I need transport officers in the regular ranks. These . . . mages might be able to send us magically through the air, but I'll wager they don't know how a convoy should be organized to pass most efficiently through those tight portals."

Aquint blinked, still groping for a reply.

He didn't get the chance to make one. "You have a background in freight hauling," the commander said. "You're not afraid to express your ideas. Fresh thinking is rare, and it's in our best interest to make use of it when we find it. I'm promoting you, effective when your paperwork is complete. That's all. You can return to your unit."

Aquint was out of the tent and walking back to his unit

when it finally, truly sank in that he was not going to be punished. When it did, he burst out in sudden, joyous laughter. Cat appearing at his side, peering at him with concern, only made him laugh harder.

PRAULTH

(1)

A SHEET OF parchment was whipped abruptly underneath her narrow nose, causing her to start violently and
nearly spill from the high stool. Having her intense study
so crassly interrupted made her bare her teeth in annoyance. Some prank? Some lower phase brat playing games
with—

"Tell me what you make of this by the end of the watch.
Wherever I am, find me. Start now."

With a rustle of his robe, Master Honnis glided past her
desk, his shrunken body moving with its usual grace. The
pure white fringe of what remained of his hair stood out
starkly against his richly dark flesh. Master Honnis was the
oldest individual at the University, one of the oldest people
Praulth had ever met in her life. Yet within that small, bony
shape burned an irascible vigor that had earned him a
widespread reputation as a taskmaster.

Praulth didn't entirely share that general view, though
Master Honnis's fearsomeness was evident. His speech
was often short, his manner curt. Yet she had gotten to

know the old instructor—as much as anyone was likely
to—and quite admired him. He had once told her that the
reason for his brusqueness was that he simply didn't have
time for social niceties. At his age there could only be so
many days left to him.

Praulth, a fourth-phase student of first ranking here at
the University at Febretree, was twenty-two years old.
Physically she was of average height and lean, with short
blandly brownish hair. Her trimness wasn't due to exercise. She was slim only because her diet was poor; as an
obsessive intellect she regularly overlooked meals.

She was charting a course of academic excellence,
one that was almost predetermined to secure her a post
on one of the scholastic councils. Historic studies to be
specific, since that was her field of greatest achievement.
Another tenwinter of diligence, of honing her analytical
faculties, and she would perhaps be *Mistress* Praulth.
Would she then also be blunt? Intimidating? Intellectually ferocious? Just like her mentor, Master Honnis. Perhaps.

Two other desks were occupied in the bleakly appointed
study parlor by lower phase pupils, neither outstandingly
bright; still, that they were here this late (it was nearing the
mid of night) spoke of commitment. Surely not the same
sort of commitment—*devotion*—that filled Praulth's
every waking moment, but perhaps one or the other of
these two would last long enough to reach third phase,
which was the minimum achievement necessary to call
oneself a Thinker. Praulth had already attained this standing. Her aspirations ran higher.

Both pupils had huddled low over their texts as Master
Honnis slid through the chamber. Both were now peering
with lurid curiosity in her direction, doubtlessly wondering
what dreadful task the old sadistic bag of bones had foisted
on her.

She was more than a little curious herself. Honnis re-
spected her. While that was indeed complimentary, coming

from one so high in the University hierarchy, it also carried
a price. The elder instructor expected much from her. Not
merely a regurgitation of facts or the tepid reiteration of
someone else's analyses and ideas. Honnis wanted origi-
nality from her. He wanted unique insight. He pushed her,
goaded her; and for her past six years here at Febretree,
Praulth had met his challenges, gladly, enthusiastically.
She wasn't arrogant. Arrogance was one trait Master Honnis was only too pleased to pulverize. She was instead only
dedicated.

She set aside the document she had been examining for
her own edification. It was a partial text said to belong to
the war journals of Ao'mp Dit, a minor Northland warlord
who ninety winters ago had dominated a small zone of the
Northern Continent. That was, at least, until the Five Year
Fever had come to the region.

Praulth had her doubts about the text's authenticity,
noting some terminology that didn't quite fit the age in
question. She wasn't yet ready to point this out to anyone
on the councils. The University took a great deal of pride
in its store of ancient documents, so much so that they
were under special guard in the Archive. She'd had to secure consent to see this text, in fact, a procedural detail
she'd always found most annoying. Some on the University's councils had made their names by discovering or
reinterpreting or translating those same documents. It
wouldn't do to challenge this Ao'mp Dit excerpt before
she knew if someone superior to her had a vested interest
in it.

She straightened the sheet of parchment that had been
flung down in front of her, peering at it in the steady clear
lamplight that always burned in the study parlors. Pupils
were encouraged to make use of the University's facilities
(which made the restrictions to the Archive that much
more contrary and exasperating), to explore and research
points of personal interest that were outside the curricula.
There were few things more tedious than an intelligent stu-

dent that kept strictly to the straight and narrow and merely succeeded. So said Master Honnis, though Praulth had heard the sentiment echoed by other instructors.

The map on the parchment was quite detailed. Small blocks of neatly printed text marked various sites. Arrows in red ink showed advancements. It was, of course, a map of battle. Felk was the Isthmus's northernmost major city-state, and its military had recently launched successful hostile actions. Word had spread far southward, here to Febretree. Praulth had been eager for more news of the conflict. It might be that this would flourish into large-scale warfare. The Felk were also said to be using magic to aid their campaigns. That was most unusual. And most intriguing.

How different—and more interesting—that would be compared to the modern pedestrian contests that occasionally heated up amongst rival Isthmus states. They rarely developed into anything historically worthy, remaining petty squabbles that resolved little or nothing. Even this new aggression by the Felk might already have played out.

The map that Master Honnis had brought her said otherwise.

Praulth set about studying it, intently, letting her formidable analytical powers take over. Soon she had entered that nearly insensible state where external input barely registered any longer. Her bland, brown eyes still stared down at the parchment, but she had absorbed its information already. Now she was cogitating. Once a fellow pupil had pricked her arm with a pin when she was in this meditative attitude; she hadn't found out about it until afterward.

Sometime later she hurried from the parlor. Now only one of the other desks was occupied, and the student at it was softly snoring. Praulth's robe flew about her as she moved in unaccustomed haste. She wasn't only eager to find Master Honnis before the watch ended, as he'd instructed, she was also full to bursting with what her studies had uncovered. This was significant. It was perhaps momentous. It was at least the sort of oddity she and her kind could appreciate. Honnis, despite being uncounted tenwinters older than her and the least civil individual she could ever recall meeting, was, in a way . . . well . . . her friend.

Master Honnis was also the head of the University's historical war studies. *He* would definitely appreciate what she had found.

SHE HAD COME to the small township of Febretree in her mid-adolescence, from her home estate in the nearby southern city of Dral Blidst. Her upbringing was a very comfortable one, at least economically, what with her family's substantial interests in the southern timber trade. However, none in Praulth's family had objected when she'd made known her desire to pursue an academic life. In truth, they had seemed pleased to be rid of her. She had never shown the least aptitude for business, and there were plenty of siblings and relations to fill all the slots in the familial concern.

Her family didn't value knowledge for knowledge's sake; and Praulth supposed she could understand their view, since the sort of education she was so ardently pursuing wouldn't be of any real service in furthering her clan's timber enterprise. She understood. But she also still resented the slights and ignorant indifference she'd had to suffer before leaving for Febretree, the best—virtually the *only*—facility for higher learning that existed on the Isthmus.

Her burgeoning womanhood spent at the University, however, was something quite different from her younger days. Here she was encouraged to submerge herself in study, was rewarded for her scholarly persistence and was even, wonderfully, envied by fellow students who were in awe of her ability to absorb and integrate knowledge so proficiently.

History was her passion. As little as her family had sympathized with her academic desires, they were that much less understanding of her choice of study. History was done. History was past. The future, though unknowable, was at least of abstract interest. Surely only the present, the practical here and now, had any true meaning. Yet she was drawn toward yesterdays, toward events and people she couldn't witness or affect. Why?

Praulth didn't truly have an answer for that. She doubted that an individual who sculpted in stone could satisfactorily explain why he or she didn't instead weave tapestries or compose verse. History was her focus, and within that discipline she was most obsessed by the analysis of war.

It was odd, in its way. She wasn't a violent person by any means. She couldn't recall ever, even in childhood, raising a hand in anger. She imagined that if she found herself on an actual battlefield, she would merely stand paralyzed in fear and horror until someone came along to cut her down.

Yet the *study* of war was something else entirely. Its connotations, its endless reverberations—nothing impacted history so dramatically. Courses of whole cultures were altered forever. Ways of life were annihilated. Power shifted wildly. Individuals who would have left no mark whatever on the world found themselves thrust into eminence. And of course countless others who might have made their significant contributions were prematurely erased.

That was a part of the fascination for her—examining war as a vast cultural modifier.

Praulth studied the annuls of older conflicts, large and small, those of the Isthmus and those of the Southern and Northern Continents (though these were sometimes quite sketchy in nature). She could make connections and associations among the facts she absorbed that some of her fellow students couldn't start to grasp. It wasn't always easy to see how the minor political machinations in some bygone ancient city-state could impact major war campaigns a hundredwinter later.

Through her exhaustive studies she had accrued a solid knowledge of battle strategies and methods. How engrossing it was, comparing those tactics, seeing how maneuvers and ploys were invented, then adopted by an enemy, forgotten, and resurrected years later.

Yes, it was quite interesting how dead things returned to life.

She found Master Honnis among the statuary and manicured shrubs of an atrium. Overhead the sky was black, pierced by stars and hung with the moon.

Praulth hurried out into the open-air area, sandals slapping stones, nose wrinkling at the scents of flowers and rich earth. She preferred the mustiness of paper. Seeing where Master Honnis was just now wandering out of sight behind a row of carefully pruned greenery, she scurried around to intercept him.

She didn't find him where he should be. She stood confused, the map in hand, until something small and hard glanced off her right temple. She yelped, spun, and saw the old man standing in the center of the court.

She rubbed her temple as she hurried over, not even bothering to complain that he'd thrown the pebble too hard. Such things didn't matter to her. Certainly not now, not with the incredible news she had.

Brandishing the map, she babbled breathlessly, "Here! This! The Felk attack on Callah, the positional maneuvers, see, *see,* the companies grouped here, here, and *here,* and the second assault, on Windal, see how the cavalry and archers—"

"Stop."

She did. She couldn't have gone on at such a frantic pace much longer anyway. Running up and down corridors had already rather winded her. She realized she was acting foolishly, sputtering like a child; very unlike her, she who was always so mentally organized and able to concisely express her ideas.

"State your findings first. Support them with particulars later." Honnis's dark face, set into its habitual glower, was tilted up toward hers. Though she was substantially taller than the small gaunt man, she naturally felt dwarfed in her mentor's presence. She also had the odd feeling that the elder was easily her physical match.

He was waiting. No one in all the generations that had agonized under Master Honnis's stern tutelage had ever profited from making him wait for anything.

Avidly, with all the nervous energy of a roaring river backing up behind a dam of dead wood, she stated her findings. In a single word. In a great overwrought blast that echoed in the atrium, frightening a small yellow bird into flight and flecking her instructor's bald pate with spittle.

The one word was this: *"Dardas!"*

Honnis stared up at her an inscrutable, excruciating moment. Then with an odd tone of fatalism he said, "Yes." He lifted a skeletal hand. "No, I don't want to hear your supporting facts. I don't need to. I've recognized the same patterns. His stamp . . . his character . . . it's on this." He nodded to the map in her hand.

Praulth felt a frenzied rush of pride. She'd gotten it right! Not that she had doubted her own findings, but to hear Master Honnis himself say it was hugely gratifying. She tried to keep her excitement from showing.

The small robed man started pacing, indicating with a blunt gesture that she should come along. Flagstoned paths wound through the ornamental shrubbery. He was deep in thought, though most students wouldn't be able to tell this grave contemplative state from his normal, equally austere one.

After a moment he said, "You haven't considered."

"Considered?"

"*Think,* Thinker Praulth. Yes, the tactics are those of General Dardas, the Northland war commander. Unmistakably. We who have studied wars fought throughout the ages, who've devoted ourselves to anatomizing strategies, to knowing the very temperament and taste and minutiae of war leaders from all periods . . . we see. We recognize. We understand."

They turned past a plot of radiant red fronds.

"But General Dardas has been dead for two and a half centuries. How can it be that his tactics are being used by the modern Felk?"

Praulth thought that obvious enough. "Someone is imitating his technique of war."

"Imitating it well, do you think?"

"Flawlessly."

"Yes. These contemporary Felk battles fit seamlessly into the old texts we have of Dardas's military maneuvers. I won't tell you the extreme lengths I've gone to to secure detailed news of this new war. Few here in Febretree care a spit's worth about it, of course. How far away it is. How safe we are from it."

Praulth listened raptly. Honnis was rarely this verbose about anything. In fact, for him, he was nearly rambling.

"Keeping up-to-date on these new war events isn't easy." A hand came out of his robe with another parchment. "I need you to study this as well. I don't want you doing anything else. Not until I say. Study. Bring me your conclusions."

He had stopped walking. So had she. The path had circled back on itself. She looked at the paper. Another battle map. This one, though, showed an advancement by the Felk army that made no sense. It was like they'd *leaped* forward, suddenly, inexplicably, in a way no army had or ever could move.

"I should like to know why our General Dardas impersonator has decided to eradicate the city of U'delph," Mas-

ter Honnis said. "I should like to know as soon as possible.
Go now."

Praulth hurried away, unsure why her mentor's last
words had just chilled her so.

SHE WOKE WITH a sudden frightful surge. Dream im-
agery exploded as her eyes went wide. The candle was still
lit but just barely, the flame a tiny bead of yellow atop the
melted stump. Her back seized up as she rocked violently
into a sitting position on her bunk. She had diligently studied the map Master Honnis had given her until she'd fallen
asleep here in her tiny student's cell.

The Felk army could move across great distances by
magical means. The battle map said so. If it were true—
and she had to believe it was—it meant this was a new
type of warfare, something literally never recorded before
in all the annals she had ever read.

She had dreamt of the Felk. In the dream they were
overrunning Febretree, the small township surrounding the
University. They were doing as they'd done to U'delph—
slaughtering, burning, eradicating. She was hiding, here in
this same cell. She was terrified, huddling on this bunk as
her door was being hammered. They were coming *in,* they
were coming to get her.

Praulth was unaccustomed to nightmares. Her ordered
mind normally forbade such unreasonable mental indul-
gences, even during sleep. And so, hearing the *tap-tap-tap*
at her cell's door, she didn't know for several instants if it
was real or carried over from her dream like an echo.

It stopped. But by now she was sure she'd actually
heard it.

Standing was painful. Squinting in the feeble candlelight, she stepped toward her door.

She opened it onto the wing corridor. Most of the students in this annex were third phase or higher, and so these
cells were located on a quiet part of the campus grounds,

away from the boisterous and uncouth dormitories. She had no fond memories of her own time there.

Praulth looked left and right. There was a single light source some distance along the row of shut cell doors, but it was enough to see that the corridor was empty. What had caused that *tap-tap-tap*? Pranksters? Had it simply been the door itself settling against the jamb?

She ached with the need for sleep. How hard could she drive herself? Fiercely dedicated academic or not, she had to sleep sometime. It was a fact that often annoyed her.

As she made to shut the door, however, she glanced downward. Frowning, she stooped and picked up the folded sheet of vellum propped against the ceramic cup sitting on the ground. Scented steam rose delicately from the cup. She opened the paper and strained to read:

> *we all deserve the occasional luxury*
> *enjoy it, Beauty, I know it is your favorite*

She bent once more, this time retrieving the cup. The liquid inside was hot. Its smell, so familiar . . . *tallgreen.* Tallgreen tea. Yes, her favorite. She had always loved it. It was among the scarce handful of fond memories she had of her upbringing in her home city of Dral Blidst. It was a fine soothing beverage but difficult to come by. It was indeed a luxury, just as the note said.

The anonymous note. She hastily checked both sides of it. No name. Not even her own. Was it meant for her? Her mind was suddenly racing. Of course it was meant for her! Whoever had left it must know her fondness for this particular tea. She lifted the cup to her lips, took a small swallow. It was even properly honeyed.

Her head whipped as she looked up and down the corridor again. It remained vacant.

She entertained the impetuous—and wildly uncharacteristic—impulse to race off after whoever had delivered this gift, whoever had gone to such lengths . . . whoever had referred to her, in the note, as "Beauty."

And why should that be causing her heart to beat so forcefully?

She withdrew into her cell. She sat up on her bunk, sipping at the comforting, smooth tea, its intricate flavor reawakening those few pleasant memories she'd all but forgotten. She examined the note. As a document it was poorly suited for study, so short, offering no substantial clues to its source. Certainly Master Honnis wasn't responsible.

Nonetheless, Praulth read it repeatedly until her candle at last burned out and the cup of tea was empty.

RADSTAC
(1)

DO THE SMART thing first. Next, the most economical thing. Then, the safest, the most self-fulfilling, and the thing that will most confuse your enemies, in that order. Failing everything, do the stupid thing.

These Isthmusers were as amusing as they were annoying. It was an orphan culture, after all. The Isthmus knew no indigenous human life. This land was merely a bridge between Southsoil and Northland. It was narrow strip of dirt abutted by a poisonous sea on one side and an unapproachable, coral-thick coast on the other. It should never have been settled. It was a road, not a destination.

As historical happenstance would have it, though, the Great Upheavals had rendered the Isthmus useless as a trade route. It wasn't that anything had happened to *this* miserable belt of land. No. Rather, the once mighty dominions of the two continents were no more, and thus the prosperous trade between them was finished. A Southsoiler had no need to go far north anymore; and as for the Northlanders, they were all barbarians now, too busy fighting cheap tribal wars amongst themselves to worry about the Isthmus or the Southern Continent beyond.

There was no profit in a Northland war. Those people had devolved into such depravity that they fought for honor, accolades, and the revered names of their warlords. Worthless reasons to fight.

Radstac fought, yes, but she fought for appropriate causes. One cause, actually. Herself.

The bodies were mounds. They stank, and they stirred feebly beneath blankets. The coverings weren't for warmth. It was still just barely summertime, but even here on the Isthmus, north of the perpetually gentle climes of the Southsoil, it remained quite temperate. The blankets were thick, black, and they cut the meager seeping sunlight that found its way through chinks in the cheap planks of the walls. The bodies under there, rolling in their own filth, were hiding from that light, from all light, from anything that would illuminate—and therefore remind them of—reality.

Radstac didn't spend time under blankets. She felt nothing, neither pity nor revulsion, for the marginally human creatures that had reduced themselves to such states. Addictions had to be chosen carefully, but there was rarely anyone to guide neophyte users. Normally they fell helplessly and randomly into their habits, and there they stayed, their physical existences turning to shit while their souls soared in glorious narcotic realms.

It ended in death, sure. What didn't?

Radstac didn't hide her leather armor and scarred bracers beneath a cloak. The accoutrements of her trade she displayed—not proudly, practically. Being a mercenary didn't begin and end with the talent and willingness to fight. Hardly. You had to hustle yourself. Someone had to *hire* you. For that they had to know you existed.

The durable leather about her upper body was marked by past blows that had landed on her. That she was still walking around inside the armor was something she wanted to advertise. She also wore dark leggings and kid-skin boots, a small, wickedly honed blade nestled in each, inside oiled sheaths, hidden from view. On her left hand she wore a black glove, more leather. It was a snug fit, customized by a superb Southsoil specialist. It had cost her more than a few coppers, but for the use she'd gotten out of it, it had proven to be a bargain. It weighed heavily, but she was very used to its heft. Used to the feel of the small gears and sockets beneath the leather surface.

On her belt she carried no weapon. Petgrad, this Isthmus city she'd come to, didn't forbid its citizens or visitors to carry arms, but the local police made a point of harassing those who did, particularly something like the heavy combat sword she favored. She had checked the sword at the Public Armory, a civilized amenity only a city-state the size of Petgrad could offer.

Radstac had to admit the city was fairly sophisticated. It was large, well-maintained, its economy stable. It provided a health service for its citizenry, had a respectable standing military. The people weren't especially oppressed. A typical worker could live a decent life of reasonable years. By Isthmus standards, then, this was the pinnacle of culture.

Cities, of course, were bigger and better back home. Radstac's home, specifically, was the Republic of Dilloqi, located in the northern part of Southsoil. Dilloqi, a *real* nation, and the city of her birth, Hynñsy . . . beautiful. Proud. Important. With an eminent history to back up its boasts.

That Dilloqi was in truth a splintered relic of the erstwhile Southsoil empire wasn't anything that needed to be dwelt upon. Dilloqi had resurrected itself from the ruins of the Great Upheavals, as had other lands of the Southern Continent. They abided now independently of each other.

This wasn't the first time Radstac had journeyed northward to the Isthmus to sell her sword. The Isthmus was a fairly reliable source of petty hostilities between individual city-states. They bickered about farmland; they wrangled about the use of roads. They blustered and fussed and made ultimatums, and eventually they provided the wars that Radstac lived on—at least for a while. Conflicts played themselves out in rather short order here. No Isthmus state had the resources to wage sustained warfare.

That, it seemed, had changed.

The prepubescent boy, who had the overused look of a rental about him, led her deeper into the waste-smelling lair. He had appeared from the air when she stepped into the doorway of this establishment, the barest glint of silver showing in her palm.

She had surrendered one silver to the boy, who made the coin disappear the instant it touched his tiny fingers. She still held another in her palm and had more money in pouches no pickpocket would ever find.

Her eyes had virtually no color, just a tint of pale yellow to the irises. Those eyes, small in a twice-scarred face, roved her surroundings without appearing to move. Her bronze-colored features were what men would call handsome, rather than pretty. Not that she lost sleep wondering what men thought of her looks. Her hair was the red of rotting berries and hacked short. Another scar was visible across the rear of her skull, a line of white in the red.

It had cut through her helmet, a blow from a hulking swordsman, a death stroke. She had tumbled over the battlefield ground, rolling back onto her feet, and everything she saw then was a roaring blackness . . . everything except the face of the giant as he clomped toward her. She had snatched a throwing knife from one of her boots and launched it. It entered his gaping mouth, skewered his tongue, and poked its barbed tip out of the back of his throat. She'd never learned who had carried her away from that field. She had woken in a surgeon's tent, her scalp being sewn.

No beds, no aisles, just mounds. The boy picked his zigzagging way nimbly, into darkness that now only hinted at the human shapes on the floor. She was alert.

One stirring heap, on her right, blanket rocking back

and forth, rhythmically, too steadily—a step away, the boy passing it . . .

She pivoted. One boot heel came down on the right upper arm, just above the elbow. She drove the toe of her other boot into the mound's side, a toe reinforced by a wedge of iron under the kidskin. A rib broke under the blanket.

If it was just another mud-brained addict, the proprietors wouldn't care.

In the dark, low and ahead, she heard, *"No sword."* Which the hisser evidently thought meant she was weaponless. So be it.

She delivered another kick, one that would immobilize the lungs for a while, and hopped off. She caught only the vaguest glimpse of the boy vanishing, but where he'd been there was now a charging figure. Blade in fist.

Brute attack. It might have worked in the daylight, where the victim would see the armed shape looming and lunging and then freeze in fear. It might have worked here, in this stinking dimness, against someone who didn't have a decade of combat experience.

She snapped her left hand outward, fingers stiff and spread. The sound of sliding metal rang on the foul air. The weight of her glove was redistributed.

Her right hand jabbed forward and punched the hand that held the knife, a hard painful shot, distracting the charger. But it was her left hand, of course, darting and singing a few thin notes of metallic mayhem as it shot through the air, that did the job. The two prongs—fine, solid, as sharp as anything she ever carried—were extended from the back of her fist. They each tore away a patch of her attacker's face. She did all this during another pivot that got her out of the way of the pouncing, bleeding, screaming figure that hurtled past and onto several of the mounds.

Into a crouch, sinewy legs splayed. Her hooks dribbled.

The figure under the blanket to her right was gasping in excruciating pain.

Noises ahead still. The one who'd hissed *"No sword."* Maybe there were others. Her charger was still screaming on the floor behind her, high-pitched, sounding nearly insane. She must have hit an eye. Stupid Isthmuser.

Her right hand flipped a blade up from her boot. It was a flat, thin slab of hammered metal, with no hilt. Made for throwing. Her fingers balanced it. She was holding her breath, listening to the dark, waiting to see what followed.

The boy reappeared, a little grey smudge in the robe he wore, a smooth face that would be inscrutable even in the best light. In some other part of the cavernous room footsteps retreated, stumbling. The mounds, even those the charger had blundered onto, remained silent, making only their irregular twitches and jerks.

Radstac slotted the throwing knife back into her boot, but kept her glove's prongs extended. The specialist who had made the contraption had lived in a village nearby her home city of Hynñsy. He was a middle-yeared man, and he was dying, consumed from within by a corruption that ate the meat of him, leaving him a sack of yellowing flesh. He couldn't move about without the assistance of others, and so chose to rarely move from the worktable where he had invented her glove. She had envisioned the device, had struggled to explain it. It had, after all, come to her in a violently vivid dream of combat and so wavered in her mind.

The man had listened, eyes serene and protruding from a shriveling face. She talked, describing the imagined weapon she wanted this man to make. Every time she ran out of words, he made her carry on, until she was hoarse, until her vision of the dream device smeared into nonsense. Then he took her money, sent her away, called her back on the day he had promised to, and presented her with the glove. She had stayed on in that quaint little village for the two additional days the man needed to die. She wanted to attend the funeral rite. She had also entered his house by

night to satisfy herself that nothing about the glove's work-
ings had been committed to paper. She needn't have worried. The craftsman had never drawn a design in his life.

Radstac stared at the boy's dim outlines, letting herself
breathe again, the breaths even and calm. She nodded and,
leaving the blood-wet prongs extended, followed him farther.

SHE HAD DONE the smart thing by coming north for
this war. She was a mercenary, and here was a great opportunity for work. The economical thing—next on her
list of personal statutes—would be to find herself inex-
pensive lodgings. That could wait a watch or two, though.

She peeled the gummy, deep blue leaf away from its
wax paper, bit away a third of it, and returned the rest to a
secret pocket beneath her leather armor. The initial sensation was a profound ache in her teeth. Addicts—the truly
lost ones, like those living underneath blankets in that
users' den—had their teeth professionally removed or
worried them out themselves one by one. They sucked
their *mansid* leaves, occasionally gummed food, and
avoided the light.

Weaklings.

Radstac clamped her molars together as the discomfort
peaked and passed. She paused to lean on a wall, propping
herself carefully, staying on her feet as the wave of gravity
struck. She was pulled, compressed, elongated, resettled.
Like the ache to her teeth, it passed. Equilibrium restored.
Improved.

The street around her started to make sense.

She pushed off, walking her prowling walk. Petgrad
was well populated, and its streets didn't seem to tire.
Some distance ahead, towers loomed. Squared shafts of
stone and mortar, capped with decorative top pieces of
metal. They were impressive, she admitted. No point in
denigrating this city unnecessarily. She was here to sell her

sword. With luck, she would soon be defending this place against . . . who was it? . . . Yes, the Felk.

They were the aggressors in this; so went the news that the traders had brought back to the Southsoil. Radstac preferred fighting on the side of the antagonist, but here that was impractical. The city-state of Felk—and even the newly captured Felk territories—were simply out of easy reach. She had come to Petgrad by buying her way onto a wagon of like-minded Southsoil mercenaries who'd heard the sweet call of war. She'd made no friends during her travels, though one night she had fairly raped the wagon's hired driver, a bashful blond lad who'd shed his trousers at knifepoint, then done everything else quite willingly—and enthusiastically.

The aroma of war was on the southerly wind. Those Felk were sweeping southward. It was war like she had never seen in her lifetime. War as the Isthmus hadn't known it for hundredwinters, if ever. No feud this, no petty strife. The Felk had absolute conquest in mind. Any fool could see that.

She wasn't deterred by the panicky stories circulating about the Felk using wizardry to aid them in their campaigns. Magic was not feared on the Southsoil, though its practitioners were highly rare. After the Great Upheavals, wizards, once quite visible as healers, retreated into hermetic cloisters.

She had of course retracted her hooks into her leather glove, after wiping them meticulously clean. She had once fouled the tiny gears with blood. It hadn't happened since.

Most narcotics were not illegal in Isthmus cities. Substances were declared unlawful only when those in positions of power wished to profit from their distribution exclusively.

Radstac could have purchased her *mansìd* leaves in the market. Could have laid out twice the silver for the three leaves she'd gotten at that fetid lair, paying the merchant's licensing tax for him. But the quality would have been mediocre. She didn't need to actually sample any of these legitimate leaves to know this. It was the way of things. Drug dens, like the one she'd visited, depended on the return business of addicts; addicts, having built up inhuman tolerances to every recreational poison in existence, required the highest potency. Thus, better profits were made by the lairs' proprietors—who got their product through the black market—than by licensed merchants in the marketplace.

Ah . . . and it was fine stuff, she thought, still chewing the blue leaf. Clarity, clarity. The *sense* of things, unfolding all around her now.

As she walked, she didn't examine that thought that surfaced, that nagging one . . . the one that said she only came north to the Isthmus because only here could she find leaves of this quality. After all, the *mansìd* that the narcotic traders brought back to the Southsoil at the end of every summer were dry, stale, their potency gone. *Mansìd* leaves did not grow anywhere but on the Isthmus.

The thought didn't last long. She turned off the street, into a pub. She ordered tea and took a table. Spirits were for weak people looking to be strong by killing those perceptions in themselves that proved, day after repetitive day, that they were powerless. She did not drink. Wine and the like provided an illusion of clarity, when in truth clarity receded with every sip, until everything became a false comforting lullaby.

The pub was fairly crowded, and that crowd was talkative. Radstac listened.

The landlord apparently didn't care for her taking up a valuable seat while drinking only her single cup of tea, which she nursed nearly an entire watch. When she finally grew tired of his malevolent glares, she crooked her finger at him, put her head close to his, and told him that blood that spurted from a suddenly opened heart was much darker than what one saw when, say, a face was sliced

wide. Then she smiled, which she knew was her most unnerving expression. The man hadn't come near her since.

In the meantime the effects of the small bite of the *mansìd* leaf had mostly worn off. As with everything else about
the narcotic, she handled the comedown ably.

"U'delph is a story. Something to frighten children. It
makes no *sense*." The overdressed merchant sported
ridiculous, elaborate facial hair—shaved here, waxed to
points there. Must have taken him the better part of his
morning to put his face together, and he was still old and
ugly, despite the fine clothes. Actually, Radstac thought,
most of this pub's clientele looked to be on the affluent
side.

Radstac had listened to the talk. It was dismaying. It
was intentional blindness, not to see what was so surely
coming. Sook was doubtlessly the next target for the Felk.
It would put them one more city-state closer to Petgrad,
though still some distance away.

"It's reliable news," said a man in a grey cowl. His
voice was strong but neutral. Radstac hadn't been able to
get a good look at his face, but his body was firm, and he
moved in a way that spoke of sword training.

"Reliable." The merchant made it a contemptible word.
"What does that mean?"

"It means credible, believable, trustworthy." His tone
was as flat as before. The effect was droll, and a few titters
rose among the assembled drinkers. A pair planted in one
corner was playing a round of Dashes—one of those juvenile Isthmuser games of chance—as if to emphasize their
blasé attitudes.

The merchant's face moved in a way that caused the
points of his mustache to sneer. "I know the definition,
lad." Half to himself he muttered, "By the sanity of the
gods, when I was a youth, we didn't handle our elders so."
He took a swallow of beer, fixed the younger man again
with scornful eyes. "What I question is the degree of credibility, believability . . . and trustworthiness."

It hung there for a heartbeat, like a challenge.

"I don't bring the news personally," the hooded man said, utterly unruffled. "I comment on news we've all heard. Everyone, here in the city."

"To hear rumor and tradespeople's gossip is not to hear truth." The merchant pronounced this like he was quoting a verse of sacred wisdom.

Something flared red in Radstac's almost colorless eyes.

"And to spew shit like that," she said, a low growl that carried into every corner of the place, "is to say *nothing*."

She had sat still and quiet for quite some time now. She had come into this reasonably posh pub specifically to take the pulse of these merchants—these people who had much to lose if Petgrad were invaded and captured by the Felk. And now had heard enough.

Every head turned, including the one under the cowl.

Radstac pushed off her seat, standing, finally allowing her pent-up contempt to show on her scarred features.

"I can't make up my mind if you're all ignorant, out-right stupid, or just cowards."

"Now that's—" It was the landlord, lumbering over, not about to let her go on insulting his spending customers.

She whirled, reached out over the bartop, clamped his knobby pink nose between her thumb and a knuckle of her forefinger and *twisted*. He yelped, then disappeared below the level of the serving counter. If he rose with a weapon, she would know it before the top of his head came back into view.

She wasn't done addressing the assembly, and they were all still staring. Some had the good sense to look scared.

"The war news comes. You all hear it. It washes down from the north, no different than news of crop failures in other cities—stories you place great faith in, seeing how there's a potential for profit there for some of you. You know what you hear of the Felk is true. You know this war is categorically different from those you've known in the past. Different from those your grandmothers and grandfathers knew. This is a war beyond the scope of you childish Isthmusers. And yet it's real. And it's coming this way. Frightens you, doesn't it? Petrifies you. Because by the time the Felk reach here, they'll have absorbed the manpower and resources of gods know how many city-states. You'll be calling it the Felk *Empire* by then. And they've got magic on their side, and that's maybe most terrifying of all to you. They'll be unstoppable. Certainly more than a match for your army as it now stands. And you—you people of some wealth, maybe of some rank and power— what do you do? Sit on your asses, swill beer, and reassure yourselves that the danger doesn't exist. Stories for children you said, you pathetic fop?"

She might have spat then, might have hurled her cup into the faces turned her way. But her tirade had done nothing but make her disgust rise to a boil. They were still staring, still in shock. It was a fair guess that these merchants and landowners weren't often spoken to in this manner.

The landlord with the tweaked nose stayed out of sight as she marched out of the pub, using the exit that led to the latrine.

Evening had settled over Petgrad while she'd wasted time in the pub. Late summer light grew paler. High clouds were discussing the possibility of rain. Still, autumn was very near, maybe already here. It might be a winter war, depending on how long it lasted.

Insects buzzed out of her way as she emerged from the latrine stall.

She heard footsteps—someone not trying to move stealthily, someone waiting to use the pisser . . . or waiting for her.

He was turned from the spray of waning sunlight that spattered down into this unroofed nook alongside the pub. The grey hood showed only a solid jaw, the suggestion of lips twisted into something resembling a smile. He stood well, balanced so as to move in any direction, though the stance would appear entirely casual to a citizen's glance.

"The barkeeper asked me to see if you would give him his nose back."

"I dropped it in there. There's a hole in the floor, and it doesn't smell good down there."

"Well, Noseless Solly isn't such a bad moniker."

"Are we going to fight, fuck, or are you going to show me that face, you've been hiding and explain what you want from me?"

She smiled, that same disquieting expression.

He raised his hands, rolled the cowl off his face, and returned the smile. His was quite disarming. His face was what women would call rugged, not handsome. They stared a moment.

The moment lingered.

THE RUGGEDNESS OF his features, which offered soft bewitching blue eyes among hard planes and heavy bones, extended to his body as well. A solid physique, lean but wiry. Snaky muscles that coiled. Dueler's scars on the upper arms. Roughened hands.

Radstac liked how those rough hands handled her. She liked that Deo—so he gave her for his name—enjoyed being handled back. Males who imagined they were the unquestioned orchestrators of sex were the most tedious of partners . . . unless they changed their attitudes under her not especially gentle ministrations.

Deo had brought her to this opulent room. Carpeted floors, frivolous and costly looking art on the walls. A monstrously big bed. They had made use of its entire surface.

He wasn't, evidently, a postcoital cuddler. She was glad of that. Being nuzzled and having useless declarations murmured at her once the event had . . . uncorked—so the expression went—was irritating enough sometimes to cancel out the pleasure of the whole incident.

Neither, though, was Deo one of those that fled the scene immediately afterward—or, in this case, one that would evict her without delay. Instead, he climbed from the bed, stretched his naked body, pulling taut muscles even tighter, and padded over pale carpeting to a circular stone table where several colored bottles stood.

"What would make you happy?" His fingers lifted a varnished wood cup.

"Water."

He didn't give her a look, poured it, poured something dark purple for himself, and returned to the bed.

She took the cup and swallowed. She guessed him to be about her age, just at the start of his fourth tenwinter. His years hadn't been pampered; so his body attested. This room pointed to wealth, but he wasn't swollen and lazy. Wasn't like those wretched merchants in the pub, too afraid to even consider the possibility that their comfortable positions might be in jeopardy.

Deo had spoken against that one merchant, the one with the face hair. Well, maybe hadn't spoken *against*; more, he had acknowledged the legitimacy of the war news from the north. She had learned in that pub that Petgrad's military, despite the threat of the Felk, hadn't even been mobilized. Apparently this whole city was under a spell of obliviousness. It was infuriating, not the least because it was going to make it hard for her to find work here. She might have to push on farther north.

"Do you object to the word *mercenary* . . . or should I find another?" Deo asked.

"It's a perfectly fine word. I can never get *sell-sword* past my lips without lisping it."

He drank. She could smell it. Something alcoholic, but it didn't reek; an undertone of berries to it.

"You've seen more than one campaign."

"And you've outlived a duel or two."

He looked at her scars; some were more dramatic than others. She looked at his, tiny white stripes across his sleek, hard arms. She never minded anyone looking. Some got terribly aroused by the sight of her mistreated flesh. Once one of this particular ilk had turned dangerous. He would never be so again.

Her clothes—everything, armor, boots, her leather glove and its hooks—were scattered from the doorway to the foot of the bed, along with Deo's cowl and underclothing. No weapons in reach. This didn't bother her.

Staying here in the city would be the safe thing to do. That was an article of her personal code, the rules she had devised, the rules that her particular life had taught her. They wouldn't work for others. Most people didn't pay enough attention to their lives, didn't try to understand the *sense*; they just muddled along, not even aware enough to see how easily it could end. How quickly. How simply.

She sipped more water. It was purer even than the relatively clean supply in the public cisterns. She stretched her supine body on the immensely soft bed, hearing a vertebra pop.

"I like that. The smile. The real one."

She floated her eyes toward him. Do the safe thing. The safe thing was to stay in Petgrad and wait until someone purchased her services. Striking north now was risky. So was crossing over to the Felk side to sell her sword. The Felk didn't need mercenaries, not at this point, not after they'd absorbed substantial troop numbers from their earlier conquests.

"I wasn't aware I was smiling," she said.

"Exactly. I also like your accent."

"We don't have accents. You do."

"Fair enough. It's very subtle. I've met Southsoilers, a lot of them. I've always wanted to hire one as a storyteller, just to hear that enunciation. Wouldn't matter in the least what the story was."

"Must be amusing to be able to afford a . . . storyteller."

"Said I wanted to hire one. Didn't say I had the money."

This wordplay was, she thought, almost as enjoyable as the sex. How odd that was. And how fantastically rare. Good lovers almost never made good conversationalists. Deo drank more of his purple drink, lounging back on a few of the bed's abundant pillows.

"What *is* the matter with these people?" she asked, as if picking up a thread of conversation from earlier. "Those merchants in that pub . . . don't they realize a Felk onslaught is inevitable?"

"Do you actually think resistance could be successful?"

"I don't know. I don't make it my business to know. I don't hire myself out as an officer or a strategist. I'm a fighter. Personally, I'm quite successful."

"Always pick the winning side?"

Her barking laugh was, she knew, something like her normal smile—disconcerting.

"Hardly," she said. "But wars don't go on until every last soldier is slain. One head of state or the other surrenders or capitulates to terms, usually well before the slaughter gets irreversibly messy. I fight for whichever side hires me. I fight well. I fight till someone says stop. I don't win the wars or lose them. I participate."

His laugh was much warmer than hers. His blue eyes moved over her body again, not lingering on the scars.

"Everyone's afraid," Deo said. "Yes. Everyone. It's war, but it's not war that we recognize. You pointed that out yourself, rather articulately I thought."

"I thought so as well."

"I was in disguise at that pub for the same reason you were there—to sound out the views of the people. I've been doing it a lot lately and keep encountering the same thing."

"How can that be?"

"The people have good lives here in Petgrad. We've had generations of reasonable prosperity. We like things stable, grounded. Why upset a good thing? This war, these

Felk . . . they'll upset it. Most certainly. But the people won't face it."

"So"—her hand glided out, her finger tracing a vein along his firm shoulder—"I've wasted a journey here."

"Wasted?" He gave her a wry, mock-injured look.

"An unhired mercenary is somebody walking about with a sword and nowhere to stick it."

"Where *is* your sword?"

"Public Armory." She felt a yawn overtake her. The bed was ethereally soft and comfortable.

"You'd better go retrieve it, then." Deo's gaze pulled her drifting eyes back open. "I wish to hire you. I should also tell you who I am."

"Someone with the money to afford a mercenary, I hope."

"Yes. That. I am also Nâ Niroki Deo." He hadn't expected her to recognize the full title. "I'm the nephew of the premier of Petgrad."

RAVEN
(1)

"WELL, GO ON. Walk through it."

Raven recognized the bullying tone even before she identified the voice's owner. This wasn't the first time she'd been harassed.

The mocking command was followed immediately and inevitably by a firm hand backed by a strong arm that shoved her face-first into the corridor's stone wall. The stone was cold. It was always cold, even in summer. This was Felk, after all, the Isthmus's northernmost city, and its climate wasn't as gentle as it was rumored to be in the south.

There was nothing gentle about this place in particular. This was the Academy.

Raven didn't try to turn her head. She heard laughter and counted at least three among her assailants.

"I can't," Raven said, slowly and deliberately. She knew it did no good to show either fear or defiance.

"Of *course* you can," said the girl who now had her

tightly pinned. The girl was called Hert, and she certainly lived up to her name. "You're a wizard, aren't you?"

"She sure thinks she is," said one of the others. More laughter followed.

"I'm not," Raven said, as steadily as before, keeping control over her fear. Discipline was key to everything. "I'm in training. Just like you."

"Oh, but you're so smart," said Hert. "So talented. You're the one who always wants the toughest exercises. If it was up to you, we'd all spend every watch studying and practicing. No sleep, no food. Not even a piss break."

It wasn't true. But Raven didn't expect the others to share her zeal. Many of the Academy's students behaved like undisciplined children. She behaved like a student who meant to graduate to greater things. Much greater things.

The hand pressed her harder. Raven's forehead and nose were now being mashed against the wall.

"I said, walk through the wall."

"I can't." Raven could barely get the words out. She tasted the wall's stone on her lips.

"Oh, come on," Hert said. "It's just a transport spell. You can do it. And we want to see." The laughter that followed was louder and crueler.

Raven sighed. She didn't have time for this. The long day's lessons were done, but she had studying to do in her room.

Just a transport spell. That was laughable, though Raven certainly didn't join in the laughter. The Far Movement magic that opened the portals through which people and even military equipment (so the gossip went) could be moved was very powerful. Only highly skilled and specialized mages could work it, and it required more than one wizard to do it. A mage had to be present at both ends of the transport corridor; the two had to be working in perfect harmony; they had to call upon powers far beyond Raven's present abilities. And even with all these efforts, they could only open portals that were very narrow—just enough, say, for a wagon to get through—and those portals could only be sustained for a limited time.

There was no point in mentioning any of this to Hert, however.

"Do it," Hert was saying, and now her tone turned darker with the promise of impending violence. "Do it!"

There were monitors who patrolled the corridors, but none were nearby at the moment. Of course.

Raven was going to have to do *something*.

She sighed again, then started gathering herself. She focused her mind and reached for those forces that aided in the acts of magic. Those forces, she'd been taught, were natural and always present. It was just a matter of tapping them, though it required a certain inherent talent and a great deal of discipline. Raven possessed both those ingredients.

She felt the power move through her in a kind of giddy rush.

Suddenly a discharge of sparks burst around her head. Her unbecoming dark hair rose up on end.

The hand left her back. Someone gasped sharply.

Raven let the minor spell dissipate. At last she turned, being careful to wear an apologetic look on her somewhat homely face.

"I'm sorry," she said. "I tried but I couldn't get through the wall."

Hert, who was as large as Raven but far more muscular, retreated a step, then caught herself. It wouldn't do to show any weakness in front of her cronies. Probably she would punch Raven now, just for good measure.

But luck, finally, was on Raven's side. A monitor came around the corner at that moment, waving one of those paddles they so generously used on students' backsides. Everyone scattered. Raven made straight for her quarters.

o   o   o

RAVEN LEANED BACK on her stool and rubbed her burning eyes. She had no idea what time it was or how long she had been poring over her studies, and she really didn't care. She was determined not to sleep until she had mastered the lesson they'd spent the day studying.

Though there was no test scheduled for tomorrow, that was no guarantee that there wouldn't be one. Unannounced tests were the norm, not the exception for magicians in training. What was more, since the tests were often of a practical rather than a theoretical nature, failing one could be injurious, if not actually fatal.

Rising to her feet, Raven stretched and walked a few steps, all the movement her cramped cubicle would allow. Students' cubicles were designed to be utilitarian, not comfortable. Hers was barely large enough to accommodate a sleeping pallet, her study desk and stool, and a chamber pot.

There was no mirror. The Academy didn't provide one, and Raven had seen no point in purchasing one for herself. She already knew what she looked like.

Her mother had named her Raven in hopes that the girl child would grow to match her own grace and beauty. The truth was, her mother had always been very proud of her own good looks. It was her beauty that once caught the eye of a rich and powerful man of the city of Felk and moved him to relocate her from her small village home into his bed as his mistress.

She had fulfilled that role willingly and with enthusiasm for many years, until she had become pregnant. At that time, her lover "retired" her, but with a stipend that enabled her to return to her old home and set herself up comfortably without having to work.

As her looks began to fade at last, she had hopes that her daughter would blossom and follow in her footsteps.

Unfortunately, it was not to be. Raven had been a chubby baby, and rather than melting away when she matured, her baby fat solidified and grew. Despite her mother's admonishments to "stand up straight" and "arch your back, don't sit there like a lump," Raven grew from being a plump, awkward girl to being a plump, awkward young woman with stringy dark hair. She had also never grown beyond a very modest height.

Friends might have made her situation bearable, but she didn't have any. Her mother always held herself aloof and apart from the other villagers, feeling her years among the rich made her better than the rustic, rural folk she had grown up with.

The villagers responded to this attitude with undisguised scorn, which their children emulated in their own fashion by taunting, teasing, and socially debasing the young Raven every chance they got.

Denied any affection by those around her, Raven had retreated into her fantasies. Her mother had insisted that she learn to read, believing it was prerequisite for anyone hoping to someday move among the nobler set, and Raven proved to be an eager student. Quickly mastering the basics, she devoured any text or writing that came her way, and took to writing her own when the limited supply of new material was exhausted.

Turning a blind eye to her actual surroundings, Raven fashioned a dream world she could retreat to at will, a world built from bits and pieces she had heard or read about, other lands and the Isthmus's various city-states. The nearest city to her little village was Felk, where her mother had once lived with her father. It was an old city, and a large one, and thus fascinating to the lonesome, homely girl.

There was one fantasy in particular that she cherished and held dear: Someday she would seek out her father, and he would shower on her the affection and approval that her mother never gave her.

That fantasy had particular allure, because, if her mother were to be believed at all, her father was none other than Lord Matokin himself.

As early as Raven could remember, the mage was known as one of the most powerful men in Felk. Now the entire city-state belonged to him. He had risen to power rapidly, promising great things for Felk's future, promising to expand the state's territory.

The people had embraced him, investing him with the power to build up the military. Matokin was a magician and did nothing to hide his prowess at wizardry. In fact, he displayed it boldly, despite the Isthmus's cultural tradition of shunning the art. Magic, he had promised, was the key to Felk's ultimate triumph. The people believed his promises, and look how mighty Felk had grown! The army had gone southward, capturing other cities, swelling Felk's borders.

The very thought of being accepted by this potent man as his daughter was enough to give Raven added determination to see her dream come true.

When she had finally announced her intention to travel to Felk and apply to the school for magicians that Matokin had founded, there was surprisingly little resistance. Her mother had long since given up any hope of her daughter becoming a beauty and was increasingly at a loss to envision a role for her in life.

Raven's idea, though something her mother had never considered herself, had no small merit. Even if her daughter proved to have little or no talent for the magical arts, there was a far greater chance of her meeting someone to take care of her in Felk than if she remained where she was. As such, she sent Raven off with a small but respectable purse of silver that she had been saving, and far more enthusiasm than Raven had ever seen her display in the past.

Folklore had it that natural magical ability tended to appear most often among the nobility. This was supported by the fact that Matokin's closest political underlings were almost entirely picked from Felk's aristocracy. However, hidden talents turned up in odd places, and this seemed particularly true of magic.

Raven rested her head briefly on her arms and smiled at the memory of her own naïveté when she had arrived in Felk and first presented herself at the Academy for testing. She recalled being puzzled when the testers showed surprise at her voluntary effort to enroll.

Of course, at that time, she was unaware of the rumors that were now virtually accepted as fact. Specifically, that those having some capacity for magic, but of insufficient degree to invest training in, had a way of disappearing or suffering fatal accidents shortly after they were rejected.

It seemed that Matokin was disinclined to have unaffiliated magic potential wandering the lands he controlled, however minor that potential was deemed to be. As a result, the number of those willingly submitting to the testing dwindled to a trickle and finally all but ceased entirely, requiring the implementation of roaming testers to find new students for the Academy. These feared individuals traveled the countryside encompassing Felk.

Far from being repelled by these methods, Raven was struck with awe. How powerful a man he must indeed be, how sure of his vision, to act so drastically and decisively.

The Academy itself was a grim affair, a campus more resembling a fortress or prison, than a school. A high stone wall circled it, and the buildings within those walls that held classrooms and living quarters had a dull sameness about them.

The growing empire needed magicians, and students were hurried and badgered through their lessons and tests to fill that need. Felk was growing. The war had begun its southward push to take all of the Isthmus; for that was Matokin's goal. It was a heady thought, an exciting time to be alive . . . if one could remain so.

What was more, as they were learning to manage and control the powerful forces of wizardry, they had to also constantly affirm and reaffirm their loyalty to Matokin.

Students were bound to the Academy by blood vows, literal ones, where blood was taken from a deliberately pricked finger, labeled with the student's name, and stored. It was said the blood could be used to bring harm or death to its source from then on, no matter where he or she was. It was a fine means of encouraging loyalty.

Raven, of course, had gladly surrendered her sample. She was already bound to Matokin by blood, she thought secretly, or at least, so she believed. Let her mother have been right about that one thing!

The students were also encouraged to inform on each other and even on their instructors, reporting any comment or action nonsupportive of empire policy, no matter how innocent or jesting. If it was learned that a student had failed to report such a comment, they were judged as or more guilty than the person offering the original offense.

At the age of nineteen, after two years of training, Raven was adept at dealing with the wariness and backbiting that was so pervasive in the Academy. If anything, her childhood had given her a head start at adapting. She didn't have to unlearn the habits of friendship. The bullies at the Academy weren't especially different from the ones in her home village, so they were fairly easy to ignore when they weren't directly harassing her.

She certainly had no difficulty devoting herself entirely to Matokin and the empire policies he set forth through his administrators. Before arriving at Felk, she had decided to keep her belief that she was his daughter a secret. To announce it upon her arrival would appear too much like she was trying to curry favor.

Instead, she sought to be noticed for her devotion and growing skills. When and if she was ever singled out for his personal notice, that would be the time to mention her kinship. More than anything, Raven wanted her sire to be *proud* of her. Keeping her relationship to him a secret until she had proven herself could only intensify that moment.

Raven's head came up with a start. There was predawn

light showing in the corridor outside her cubicle! Against all her good intentions, she had dozed off.

Panic and self-recriminations were useless. Her disciplined mind swung smoothly into dealing with this new set of circumstances. She had yet to master yesterday's lesson, a slightly more powerful version of the static electricity spell she'd already learned. If a test were sprung upon the class, she would perform poorly.

For her own safety and continuation at the school, she would have to gain some time. Perhaps some kind of a diversion.

She could denounce someone. She always kept a few choice incidents in reserve that she could produce if necessary, and the removal of a student or instructor usually threw the Academy into a turmoil for at least one day. Still, if one did that too frequently, it simply tended to cast suspicion on the accuser.

Maybe a training accident. They were not uncommon and not that difficult to arrange. Something that would make them empty the classroom or the entire school for a watch or two. In two years here, she had learned more than just her lessons.

It might look suspicious if Hert was the one involved in the accident. Then again, the girl bullied many students, not just Raven. Frowning with concentration, Raven continued to review her options. Only one thing was certain. Absolutely nothing was going to stand in the way of her earning her father's love.

BRYCK
(2)

HE KEPT THE grey at a calm lope, even as he spied the soldiers ahead at the entrance into the city. He had gained some practice in exuding the cool of a seasoned wanderer, though in his previous life he'd done little traveling—and when he had, he'd been moved about in appropriate style. With an entourage, in the comfort of an enclosed coach; certainly not rambling alone on horseback, a bedroll beneath the stars more often than not his berth for the night.

Many days' determined riding had brought him deep into the territory of the Felk. Now he was at the entry into Callah, the first of the cities to have fallen in this war.

He shifted the vox-mellifluous slightly with a shrug of his shoulders. He was by now rather accustomed to having the instrument strapped across his back. It twanged faintly with each step his horse took, knocking softly against his backbone.

He'd bought the instrument at a roadside inn. As a part of his daily routine, he made sure to practice. It wasn't just a matter of reacquainting himself with music-making and the lyrics that went along with the songs he knew; it was acclimating himself to this particular instrument.

A troubadour and his implement should seem as one, Bryck knew.

Since he had started moving north, he had played the stringbox at several inns along the way. It was one thing to play for his horse, which was courteous and attentive; another to play for an audience. The first time he'd started cranking the winder and fingering the strings, he was nervous, aware that he had everyone's ear in the place. Once that would have been the natural state of things.

Bryck of U'delph, playwright and noble, was often the focus of any gathering of people—be they guests to his villa or companions at the taverns he frequented. His store of anecdotes and witticisms was effectively inexhaustible, and his ability to keep people laughing in the flesh was perhaps as keen as his talent for amusing the audiences of the theatricals he penned.

But Bryck of U'delph was, figuratively, no more. Just as U'delph was quite literally no more.

The city-state had originally been laid out in a spiral, a single uninterrupted chain of structures that started at the east end and wound continuously inward. During U'delph's long, proud history, many other buildings had been erected, jostling for space as the city prospered and grew. That original fanciful spiral was all but eradicated and made sense only when one studied a map, eliminating every structure put up during the past hundredwinter or so.

The city had been built on a broad prairie. With each and every multistoried building and tower now out of the way, Bryck had seen the spiral traced out clearly in the scorched foundations that were the blackened bones of his home.

He had made the return journey in something near to half the time it had taken him to get to Sook. He had run his horse brutally for home, stopping only for a single watch when his vision had come over white and he fainted, exhausted, in the saddle. He'd encountered no Felk along the way—perhaps miraculously, perhaps merely due to blind luck.

Rain had come, and no smoke rose in the windless midday. There was nothing left down there to burn anyway. The smell was terrible.

Six days of safety before the Felk arrived. Six days, the scouts had said.

His villa was down there on the blackened prairie as well. Involuntarily his eyes strayed toward the spot, in the city's affluent westward quarter. Yes, there it was, with scarcely one stone standing atop another. Ashes and rubble.

He could have searched that debris. He could have entered that maze of rubble and sifted the wreckage. He could have uncovered, surely, tiny fragments of memorabilia, items scorched beyond recognition to any eyes but his. He would find remnants and shards. He would pick out pieces of furnishings and know what the articles had once looked like. He would find bones and, with some effort, likely be able to identify their owners.

His wife, Aaysue. His children, Bron, Cerk, Ganet, little Gremmest.

U'delph's population had been roughly twenty-five thousand. By the madness of the gods, such a slaughter. Slaughtered and abandoned, for the Felk had moved onward.

Atop his horse and upon the mild rise at U'delph's south end, Bryck was given a fine view. A lone thought beat in his skull. Actually it was less a thought, more a raw naked impulse. Unrelenting. Potent.

Vengeance.

Against the Felk, who had taken everything from him. Vengeance, because nature demanded it of him. Were this a drama and he a player, he would be overwhelmingly propelled into the role of avenger. He would not disappoint. What he required was a *suitable* vengeance, something worthwhile, something that both matched his natural talents and would inflict the greatest damage on his enemies.

It was now half a lune since the fall of U'delph. Rumors along the road said the Felk had camped some while south of the devastated city-state, then moved against Sook, which had unequivocally surrendered. Evidently U'delph was an object lesson, and the people of Sook, led by that gaggle of ministers he'd once found so amusing, had learned that lesson well.

Such thoughts evaporated as he neared the small unit of soldiery waiting ahead. Beyond lay Callah, an impressive expanse of streets and buildings, though not as imposing as, say, U'delph, which was something near to twice this city's size. It wasn't a walled city, but no doubt each connecting road was guarded, and its perimeter probably patrolled as well.

He saw only one damaged structure, at the outskirts, a building whose roof had been burned off. A demolition crew was at work on it, salvaging its usable stones. Perhaps it was left over from the Felk's original assault against the city.

Bryck had been in Felk territory some while now. One could almost feel it, like a dark disquieting weight. Territories and state borders did occasionally shift, but rarely so dramatically. The Felk had advanced substantially southward. What had relatively recently been only a large city-state was now more the size of an empire. And still no one seemed to know what the Felk ultimately intended with these aggressive military actions. There were those Bryck had met or overheard during his travels who believed the Northerners meant to conquer the entire Isthmus. Others speculated that the future held more atrocities like U'delph's annihilation.

When Bryck had first encountered a detachment of Felk soldiers, they had interrogated him. Their job was to see that all who used the particular stretch of road they guarded had license to do so. Their real task, of course,

was to make sure no fugitives fled southward. They were
a bit perplexed by Bryck, who was riding north, *into* the
new expanded Felk territories. He explained that he was a
roving minstrel, that he hoped to continue northward, as
this was his habitual route. He made it clear that he cared
nothing about the war.

That attitude had precedent. Troubadours were traditionally neutral. Music knew few national boundaries. For
hundredwinters, even during the Isthmus's most notorious
strife-filled times, musicians of this ilk had moved unmolested. In some regions it was considered severe bad luck
to interfere with a troubadour.

Of course, he'd had to prove he was a minstrel by playing several songs.

That first contingent of Felk soldiers, though, had eventually issued him a civilian travel pass and let him through.
That pass was a sheet of vellum on which had been dribbled hot yellow wax; in the center of that congealing blob,
the Felk sergeant had imprinted some complicated shape
with a small metal stamp. It wouldn't give Bryck unre-
stricted movement within the new Felk territory, but it
would ensure that he wouldn't be summarily executed.
The army was on alert for dissidents, deserters, and other
runaways. Troubadours apparently weren't viewed as a
threat.

Bryck now reined in his grey steed. He felt fortunate
that no one had conscripted the horse. He raised an empty
hand in the customary traveler's greeting. His other hand
reached slowly into his coat to withdraw the wax-blotched
sheet of vellum.

There were five soldiers in the Felk unit waiting at the
road's terminus. From the deep ruts in the packed earth
under his horse's hooves, Bryck guessed that this was a
major transit artery—or had been; there certainly wasn't
much traffic on it now. Surely the Felk occupation had disrupted or even ended normal trade and travel. Indeed, he'd

seen no other civilians at all on the road for days, this far
into Felk territory.

Despite the disquiet of being so deep inside enemy
lines, he'd seen no fighting, and the soldiers he encountered were occupiers, not combatants.

Fields of summer-yellowed grasses lay on either side of
the roadway. Stones were gathered to make a fire pit, and
there was presently something aromatic simmering in a
bell-shaped pot over the flames. There was a water tub,
laundry swaying in the breeze. Two of the soldiers were
playing Dashes atop a small makeshift table contrived
from a pair of supporting rocks and a shield laid across.
Dashes was a game one played with cards, dice, and a
good deal of underhanded cunning. Bryck had once been
quite a deft player, even when he didn't sweeten his odds
with a little subtle wizardry.

The five-strong unit looked like it had been at this post
some while. It appeared to be rather light duty. They had
shed most of their armor and made do with uniform tunics,
though all were wearing their swords. The sergeant strode
forward for Bryck's offered travel pass, barely acknowledging his presence with a swift sweep of her bland eyes.
Behind her another of the Felk soldiers—this one male,
nearer Bryck's age, with an intense air about him—eyed
him more keenly.

The imprint in the yellow wax was complex and would
have been difficult, if not impossible, to counterfeit. A
glance seemed to convince the sergeant of its authenticity,
but she held on to it anyway.

"Get off that horse." She sounded bored, not hostile.

Bryck climbed off. The other soldier continued to study
him in a way that was becoming uncomfortable.

"What is that?" asked the sergeant, peering over his
shoulder.

"Vox-mellie." No self-respecting troubadour would
refer to the instrument as either a "vox-mellifluous," its

formal name, or "stringbox," the nickname anybody but a troubadour would use.

"So, give us your best." She gestured for the attention of the pair playing Dashes and another soldier lethargically whetting his sword blade on a stool by the cooking fire.

Without lifting off the canvas tether, Bryck worked the instrument around to the front of his body, pausing briefly to tune a string, then launched into a number. His relentless practicing was paying off. Already his fingering had improved measurably. More important than that perhaps, was that he could now play on demand. He didn't need the spirit to move him, didn't need to be in a musical mood; if someone gave him coin (or in this case, ordered him), he could produce an entertaining song.

Which is what he proceeded to do, wishing as he had several times recently that his repertoire was more extensive. He knew a fine abundance of suggestive drinking songs, but a knowledge of some more traditional verses would strengthen the illusion of his being a professional songster.

He wasn't entirely over his stage fright. But he'd recalled a bit of sage advice thespians gave each other to combat such nervousness. Play your role to a lone individual in the audience and ignore everybody else. The first time he'd played at an inn, he'd done just that, picking out a child, a girl, apparently traveling with a family of merchants. She was staring at him, large eyes following the movements of his somewhat bumbling fingers with fascination.

Bryck had played for her and her alone, and that somehow steadied his fingering of the strings, evened his voice. Actually his singing voice wasn't entirely miserable; it even had a certain flair, after a fashion. He performed a few of the more respectable ballads he knew, in deference to the young girl—three or four winters old—who was his audience. It definitely wouldn't do to belt out "Silda's Maidenhead" or "Man Drowned in Ale" for her. The girl seemed thoroughly enthralled, clapping small, chubby hands, giggling loudly. That, Bryck found, was gratifying.

So were the extra coins that appeared on his table as he'd played onward, enough to buy him a bed for the night, though he still had quite a few coins secreted in the lining of his coat. Aaysue had insisted he take the money with him on his heroic venture to Sook.

It was also gratifying that day that his audience had accepted him as a legitimate troubadour. It was essential to his entire scheme that he pass as one.

It was a full day later, riding north once more, that he had realized that the little girl at the inn reminded him of his daughter, Gremmest. That had made his throat go hot and thick. His youngest child had also enjoyed watching him play the stringbox.

These Felk soldiers didn't appear to care overmuch what Bryck played. They seemed interested in him only as a distraction from what must be a dull, if soft, assignment. The ribald wit of the lyrics he sang got an occasional chuckle, but by the third tune, the pair were back to their game of Dashes, and the soldier on the stool was stirring the pot over the fire.

Only the man standing behind the sergeant was still paying close attention. This was hardly Bryck's first checkpoint; he knew enough how to behave in the presence of armed warriors.

In the presence of the enemy . . .

The thought beat—controlled but indestructible—behind his carefully flat expression. These were Felk soldiers. As ordinary and perhaps benign as they appeared here, these were the same creatures that had laid waste to U'delph, sparing only a handful of witnesses who had spread the stories of the city-state's destruction. Bryck had heard the stories on the road, tales of the Felk army appearing impossibly from the very air. If it was indeed magic, it was of a kind far beyond any he knew.

That these five particular soldiers had likely been manning this same post when U'delph was being annihilated meant, ultimately, little. Perhaps nothing. Felk were alike. They had to be. For the purposes of his vengeance they were as one. His hatred for them was expansive enough to accommodate them all.

Hatred. For what had been done to his home, his people, his family. That hatred had sired his thirst for vengeance. Killing all five of these soldiers—though he had no weapon with which to do such a thing—would be entirely justified, when compared with the numbers slaughtered at U'delph.

But his plan called for a different procedure; and so he played on until the sergeant brusquely returned him his travel pass and turned her back.

Bryck had at first been quite surprised how relatively easy movement was for him. He had yet to be thoroughly searched at any of these checkpoints, which was why he retained his cache of coin. Surely the folk taboo about meddling with a minstrel couldn't account for it. Then he'd realized that his masquerading as a troubadour was only an effective means of moving *one* individual within these Felk-held lands; for what damage, must be the thinking, could a lone individual do?

So he had asked himself when he'd concocted his scheme.

As he made to mount his horse, the older male soldier stepped forward.

"You play it well."

Bryck nodded a civil bow but said nothing.

"You'll have to present yourself at the Registry," said the soldier. He recited the street where it was located. "How long will you be here in Callah?"

Bryck had been questioned about his plans a number of times by now. "Stay until winter. As I've done this past tenwinter and more."

The soldier was still studying him intently. "I don't recall you," he said eventually.

Again Bryck kept silent, though now he felt a cool wave of uneasiness wash over him. The others, even the sergeant, were no longer paying him any attention.

"I am . . . from Callah," the soldier said, finding some difficulty with the words. Bryck imagined he understood. The man was a Callahan, a native to this first city the Felk had conquered. He had evidently been absorbed into their army. That he'd gone happily or even willingly was unlikely; yet here he stood, in a Felk uniform, serving the military apparatus that had subdued his homeland.

At least that home hadn't been burned to the ground and nearly every inhabitant butchered, Bryck thought grimly, noting the mostly intact buildings in the background, the denizens scurrying about the streets, very much alive.

"I knew quite a few of the troubadours that paid regular visits to the city," the Callahan went on. "What is your name?"

"Goll." Bryck had chosen the false name on a whim. It belonged to a very minor character from one of his own earliest theatricals. During this past half-lune he hadn't spoken his true name aloud to anyone. He was content to go unrecognized as Bryck of U'delph, renowned writer of stage comedies. Certainly he never intended to pen another. His life as a dramatist was as dead as his home.

"I don't recall you," he repeated.

Sweat was gathering beneath the collar of Bryck's coarse coat. The breeze rose, cooling it and chilling him. He itched to step his foot into the stirrup and ride onward.

Suddenly the man from Callah was patting the pockets of his tunic. A brass coin appeared in his hand. He held it out toward Bryck.

"Here." His eyes were moistening. He spoke in a hush that none of the others would overhear. "Had you come to my city . . . to my beautiful Callah . . . and had I sat and listened to you weave your music, as I once enjoyed listening to so many others of your kind, I would have applauded you. I would have given you this same coin."

Bryck accepted the brass, at an utter loss as to how to respond. Luckily he was spared the difficulty as the Callahan/Felk soldier turned sharply away.

Bryck at last climbed into the saddle and rode on into the city.

DARDAS
(2)

IT WAS GOOD to be at war. Even a war like this one, even with wizards everywhere underfoot, even (this was most galling) with those same magicians providing Dardas with the most amazing resources he'd ever known in combat.

Still, he didn't enjoy explaining himself, even second-hand, to Matokin, the leader of the Felk. The feats of his army's communication mages were remarkable. They called the magic Far Speak, and they could pass messages instantaneously across great distances, all the way back to Felk itself. It was a less strenuous, but ultimately no less impressive, accomplishment than moving troops, horses, and equipment through those portals.

However, it meant that Dardas couldn't get free of Matokin, not even here in the field, where he was well accustomed to having an absolutely free hand.

In his time as a Northland military leader, he had answered to no one at all. He hadn't represented a monarch or a sovereign state. His army *was* his nation, and his companies of fierce warriors were his nation's population. He had led them to glorious victories on the Northern Continent, and their loyalty had been total.

Now, he was commanding an army again, two and a half hundredwinters after his own death. Once again, he was proving himself a successful commander, as his victories attested.

Sook had surrendered unconditionally without offering the slightest resistance, leaving Dardas with an army that was geared to a fighting pitch and no enemy to match itself against.

Objectively, it was the ideal situation for a commander. To accomplish one's goal without a single casualty or fatality.

While he had acknowledged the possibility, Dardas was nonetheless caught unprepared when the delegation of eight ministers from Sook had appeared, throwing the city-state on his merçies. Instead of dealing with scouting reports, skirmishes, and preparations for a siege, the general had suddenly instead found himself plunged into the details of taking control of a city-state that was intact and cooperative.

Occupying territories had never been his forte in his previous life. For Sook he had merely implemented the rules of occupation already in place for Callah and Windal. His army was presently encamped outside the city.

He was disappointed. What was wrong with these gods-damned Isthmusers? Didn't they have any backbone? Didn't they understand that if they didn't resist, he would subdue this entire land for Matokin?

And then . . . what would happen to him, once the last battle was fought and the army didn't need its general anymore?

I don't think the officers are in total agreement with your theories about sharing the food of the common soldiers.

By now, Dardas was used to his host-mind's thoughts

intruding on his own. As weak as the voice and the personality behind it were, they was still present in Dardas's head.

It was truly amazing that Weisel was still dwelling on the issue of eating troop rations.

They may not agree, Lord Weisel, but they'll go along with it . . . and be better officers for the experience.

It was a subdued gathering, not at all like the high spirits that had followed the slaughter of U'delph, when most, if not all, of these officers had gotten their first real taste of blood lust. That had been more than half a lune ago now.

Dardas covertly studied the senior officers assembled around the campfire as he busied himself consuming the soldier's rations on his plate. They were talking quietly together in groups of two or three, or sitting alone lost in thought as they addressed themselves to their own lackluster meals.

I should think you'd want your officers to be happy. Happy officers are less likely to mutiny.

Happy is one thing. Smug and complacent is another. Besides, new officers have to be taught what they should be happy about. Wallowing in special privileges is pointless if the troops under you are discontent.

He eyed the small knot of magicians standing together at the edge of the gathering. As usual, they rarely spoke, even to each other, and almost never smiled. *There's a group that's primed for mutiny, privileges or no. If I were Matokin, I'd be keeping an eye on my underlings, and sleeping very light.*

But the magicians are supposed to be unswervingly loyal to Matokin. I've heard they were screened for loyalty before being admitted to the magic school, the Academy. Besides, they're all bound by blood oaths and wouldn't dare to move against him.

That may be so, but I know discontent individuals when I see them.

Perhaps. Who knows how wizards think?

Weisel's thought was dismissive, almost indifferent.

He was an idiot, Dardas thought, but Weisel would never be aware of the thought. Dardas had surprised himself with the strides he'd made in acclimating his resurrected self to living in this new body. He had gradually raised mental blocks against Weisel, exerting his will in ways he hadn't known he could. By now the Felk noble was boxed into a corner of their supposedly shared mind.

What was more, Dardas was certain that Weisel wasn't even aware of the situation. The man had effectively lost himself and didn't know it. Dardas felt that soon, very soon, he would, if he so chose, be able to simply snuff Weisel into nothingness.

But there was no point in hastiness. The idiot might be useful for something.

"Berkant," Dardas called, having finished his meal.

The mage, a youngish man with an honest unaffected expression on his face, looked up sharply. He, too, was done eating. He came quickly but uneasily toward the general.

"Yes, General Weisel?"

Dardas kept his tone casual. "Any communications from Felk?" He knew there had been none. Berkant was in charge of relaying Far Speak messages directly from Matokin, and he naturally wasted no time delivering them. These wizards, loyal or not, plainly lived in fear of the Felk leader.

"No communications, General," Berkant said.

Dardas nodded. "Come with me—oh, if you've finished your meal?"

Berkant blinked at the general's unexpected magnanimity.

"I have, General."

"Good. Come to my pavilion. I may be charging my officers to eat regular rations, but they're free to drink whatever they can procure for themselves. As it happens, I myself have a fine bottle of something." Dardas was aware of the curious stares of the other officers that followed as they strolled to the tent.

Berkant was nervous, but Dardas wasn't without charisma and charm. He poured out two glasses, and they sat.

Dardas kept the talk initially about military matters, specifically communications. Far Speak mages had been installed in Callah, Windal, and now Sook, naturally, so that Matokin could receive direct reports about the status of the occupied cities of his growing empire.

Berkant relaxed a bit. The liquor was strong, but had such a mellow taste it snuck up on a person unprepared for it.

"Berkant," Dardas said finally, "it may be you can't answer what I'd like to know. I don't know if Matokin has placed restrictions on what information I should be privy to." He shrugged, as if to indicate that it was all right with him if he was so restricted. "But I would like to know something about magic."

"Magic?" Berkant said, his open face suddenly closing tightly.

Yes, thought Dardas darkly. That Felk bleeder Matokin meant to keep him ignorant.

These thoughts didn't show on Dardas's face. "Not the mechanics of magic," he explained airily. "It makes no difference to me how you wizards work your spells. I'm impressed by it all, to be sure. But, no. I'm interested only in the *history* of magic. It wasn't a field of study my tutors made much fuss about."

"I see, General Weisel." Berkant mulled it over a moment. "Well, perhaps I can enlighten you. Magic, of course, is a purely natural talent, one that has been with our species since it learned to speak. Maybe before. It—"

Already he was warming to the subject. Dardas let the mage ramble awhile. He seemed to enjoy holding forth. Probably Dardas was the only member of this military outside the circle of wizards who'd ever engaged him so in conversation. The animus between the army's regular numbers and its magic-using squads was quite strong.

Maybe, like Dardas, they were simply unsettled by the presence of so many wizards. Matokin might have shown true brilliance in recruiting powerful mages into his new military (not to mention using magic to resurrect the general who led it), but did he truly grasp the tension he'd also created within these ranks?

"Before the Great Upheavals," Berkant was saying, "things were different."

Dardas perked up, paying closer attention now.

The Great Upheavals had occurred even before Dardas's day. Once, mighty empires had thrived on the Northern and Southern Continents, but they had both crumbled from within. Before that time, however, wizardry was relatively widespread. Both the empires of the Northland and the Southsoil had made efforts to develop the sciences. The best practitioners were kept at the ruling courts.

"When those continental empires fell, it was a time of much fear." Berkant was showing the effects of the liquor, though, like any amateur drinker, he didn't seem to know he was getting drunk.

"I see," Dardas said, refilling the wizard's glass.

"Rumors abounded that occult forces were responsible for the empires' collapse. Magical practitioners went into hiding or renounced their disciplines. Some fled to the Isthmus. In the Northland, a very few attached themselves as healers to the armies of the new warlords."

"Fascinating," Dardas said. He, of course, had been one of those warlords. "But what about *here,* on the Isthmus?"

"The Issh— The Issh—" Berkant actually giggled, then reined himself in. Overenunciating, he now said, "The Isthmus once served only as a trade route between the continents. When the Upheavals came, many trade clans were stranded here, and they, as you know, settled this land."

"Yes," Dardas said, hiding his annoyance. Soon the

liquor would make this mage useless as a source of information. "But what about the magicians?"

"The wealthiest and most powerful of the trade clans had the insight to give shelter and succor to the suddenly outcast wizards. They recognized magic's value, its potential advantage. They didn't fear magic as did the rabble."

Berkant drained his glass in one heroic swallow. This time Dardas didn't refill it.

The mage continued, "The wizards were absorbed into these newly founded wealthy houses of the Isthmus. They took mates and entered the families, and the penchant for magic was passed through the generations, though often the lore of it was distorted or outright forgotten, and the strength of talent weakened, in some cases all but disappearing."

That explained why magic ran strongest among noble families, Dardas thought.

"Very well, Berkant. That's enough for now. Dismissed."

Berkant teetered up onto his feet and exited the pavilion, managing to stay upright at least until he was past the flap.

Dardas sipped meditatively at his own drink, savoring the flavor, as he did all of life's little pleasures now.

Portal magic. Far Movement magic. *That* was what he needed to know about. It was a powerful tool in his arsenal, and it was completely at his disposal as this army's commander. But . . . he knew nothing about how it worked, and Matokin had evidently given orders to these army mages that Dardas remain in the dark.

He called for his aide.

The officer appeared immediately. "Yes, General Weisel?"

No one addressed him as Lord Weisel anymore. Apparently word had gotten around.

"We'll be moving in the morning," Dardas said. "Inform the senior staff."

"Yes, General Weisel."

To the south lay the city-states of Ompellus Prime, Trael, and Grat. All three were some distance away. But, of course, Dardas need only order a squad of Far Movement mages to scout ahead, and the army could transport itself to any of those cities' doorsteps.

Those portals. What sort of place, exactly, did they open up into? Did that strange, milky world have inhabitants?

Dardas had seen none when he'd passed through with his army on the way to level U'delph. But he'd barely gotten a glimpse of the place, so distorted was everything, so overwhelming the sense of *otherness* there.

Yet, very strangely and despite its alienness, something about that realm had seemed . . . familiar. It was as if he recognized the place without having any memory of it at all, as if he was remembering something from a dream. It made no sense.

Yes, a strange war this was. But it was war, nonetheless. And war was the environment in which Dardas thrived. It was, in fact, the only state of reality in which he felt at home. That was why he had risen to such heights as a military commander in his first incarnation. The Northland had provided him with a virtually endless series of adversaries, peoples, and rival armies to be conquered.

He *loved* war. And he would do anything to preserve it. He had never wanted a final victory, never wanted to see the end of all hostilities.

Naturally, he did not wish to see the end of this war. But if war was to continue, he needed a foe, some force to stand against his growing army.

U'delph's ruthless destruction had real purpose. It was meant to horrify the remaining Isthmus states, yes, just as he'd told Matokin. But Dardas didn't want to provoke surrender. No. He wanted to goad the remaining city-states into action.

Perhaps you could requisition a student directly from the Academy.

Weisel caught him off guard, but he quickly recovered, assured that the Felk nobleman hadn't overheard his thoughts.

What's that you say?

You were wondering about magic and magicians. Someone straight from that Academy in Felk where they train them might be able tell you what you want to know.

Dardas considered. It was, he had to admit, a sound plan.

That's a fine idea. My thanks.

Glad to help.

There was no mistaking the preening tone of the thought. Weisel *was* an idiot, but Dardas wasn't one to reject a good scheme simply because he didn't like where it came from.

He finished his drink. Then he called again for his aide and told the officer what he wanted. The comely young woman was brought to him immediately. She was different than the one he'd had last time, which was good. Life offered many possibilities, and Dardas, now that he was alive again, meant to enjoy as many of those possibilities as he could.

AQUINT

(2)

'STAND EASY . . . AQUINT, is it?"

"Sir?"

Aquint maintained his rigid stance, unsure of what the order meant. He was still getting used to this military lingo. It was ironic that, though he still didn't really consider himself a soldier, he had nonetheless been promoted.

"Relax," the officer expanded, waving at the seat opposite his desk. "Sit down. You make me tired just watching you. We're not as spit and polish here in the quartermaster's as they are out there in the field. Make yourself comfortable while I read these orders."

Aquint did as he was instructed and peered curiously about as the officer pored over the scroll he had just been handed. Aquint had been ordered to report to this warehouse in the city of Sook. Not much of a city-state, he judged. Shabby, in fact, compared to Callah. But it was now a part of the growing Felk Empire, owing to its recent unequivocal surrender. Apparently spines didn't grow strong among the people of Sook. Callah, at least, had put up a decent, if inadequate, resistance before giving in to the Felk.

The warehouse looked pretty much like any other warehouse he had been in, including his own. There were stacks of materials with aisles running between them, and men and women wandering about in seemingly aimless patterns loading and unloading wagons. Much of the material was more war-oriented than he was used to seeing, with stores of weapons and armor, and there were wizards present, but other than that, he had the strange feeling of coming home.

He had been surprised by this posting, thinking a "transportation officer" would remain in the field with the wagons and equipment. But of course supplies had to come *from* somewhere, and this warehouse was one of those places.

"Brand new officer, eh?" the man said, glancing up from the scroll. "Well, no matter. We can use any help we can get right now. I notice you aren't wearing an officer's uniform. Why is that?"

"I was told I was being transferred here to take a posting as a junior officer," Aquint said. "Nobody told me if the new rank was effective immediately or after I started work in the new position. I thought it better to dress the part too late rather than too early."

"Mmm. Probably the wisest course," the officer nodded. "Have you had any previous experience?"

"Not in being an officer. No, sir," Aquint responded.

"Well, no matter. I was a shopkeeper in Felk myself before this war started. You'll catch on quick enough. Tell me, what do you think the job of an officer is?"

Aquint hesitated, then shrugged. "As near as I can figure, it's like any other manager or supervisor. You do as little as possible by delegating everything to others . . . sir."

The officer gave a quick bark of laughter. "Well put. And better than most answers I've heard." Then he sobered slightly. "Of course, there's another side to it as well. You also get to take the blame for anything that goes wrong in your command. I should know. I just spent the morning getting chewed out by my own superior for something I have no control over."

"Sir?" Aquint said, curious in spite of himself.

"Lost material," the officer growled.

"Lost? Between here and the field?"

The officer nodded. "We send material *directly,* if you know what I mean."

Ah. The wizards, Aquint thought. They were transport mages, and they sent supplies to the troops in the field through those portals. It was an impressive way to keep an army supplied.

"And still they're saying that the shipments are coming up short, despite the spot check inventories I've implemented," the officer said unhappily.

"How much is missing?"

"According to the numbers people, about ten percent."

"That's too much," Aquint said thoughtfully, an idea starting to form in his mind.

"That's exactly what my superior said," the officer said, peering closely at his new charge. "It sounds like you know something about this kind of operation."

"I used to run a freight and hauling outfit in Callah before the Felk came," Aquint said. "You expect a certain amount of loss to pilferage from the help, stuff that 'falls off the wagon.' But ten percent is too high for casual theft. It sounds like someone is running an organized ring right under your nose."

"I see," the officer said, rubbing his chin. "You know, Aquint, it sounds like you can be a lot of help to me after all. Any suggestions as to what we can do?"

"Just one, at the moment," Aquint said. "Does anyone except you and me know I'm being assigned here as an officer?"

"Didn't know it myself until you handed me the scroll."

"Well, let's keep it that way for the time being. Give me the rest of the day off so I can look around Sook, and when

I start tomorrow, have me introduced around as a new transfer, nothing more."

"I can do that. But why?"

Aquint smiled. "I imagine that regular grunts tend to go mum around officers, if it's anything like it is between workers and bosses," he said. "I'll probably hear a lot more if they think I'm just another mud-slogger. With any luck at all, they'll try to recruit me for whatever they have going."

"I have no problem with that," the officer nodded. "Very well, we'll try it your way. As you say, take the rest of the day to get to know beautiful Sook, and we'll start first thing in the morning."

"Ah, sir?"

"Yes, Aquint?"

"I'll still be getting paid as an officer, won't I? I mean, just because . . ."

"Don't worry," the officer laughed. "We'll take care of you. Glad to hear you're still watching out for your own interests, though. Man has to look out for himself, even in the army."

SOOK'S OCCUPATION BY the Felk meant its citizens, those who hadn't been conscripted into the army, were quickly learning to obey the new laws. There was a curfew, and a list of crimes and punishments each person had to memorize. Mostly this was a way to keep the population intimidated. Judging by the nervous and timid looks Aquint received from civilian passersby as he emerged from the warehouse, it was working.

"Don't worry, sir," he said to himself, as he made his way down the street. He was smiling. "I'll be sure to remember to look out for my own interests."

"You're looking pleased with yourself," Cat said, materializing at his side.

"Cat! Hey! Good to see you! I was starting to think I had lost you for good."

In fact, Aquint hadn't seen Cat since the night he told him about his transfer to Sook. The next morning his young friend had vanished, and Aquint had actually started to wonder if their partnership had been severed as quickly and wordlessly as it had formed.

"Thought I'd run on ahead and get a feel for the place." Cat shrugged. "Camping out with the army types is one thing, but you and I know cities. The more you can find out about a new city, the better off you'll be in the long run."

"Excellent," Aquint said, nodding almost to himself. "That will fit in nicely."

"Nicely with what? And you still haven't told me why you're grinning like someone who just beat the taxman."

"We've got a potentially sweet deal going here, Cat m'lad," Aquint said. "I may actually start enjoying being in the army."

Cat slowed his pace and peered at his elder. "Don't tell me you're letting this officer thing go to your head," he said with his normal accusatory disapproval. "What happened to 'keep our heads down and serve our time'?"

"Not to worry." Aquint waved. "What I'm saying is that we may be able to go back into our old business right under the army's nose."

"How do you figure that?"

"They've got me working a warehouse," Aquint explained. "What's more, the operation has been suffering a ten-percent loss to pilferage."

"That's high." Cat frowned. "Sounds like someone already has an operation set up."

"That's what it sounds like to me," Aquint said. "And get this, the officer in charge used to be a shopkeeper. You know how easy those types were to flimflam."

"So how do we figure into this?"

"Already in motion," Aquint said. "I'm going to be

heading up the investigation to deal with the problem. Working undercover, of course."

Cat's mouth curled into a smirk.

"Sort of a 'set a poacher to catch a poacher' deal, huh?"

"It would be, except all he knows is that I used to run a freight business," Aquint grinned. "It's actually more like setting a weasel to guard a henhouse. I figure we can cut ourselves in on whatever action we uncover, and end up getting paid from both ends."

"It could work," Cat said thoughtfully. "Might be a little risky, though."

"That's why I have you, my young shadow-loving friend," Aquint said, draping his arm across Cat's shoulders as they resumed their walk. "Now help me here. That fellow we worked with in Callah . . . the fat slob with the bad teeth . . . didn't he have a cousin or something that was his contact here in Sook?"

THE DINING ROOM of the inn was furnished with modest but clean and sturdy tables and chairs and had large shuttered windows that opened onto the street for light and ventilation. Aquint could not help but think as he entered the room with Cat that it was not at all the seedy den of thieves one would think of when meeting with a black marketeer. It was midday, but the place was barely half full, making Aquint suspect either the quality of the food or inflated prices. Cat did not hesitate, but immediately led the way to a medium-sized table near the far wall, where a stocky man in merchant's garb was dining alone.

"Vahnka, this is Aquint, the man I was telling you about," he said without preamble.

The man briefly ran his eyes over Aquint. If he was surprised at the Felk army uniform, he gave no indication.

"Please, join me, gentlemen," he said, gesturing to the empty seats at his table. "So. The lad here tells me that you know my cousin Tyber up in Callah. You know, I've always envied that *grink* his looks. Tell me, is he still married to that little redhead?"

Aquint looked at him levelly.

"The Tyber I worked with is built like a toad with pimples and bad teeth. I don't believe he's ever been married. In fact, from what I heard, his tastes run more to young boys."

"Too true," Vahnka said, mopping up some gravy with a butt of bread. His rustic Sook accent was mild. "He's always been a bit of an embarrassment to the family. Still, he has a good business head on his shoulders."

"Testing me?" Aquint said. "Is that really necessary? You've got at least three men in the room ready to step in if I try anything."

Vahnka paused in his eating to peer at Aquint.

"You spotted them?"

"Haven't bothered to try," Aquint said with a shrug. "It's a precaution I would have taken if I were meeting with someone I didn't know. I just assumed that you'd do the same."

"Quite right," Vahnka said, returning to his meal. "Still, one can't be too careful these days. So, I'm told you have a proposition for me. Are you buying or selling?"

"First, I have a question," Aquint said. "Are you handling the merchandise that's being lifted from the army warehouses?"

Vahnka peered at him carefully.

"Pretending for the moment that I know what you're talking about," he said, "why should I admit any involvement to you?"

"Because if you aren't the outside man in that operation, we can end this conversation now, and I'll keep looking for the person that is," Aquint said. "If you are, then we might be able to do some business together. As a token of good faith, I'll give you some inside information right now. For free."

"Free information is usually like free advice," Vahnka said. "More often than not, it's worth its price. I'll listen, though."

"Whoever is the outside man needs to find a new inside contact," Aquint said. "The one they've got now is sloppy."

"How so?"

"He's been lifting too much too often," Aquint said. "Sook has only been occupied a short period of time, and the army has already gotten wind of that pilferage operation and has assigned a special officer to go undercover to investigate it."

Vahnka leaned back in his seat. "That is an interesting bit of news," he said. "Of course, we already know all the officers in the local garrison so whoever they assign will have trouble conducting his investigation unnoticed. Still, if it's true, it would be an inconvenience. How did you come by this information?"

"Because I'm the officer," Aquint said with a smile. "Don't let the enlisted man's uniform fool you. I'm newly assigned and newly promoted. I've only been in Sook since yesterday, so I'm not known locally. That and my previous experience with warehouses made me a natural choice."

"So you've decided to try your hand at crime," Vahnka said, thoughtfully.

"More like continue it," Aquint said. "My warehouse operation in Callah had several sidelines the authorities knew nothing of. That's how I came to know Tyber."

"So, what exactly is your proposal?"

Aquint gave a small shrug. "I should think it's obvious. I think it would be best for all concerned if I became your new inside man. Once I've gained a reputation for my honesty, I'll be able to provide you with information on all supplies arriving or departing, so that we wouldn't have to rely on simple pilferage. That is, if your contacts are reliable."

"Assume we have the contacts," Vahnka waved. "But going back to something you said, how exactly do you plan to establish your honesty?"

"By exposing the existing operation and reducing the level of pilferage to a fraction of what it is now."

"Forgive me for being slow," Vahnka said with a frown, "but how can reducing the level of pilferage increase our profits?"

"By using the information I have at my disposal to target those items that are of the greatest value. That way we can skim the cream and not bother with the low-profit dregs. Just out of curiosity, what items are most in demand right now?"

Vahnka laughed. "That's easy. Weapons and armor. Every paltry state in the south is short of almost everything needed to equip an effective fighting force. They want that gear. They know the Felk are coming. Whether they can or will put up a fight remains to be seen. Right now they're just a separated, disorganized rabble."

"Then for my first contribution, there is an order being gathered that the wizards will ship out in two days. Tents and uniforms loaded on top of swords and crossbows."

"Excellent," Vahnka said, rubbing his hands together. "I can see where working with you will simplify matters greatly."

"Enough to justify my exposing your current inside man to establish my own credibility?" Aquint said.

"He is no friend of mine," Vahnka said. "And business is business. Of course, it would be convenient if an accident befell him or he were killed resisting arrest so that he could not betray his outside contacts."

"I had already taken that into consideration," Aquint smiled.

"Just one question," Vahnka said. "You are an officer in the Felk army, but you're willing to rob your own fellow soldiers of necessary supplies and sell them to the very forces you're likely to be fighting in the near future. Doesn't that bother you?"

"We won't be taking everything. Just a little here and there. And besides," Aquint stared at Vahnka levelly, "in your own words, 'they're no friends of mine, and business is business'."

PRAULTH
(2)

BEING MADLY IN love and being in love for the first
time weren't, surprisingly, the distractions one might
imagine them to be. In truth, she felt *more* focused than she
had before Xink had appeared in her life. He—through his
caring, his passion and compassion, through his simple
steady presence—settled her mind and spirit . . . settled
those restless and longing parts of herself she'd not even
been aware of before Xink's advent.

Yes . . . that and all the fabulous, wonderful, glorious
sex they were having! That, too, had settled and centered
her.

Over the blur of the past several days so much had
changed. And yet she was still ardently pursuing the mas-
sive assignment Master Honnis had burdened her with. It
was an intellectual challenge she welcomed, yes, but still
it was onerous.

However, that her elderly mentor had chosen her made
her . . . proud.

Master Honnis was still receiving current intelligence

about the war in the north. The Felk were moving once more, having settled the occupation of Sook.

Honnis hadn't shared with Praulth any details about the source or sources of his information, and she didn't have time to speculate. She had spent the past quarter-lune poring over the battle synopses. She had submerged herself in the study.

She was envied for her talents by her fellow pupils. They saw how deftly she absorbed lessons, grasping the material and adding to it her personal insights, rather than merely making restatements. What most of those average students didn't understand was the effort she put forth.

Praulth didn't simply study surfaces. She virtually assumed the personas of those she studied, even the "personalities" of historical events and locales.

History was not inanimate. Praulth accepted it as a kind of ultra-reality, weighing over the present, influencing, directing, birthing events as surely as women brought forth their generations of children. The past did not die.

If any wished to argue the point, she now had proof beyond her convictions. Dardas. The famed (at least among war scholars) general of the Northland. *He* lived. Almost impossibly, but it was so.

Praulth of course didn't believe that the two-and-a-half-centuries-dead war commander had reconstituted himself from moldering meat and bones and was now leading the Felk army in its southward campaign to claim the Isthmus. The dead didn't need to parade about before the living to prove her point that history was immortal.

Dardas was dead. Yes. But his tactics, his unprecedented brilliance on the battlefield, survived him. Weisel. Lord Weisel of the Felk. That was the vessel that was carrying Dardas's . . . well, *spirit,* she supposed, though her rational mind immediately balked at the term.

Praulth had marked Weisel's name. History was occurring now, history that even the ignorant and indifferent would remember. The Felk meant to conquer the Isthmus.

This she knew. They had the means, and they had chosen the proper time for the move. No other state stood strong enough to oppose the Felk. The Northerners had amassed a powerful army and were adding to it with each city they subdued. They were using wizardry, a practice that was changing the face of warfare forever. She had learned of Matokin, a mage. Evidently he had established himself as the ruler of the Felk and had fostered this war.

Master Honnis had wanted to know why the Felk had obliterated U'delph. She had dutifully examined the battle précis. She had reached her conclusions.

U'delph's eradication seemed meant to incite *resistance*. Not—as at first seemed obvious—to intimidate the Felk's future opponents into surrender.

She had immersed herself in this Lord Weisel, who himself was effectively embodying the long-dead Dardas. Weisel was plainly an exemplary war scholar to know the Northlander general's methods so well. Praulth could only imagine how rewarding it would be to sit and talk with him, for days on end, trading historical insights.

She sighed.

What had occurred at U'delph was certainly deliberate. Atrocities, historically, were often unplanned, happening sometimes despite all efforts to prevent them; but U'delph wasn't like that.

Dardas, in his day, had been known to commit similar acts of annihilation. These always occurred when his enemies were most disorganized, and the effect was almost always to rouse those adversaries into action.

U'delph's annihilation might not necessarily be a demonstration of power. It could be taken for a challenge. A dare. U'delph might have been so ruthlessly destroyed in order to cause outrage, horror . . . and to impel defiance.

Praulth didn't understand why Weisel might be doing this, but deep within she felt certain of her findings. She was operating on a level of logic so advanced it could contrarily be misunderstood as instinct. Or magic.

She had of course told Master Honnis her conclusions. He agreed. Just as he agreed with her larger assessment that the Felk's ultimate intent was to capture the entire Isthmus. As General Dardas before him, Lord Weisel desired total conquest.

And so eventually the war would come here to the deep south, to Febretree. Perhaps this was why she was able to care so little about neglecting her other studies in favor of this assignment, despite the fact that she was straying dangerously from the path toward academic success and security.

But such deviating was encouraged, her coldly capable mind argued. Iconoclastic thinking was a far surer means of advancement within the University than sticking rigorously to the curriculum. That made her actions and behavior matters of pure logic, which pleased her.

What pleased her more, though, was Xink.

She liked the campus's Blue Annex. The quarters of a sixth-phase Attaché were indeed superior to her old cell, and a palace, when compared to conditions in the dormitories. It was roughly four times the space she'd had before. The floor was finished wood, not stone. (She even recognized the type of wood—blood-ash, a fine wood—and was surprised and amused that she retained any knowledge of timber from her Dral Blidst childhood.) There was a brazier where she heated water for tea—the tallgreen tea, of which Xink seemed to have an unaccountably inexhaustible supply.

The two most important furnishings in the chamber were the desk and the bed.

It was a broad, solid desk, and the chair was upholstered and quite comfortable. The bed was to her old bunk what . . . well . . . being sexually experienced was to being virginal!

She hummed a bright little laugh to herself at the thought. That was something she was having to get used to. Laughter. Also smiling. Lately, when Xink fixed her with that gorgeous smoldering stare of his, she was able to return what she thought was an equally wanton look. She laughed a bit harder now, thinking of their first kiss and how awkward she had been, nearly swooning—not from passion, but from abject terror and uncertainty.

It was incredible to think that before Xink no male had ever touched her in the least lustful way, had ever expressed the most minute carnal interest in her. She did not feel slighted in hindsight by this inattention. Quite simply, she hadn't known what she was missing out on. Whatever normal curiosities she might have experienced in her life had been ground under by her deep-seated social timidity and her overwhelming academic urges. Those had served to effectively bank her hormonal fires for all those years. It had taken Xink to awaken everything in her.

He'd done a fine job. Her laugh turned to an outright snicker.

"Did old Honnis bury a joke in there somewhere?"

Praulth looked up from the papers. The desk was broad enough that she could spread them out. She had the detailed maps of the Felk battles arranged chronologically.

Xink was rather pleasingly arranged himself, slung across the wide mattress of the bed, his robe on a hook near the door, next to her own. Since the brazier was lit several times a day for her tea, the chamber remained constantly and comfortably warm. She wondered how it would be in the winter. Surely warmer than any accommodations she'd enjoyed since arriving at Febretree six years ago.

The gauzy shift—like those they all wore beneath their robes—clung to Xink's sleek, but muscular body. He was long-limbed, long of finger too. His hair was wildly overgrown and so dark it seemed to suck the lamplight from above. (That was another remarkable improvement about these lodgings—an actual clean-burning lamp; it hung from a bronze hook in the middle of the room, and they never seemed to run out of oil.) And his face, oh, his face . . .

He was so beautiful, it defied all reason. His brows were thin but as dark as his lush, cascading hair; his eyes were limpid blue flecked with gold and seemed to see always right through to her heart. His cheekbones were high, elegant, he had an angular jaw, and the sweet soft lips of his luscious mouth . . .

He had said something, asked a question. With a start, she made to answer. She loved him, yes, loved him dearly and desperately; but she didn't want to appear foolish in any way in front of him.

"No, no joke," she said hastily. "Umm . . . just more of the usual."

He was smiling easily, so at ease with himself, so confident. He had been glancing over some of Mistress Cestrello's papers, which he needed to organize by the end of the next watch. It was nice that Xink sometimes came here to their quarters to work, since here was where she was throughout the day, and where she sometimes missed him terribly, waiting hungrily for the night, and bed. Bed had once meant only sleep.

"What new doings of your Lord Weisel?" he asked casually.

He knew of her assignment. Of course he knew; of course she had told him. How could she not share everything about herself with him? She wanted to give herself, utterly. How sweet the surrenders so far.

"It's not what he does, it's what he will do," she said, trying to match his effortless smile but knowing hers was more of a giddy grin. "That's what interests Honnis."

Knowing that Weisel was imitating Dardas's war techniques, Honnis had charged her with predicting the future movements of the Felk army. Weisel was presently within striking distance of three different city-states. Trael, Grat, and Ompellus Prime.

Praulth had already had some success in predicting this

war's smaller engagements, the military operations that overran the lesser burgs among the larger city-states. Since the Felk had moved on from Sook, she had calculated those moves that sacked villages and captured roads.

Sometimes her deductions had the taste of intuitive leaps; yet they were not. She was always able to prop up these "feelings" with the hardest facts. She felt obligated to do so—to prove to Master Honnis that none of this was guesswork and, perhaps, to remind herself of that same thing.

The surface of the desk started to blur slightly.

She shifted on her chair. Comfortable or not, sitting in it watch after watch was its own sort of ordeal. Her body, beneath her own gauzy shift, felt stiff. She returned her gaze to Xink.

She saw his bulge then, growing. She saw the new look in his eyes, one she recognized, one that set her blood singing. Suddenly her throat was dry, where elsewhere she suddenly was not. Longing that was agony, and bliss stole over her. She was rising to her feet, and he was there, waiting, ready, on the bed. Wanting her, needing her. So much she had learned. So much he had taught her. He was twenty-five to her twenty-two years. He had knowledge, worldliness, *experience.* Just as she now had experience, a dizzy mental satisfaction that complemented the bodily gratification so sublimely.

It was a vast new vocabulary: manhood, nipples, engorgement, clitoris, ejaculation, contraceptive. How confused she had been when he'd first fit on that small tube of animal bladder, until he'd explained the function, until she understood that only ignorant country maids need bear children that they didn't want.

She lay down on the bed. He buried himself in her, and it seemed to go on forever.

IT WAS HARDLY unheard of for two students to cohabitate, but Praulth had never imagined she would find herself doing so. Had never successfully imagined so many things, in fact.

How quickly Xink had come into her life. Less than half a lune had passed since he had first left that cup of tall-green tea and the note outside her door. And now she was living with the handsome student who had achieved the academic rank of Attaché, a fine intelligent individual with a bright future, currently serving the University's sociology council and Mistress Cestrello in particular. Incredible.

She was happy. Impossibly happy.

He had made it all so easy, from the first moment he introduced himself in one of the study parlors. He had confessed to bringing her the tea and to having had an infatuation for her for some while.

She couldn't remember ever having seen him on campus before, but she wasn't one to focus on people. At least not people who weren't part of history.

Later she returned to the desk, spent and thoroughly refreshed all at once, and knowing that the city-state of Trael was Lord Weisel/General Dardas's next logical target.

RADSTAC
(2)

SHE HAD NEVER been so high off the ground in her life. They built magnificent tall buildings in the Southsoil's grander cities, to be sure; but these Petgradites had something of a mania for towers, it seemed. In this administrative district of the city, the great stone spires punched toward the sky. This was evidently the tallest of all.

She was looking out through a wall made of glass—expertly cut, no warps—and it made for an extraordinary view. She had chewed a corner of a *mansìd* leaf before making the formidable climb up this tower's endless stairways. Petgrad's lights winked with individual clarity and life as she looked down on their array.

She would need to procure more leaves soon.

"There you are."

This level was near the top of the tower, perhaps the very top, just underneath the cupola of luminous metal that capped the structure. Deo had undertaken the climb with her, not needing to pause to rest any more than she had.

She saw the indistinct reflection in the glass and turned.

The chamber was large and stylishly under-furnished, its every surface polished to a high gloss. Dusky red stone underfoot, brass fixtures twinkling from the walls here and there. There was incense burning, a cool, very pleasant scent.

Deo turned from the nighttime view of the city as well. He and Radstac had spent time together the past several days. A fine few days. He had made good on his intention to hire her, though as yet, she'd done nothing but receive the goldies he put into her hand. She had retrieved her heavy combat sword from the Public Armory. And waited. It was possible, of course, he was merely paying for the use of her body; possible even that he wasn't a relative of Petgrad's premier at all, just some rich fool out to impress his new lover.

She hadn't thought so, though. It wasn't that difficult to measure a man's character, and Deo rang true.

"Uncle," he said now, crossing the gleaming floor toward the tall shape that had entered through doors of blood-oak wood.

Her eyes went to this new figure. Tall, solid but not stocky, red hair much longer and fuller than Deo's, the same shade but shot through with a goldish blond. He wore a beard over features far craggier than those Deo had. The beard had grey in it. The blue eyes were stonier. But these two looked very much like relatives.

Radstac watched as the two men—at least two tenwinters apart in age, probably more—came together and spoke. She couldn't hear the words, but the rich sounds emanating from the older man made patterns that were almost tangible, dipping, rising, like music . . .

One had to travel to the Isthmus to get fresh *mansìd* leaves of such quality.

Eventually they turned and came toward her. The bearded one led. He wore a long lounging coat, sumptuous fabric, unsashed, its tails brushing the floor. Soft silent black shoes on his feet. The whites of his fierce blue eyes were reddened, but he didn't reveal his fatigue in his gait or the set of his coarse—and decidedly handsome—face.

"Nâ Niroki Cultat," Deo said, behind, formally, "Premier of the Noble State of—"

"I'm guessing she's deduced that by now, Nephew." Cultat halted. His hands folded themselves at his back. He looked at her, closely, briefly, then shifted his gaze past, to the panoramic window.

She had surrendered her weapons before being admitted to this chamber, including her glove. Deo had told her to do so, and she was working for him. There were also quite a few guards on the premises.

This Cultat was a fighter. She didn't need any *mansid*-inspired clarity to see that. Deo had dueling scars on his arms. She would wager that his uncle had them as well— and that whoever had put them there hadn't had an easy time of it.

"What do you think of our city?" He had a voice comfortable at command, but this was just a question, an honest one.

"Attractive. Clean. Prosperous."

"Better cities back home, I'd guess. Home"—a thoughtful hum rumbled briefly in his throat—"I daresay . . . Republic of Dilloqi. Yes?"

Her colorless eyes widened. She hadn't told Deo the specifics of her origins.

"Thought so. I went south once, before my University days. To the Southsoil, with a pair of comrades more reckless and fearless and asinine even than I. I abandoned my duties, my family. We rode to the city of Ichuloo. We were there for Modyah Te Mody's abdication of her rule. Heard the criers in the streets. All three of us grotesquely drunk. Stumbled our way to the palace to see. I vomited out my guts on the way. Saw the soldiers turning back the crowds. Screaming, hysterics, violence—"

"A dark episode in Ichuloo's history," Radstac said, trying to equate this poised premier with the rash young idiot he was sketching for her.

"Indeed. Was a beautiful city, though." His gaze was still past her, through the glass. "What do you think of our people here?"

"As a people . . . blind fools. Individually is another matter."

"Yes. It's always that way, isn't it? When my two friends and I rode back, my father put me in a cell. He had a legal order for it. I'd reneged on my duties, you see, though to me at that age everything that was ever asked of me was a vast imposition. I was a premier's son, and I wanted, essentially, to be thoroughly indulged until the time came for me to assume my father's place. The burden of the premier's post is often lifted from a parent's back and set on that of its child. But it is not always so. The Noble Ministry has the power to block an ascendancy, and with me, they would very likely have done so, but I was too obtuse to really see that. My days in that cell my father put me in, though—and there were *quite* some many days—along with my time at the University . . . well, it all served me. I learned. I grew."

He drew a slow breath, not lost in his thoughts, not rambling out loud.

"The game of it, then . . . how to make these people of Petgrad see reality. How?"

"I have come up against that quandary myself since arriving here," she said. In the tiny squiggly veins of his eyes she read the code of this man, this premier, this highest authority—literally—in the city. Atop his tower, gazing down on his domain. Yet he did not seem aloof. He cared for his people; yes, that was plain. But he saw them clearly, and he was troubled.

As leader of a city-state that lay in the path of the Felk, he *should* be troubled, Radstac thought.

"You expected us to be arming for war," Cultat said. "Adding numbers to our military. Grabbing up every mercenary and every farmer with an axe claiming to be a mercenary that came within reach."

Radstac said simply, "Yes."

"We do have an army, and it is maintained. At a cost the people grouse about. We've made a reputation for ourselves, you see. Petgrad, a powerful city, well-defended, a stable leadership structure. We don't lose our wars. When we're intruded upon, we set things right—successfully, decisively."

His jaw shifted beneath his beard. "In fact, no one has made a successful move against us in over a hundredwinter. You see the fatal snare of that, I'm sure."

"I do. Of course." She caught sight of Deo still lingering behind Cultat. Not nervously, though the premier's presence, even in this casual dress, was quite forceful. He must seem a titan garbed in the doubtlessly grand raiment of his office, she thought. Or wearing armor, a sword in his fist.

"My word alone isn't enough to build up and mobilize the army," he continued. "It requires a mandate of the people, endorsement by the Ministry. But first we of Petgrad must admit that we are no longer the strongest.

"Uncle." Deo stepped forward. He was wearing a sort of uniform tonight, a simple and elegant ensemble, red and gold, near the colors of Cultat's hair.

"I've seen to it my children learned proper behavior with less fuss than what I went through. Perhaps their offspring will have an even easier time of it. You, Deo, though . . . my elder sister was quite fond of you. Rightly so. She turned you out as she saw fit. Didn't want you anywhere near being a possible successor to our father. Just as she herself refused to her death to be a candidate for premier. Do you regret that?"

"Of course not, Uncle." He smiled his warm, winsome smile.

"Naturally," Cultat pronounced. "I've regaled you often enough, in agonizing detail, with tales of what this post entails. And you're so finely suited for the role you play. Handsome noble. Philanthropist. Benefactor of the arts. Make a few speeches, sweep the Ministry's daughters off their feet at state functions. The people adore you. Sensible people stay away from onerous tasks—at least those chores that others are willing to shoulder. Gods pity me, I was willing to accept mine."

"To all our good fortune," Deo said.

Cultat gazed levelly now at his nephew, somberness joining the secret fatigue he carried in his eyes. "And now there's a task for you." His rich voice was low, soft.

"One I'm willing and ready to take on."

Cultat's head dipped in a slow nod. "She's to be the one, then?"

Radstac waited, as she had waited these past several days. She watched the two men.

"Yes, Uncle," Deo answered. "You gave me leave to make my own choice."

"I'm aware of that." Something hard moved under his voice. Family they were, she thought, but this matter was serious, whatever it was, and these weren't frivolous men. "I know that even the most libidinous rascal wouldn't make such a choice on the basis of someone's performance as a bed partner."

Cultat looked at her once more, closely, still a few paces away; yet it seemed the potent heat of him brushed her scarred face. "You'd better hire her, then," the Premier said.

"I've already done so."

"And explain the task you've volunteered for . . . the one you're now dragging her into."

Without a further word or look, Cultat exited the chamber.

'I AM *NOT* refusing," she said for the third time, emphatically. "But what you're after isn't my specialty. I'm a combatant. I go into battles, face the enemy in the open. I'm not an escort."

"Understood," Deo said.

She had collected her weapons from the tower's guards, and they had descended. Now they were walking the streets, the watch growing late. Someone with a dilettante's voice and zeal was singing in a pub as they passed, with what sounded like the rest of the place coming in on the choruses.

"You're still my choice."

"It's your choice to make," she said, tone level.

"Yes. So Uncle made clear."

"So I make clear as well. You've hired me. I work for you. What you say is what happens."

"That's purely your professional self speaking?"

Her eyebrows, a darker red than his, pulled together. "Of course. How else would I say such a thing?"

"The words lovers choose can sometimes be very, very strange. I've heard my share." They were turning onto an avenue lined with shops that bustled in the day. Here the night was nearly still.

"I imagine you've heard your share and then some," she said. She looked sidelong at his ruggedly appealing features. If he aged along the lines of his uncle, he wouldn't want for carnal companionship until he was too old to care about it. "Do you think I would behave unprofessionally because of the few good fucks we've had?"

"Ah, Radstac, I do enjoy that melodic Southsoil accent."

"You adore women who speak vulgarities."

"What right-thinking male doesn't?"

They walked a bit in the silence. Wings beat the air—but not feathers. Her keen ears caught the leathery sounds. One of those flying rodents of the Isthmus. She didn't see the creature, however. Two figures in the modest uniforms of Petgrad police were walking the street's other side, going the opposite way. The female of the pair offered a salute that was more a wave, teeth flashing in a happy grin. Deo returned it with an equally casual gesture.

"When do we leave?" she asked. Her palm alit on her sword's heavy scratched pommel. It felt good to be wearing the weapon again; felt good to be *hired*. Even if the job had turned out to be something unexpected.

"Tomorrow. I can supply you with as many *mansìd* leaves as you like, or you can see to the procurement yourself. I'll be happy to cover the purchase above your work fee."

She very nearly broke stride. The small bite of leaf she'd chewed just before the visit to Cultat's tower had dissipated. Deo had sprung surprises on her from the first, but none had caught her entirely off guard.

Do the smart thing, do the economical thing, do the safe thing, do the thing you find most self-fulfilling. It was her code, presenting its points one by one.

"If you can get my leaves from the lair I specify," she said, "then I'll gladly let you see to it."

"Done." He sounded like a merchant sealing a sale or a gambler finalizing a bet. "I'll show you what supplies I want to bring. Tell me what's practical—what we should have, what we don't need."

"It's going to be quite a trip."

"Hardly compares to the one you've already made from home," he pointed out.

"It wasn't distance I was referring to."

He nodded. "You really shouldn't have misgivings about being . . . underqualified. There's a perfectly good reason Cultat or I haven't hired the proper specialist for this mission. It's that there are no experienced professionals in this field. None here in Petgrad anyway. None among our own military—men and women who bear arms and have not fought a battle in their lives. Nor did their progenitors. So it becomes as much a matter of character as one of appropriate credentials. I trust you."

"That's the nephew of the premier of Petgrad speaking,

not an overwrought lover?" She permitted herself a small trickle of her rather harsh-sounding laughter.

"Yes." His tone was solemn. "The nephew of the premier . . . cheated out of the post by his mother. And by her brother. I do love my uncle. Most sincerely. But my life has not gone as it should."

The silence returned.

Quite a trip, Radstac mused. It indeed promised to be. She would see Deo safely delivered to Trael, which was one of the city-states to Petgrad's north. It was presently—along with a few other Isthmus nations—in the path of the south-moving Felk.

There Deo would convey Cultat's message to the leaders of Trael. That message was simple. The remaining free states of the Isthmus must unite now against the Felk.

Other members of the premier's family were making similar ambassadorial journeys to other cities, seeking to create the alliance that Cultat envisioned. Petgrad was the most powerful nation in the south. It did not have to politically appease or parley with its neighbors. So long had it held this uncontested status, in fact, that it had no proper staff of diplomats. Now it was up to Cultat's relations to spread the word, for who else would be heard in those rival royal courts? And, according to Cultat, who else should bear the burden of this undertaking but his own blood?

So, to Trael it was.

Radstac shrugged to herself as she walked with her employer/lover, hand still upon her sword's pommel. So long as she got paid.

RAVEN
(2)

THE COUNCIL CHAMBER in the Governor's Palace was the largest single indoor space in the city-state of Felk. Here the governor would traditionally meet with his advisors to hear their reports and discuss plans for the running of what was at that time the second largest territory on the Isthmus, smaller only to the mighty state of Petgrad in the south.

Here, too, the governor would hold public trials and audiences once every lune, listening to cases and petitions from any who would seek his judgment or support. In those days, the space was opulently furnished and decorated, both to impress visitors and to remind them of the wealth and power the governor controlled.

Now, it was just a big room, the expensive furnishings gone, and there was no governor of Felk. Matokin was much more than that. It was said he took no hand in the day-to-day operation of his growing empire, preferring to leave minor matters to his underlings with whom he consulted in private. Nor did he conduct public hearings. He believed his time and the national treasury were better spent elsewhere, and felt no need or desire to remind anyone of his power.

Raven, both curious and anxious, paused at the periphery to survey. The space was huge, like a cavern inside this palace. It swallowed even the crowded bustle that infested the place.

The crowd of people ebbed and flowed. There were groupings of men and women huddled together in discussion, occasionally melding with other groups for brief consultation or argument before dividing again. A constant stream of messengers brushed past her, both arriving and leaving.

There was no doubt in her mind that what she was viewing was the nerve center of the empire she was sworn to serve, and she knew instinctively that there were dozens of decisions being made within her sight that would affect thousands of people.

As to exactly what her part in this was to be, or why she had been summoned here, she hadn't a clue.

Unwilling to interrupt any of the huddled planners, Raven approached a woman who was standing alone studying a scroll. "Excuse me?"

Dark eyes fastened on her, and she felt she had been weighed, measured, scrutinized, and dismissed as unimportant all in the space of a heartbeat.

"Well?"

"I was told to report here to Matokin, but I'm unfamiliar with the procedure."

That earned her three more heartbeats of examination.

"The middle door there in the far wall," the woman said at last. "The one with the guard in front of it. Give your name to the guard and wait to be summoned."

"Thank you," Raven said, but the woman had already returned her attention to the scroll.

Feeling even smaller than before, Raven undertook the

journey across the length of the room and eventually stepped up to the guard in front of the indicated door.

The guard stared at her, expressionless.

"My name is Raven," she said, trying to draw herself up, though even with her efforts she barely came midway up on the guard's chest. "From the Academy. I was told to report to Matokin."

The guard did not so much as blink.

"They're waiting for you," he said.

Turning, he banged his fist twice on the door, then stepped back, urging her forward with a quick jerk of his head.

Bracing herself as best she could against the fearful unknown, Raven pushed the door open.

Beyond was a small, unimpressive room, barely half the size of some of the classrooms back at the Academy. There were no decorations other than a large map of the Isthmus hanging on one wall. Scrolls and parchments cluttered the place, giving the appearance of a scholar's retreat, but it wasn't the room or its furnishings that captured Raven's attention. Rather, her eyes were drawn to the two men whose dialogue she had apparently interrupted.

The one behind the small desk was short and heavyset, more portly than muscular. He had dark hair and lively, dancing eyes. The soft blue robe he was wearing appeared to be more of a lounging or sleeping garment than a uniform, but there was no doubt in Raven's mind of his identity or rank. This was Matokin, the most powerful man on the Isthmus and engineer of Felk's growing empire.

Matokin's hair was dark. Just like hers. Just like her mother's.

Raven's heart beat hard. She felt almost giddy, though she would never have admitted to the emotion and showed nothing of it on her face. Here was a lifetime's worth of fantasies coming true. Here was her father! Of course, she meant to stick to her vow to keep that secret, even from him.

The other man in the room, lounging on a heavily cushioned chair, was long and lizard-lean. His soft hands had exceptionally long fingers, while his angular features housed eyes that, at the moment, were flat and expressionless.

"This must be Raven," Matokin said, inclining his head toward her slightly. "If not, the guard will regret it. Eh, Abraxis?"

Abraxis. Raven recognized the name. He was the chief of the internal security for the growing empire. He was supposedly responsible for the terminations that befell those of untrained magical ability who didn't pass muster. Politically, he was second in power.

Whether or not Matokin's comment was meant in jest was left uncertain, as the man on the cushions gave no reaction either by word or gesture, but instead continued staring at the intruder.

"I am Raven, Lord," she said. "I was told that you wished to see me." With great effort she kept her voice from quivering completely out of control.

"Yes. We've been reviewing your records," Matokin said, gesturing vaguely at the small clutter on his desk, "and wished to meet you in the flesh. You seem to be making excellent progress, though your instructors' praise seems grudging at times."

"At the school, we work at perfecting control of the magical arts to the best of our individual abilities," Raven said. "We are discouraged from comparing our efforts to those of our fellow classmates, or from seeking approval from the instructors."

"Do you find the discipline and rules at the Academy to be harsh and demanding?" Abraxis asked, speaking for the first time.

"Words like *harsh* and *demanding* are relative terms," Raven said with a shrug. "I myself do not feel the conditions at the school to be unreasonable. We are living in difficult times and fighting an expansionist war. If we are to achieve our goals, it means accepting as normal conditions that, in other circumstances, might be deemed harsh and demanding."

"And what do you think those goals are, Raven?" Matokin said with a smile.

That smile nearly undid her. Her *father* was *smiling* at her. But she kept control.

"To unite the city-states of the Isthmus under one strong rule, specifically yours, Lord Matokin."

"Yes," Matokin was nodding. "Indeed."

"We have a posting for you," Abraxis said.

Raven's already fast-beating heart gave a sharp start.

"A . . . p-posting?"

She winced inwardly, hating the timid sound of her voice. She was off guard. She hadn't yet graduated the Academy. She wasn't a full-fledged mage, not by anyone's measure. She had an aptitude, yes. She was most certainly dedicated to learning the magical arts. But she could only perform tricks at best at this point.

Had some error occurred? Had they meant to summon someone else here?

"Really, Abraxis," Matokin said mildly. "No need to unsettle the girl."

Raven felt a rush of gratitude toward her father.

"There's been no mistake," Matokin continued, as if reading her thoughts. Considering what magical powers he was reputed to possess, perhaps he was. "We know that you are still studying at the Academy. You're no wizard yet, but I'd wager you'll make a fine one someday. Discipline is as key as any innate talent."

She flushed, feeling her face heat. Neither of the men remarked on it.

"Our general in the field, Lord Weisel, has made a specific personnel request."

"He requested *me*?" she blurted.

This time Abraxis laughed, but it didn't sound as pleasant as Matokin's laughter.

"No," said Matokin. "He wanted a student straight out of the Academy. Someone absolutely fresh."

"Why, my Lord?"

"In his communication," Abraxis said, "he made mention of a desire to be kept thoroughly updated on any magical advances, so that he can immediately implement the techniques against the enemy."

"It's a lie, of course," Matokin added.

Raven's eyes widened. She of course knew Weisel's name. He was a military man, supposedly a brilliant strategist, but not a magician.

"Our Weisel wants to learn about magic," Matokin said.

Raven was confused. "But . . . doesn't he have wizards with him? A whole company of them?" Naturally many of them were graduates from the Academy.

"He does," Abraxis put in. "But they are under strict orders not to divulge any specifics about magical procedures to the general."

"Why not?" she asked, before she could catch herself.

Abraxis's flat eyes darkened. "It's not your place to ask that of anyone in this room, girl. Understood?"

"Yes, Lord."

"We're sending you to him," Matokin said, businesslike now, moving papers around on the desk. "You are free to divulge to Weisel anything you're able to. In fact, your orders are to supply him with whatever information you've accumulated in your time at the Academy. If Weisel asks about a spell, you answer him to the best of your ability."

"But that's not all there is to this posting," Abraxis said.

Once more Raven braced herself. She would obey, whatever the order. Of course she would. She was loyal. To the empire. To her father.

"You will spy on our general," Matokin said. "You will become his confidant. You will become whatever else that we subsequently instruct you to become. You will inform us via one of our Far Speak wizards what information Weisel is seeking. These are your orders."

Raven stepped forward and took the scroll that Matokin held out. Her fingers very nearly brushed his.

Her father had one last thing to say.

"Go now and justify our confidence in you."

Raven went. She would do just that.

BRYCK
(3)

FOOT PATROLS MARCHED at unfailing intervals. So regular were they—even using the same routes—that one could mark the passing watches by the movements of the Felk occupiers through Callah's streets.

Bryck had surmised that these patrols were meant mostly to intimidate, rather than do any real policing. Everyone he'd met already seemed acutely aware of the Felk and their dominating presence and didn't need the reminders.

He had just bought himself a light but tasty meal. He had surreptitiously tapped a brass coin on the tabletop, thus receiving special service from the proprietor.

Legally only scrip could be used for all transactions within the city. Paper money. *Paper.* The Felk had issued it, and at the same time they had confiscated all the hard currency they could lay their hands on, presumably to help finance the war. The funny-looking pieces of imprinted colored paper were, the occupiers said, worth precisely the same as proper coins. The scrip was marked to indicate denominations. If the Felk took a copper, they issued a red note; if they took a bronze, a green note; and so forth.

Perhaps more than anything else about the occupation, people were having difficulty adjusting to transacting business with scrip. But these were just the impotent grumblings of a defeated people.

One of those patrols was passing, booted feet clomping in a synchronized rumble. The faces of the Felk soldiers were set, hard. The squad was twenty strong and well armed.

People immediately found somewhere else to be. Some shrank into doorways. All traffic halted till the soldiers were past.

Bryck, too, quietly stepped aside. He had been in Callah some days now. He knew its ways. He had also noticed the superficial differences from his home of U'delph, the variations in architecture and style of dress. Fortunately his traveler's clothes were neutral enough they didn't make him stand out.

Even his meal had been unusual—the curious variety of vegetables, the pungent tea he'd sipped only once. Everything was recognizable but also odd, exotic. The way familiar things were made strange in dreams.

On arrival he'd been ordered to report to the City Registry, where his horse had finally been conscripted. He was only surprised that he'd managed to hang on to the animal so long. The horse had been with him since he'd ridden from U'delph, seeking aid from neighboring Sook. Bryck wouldn't even have earned the privilege to ride if he hadn't trifled with those dice, manipulating their outcome with a little wizardry.

At the Registry he had exchanged the small number of coins he purposely kept in his pockets for local scrip, not protesting the trade. His larger cache of coins stayed secreted in his coat's lining. He had used the money to secure himself lodgings, which was where his vox-mellie was currently stored.

The Registry was a large municipal building of white-washed stone at the city center. Evidently it had been the seat of the city's government before the Felk arrived. There Bryck had also surrendered the civilian travel pass that he'd been issued on entering Felk-controlled country. It was replaced with a temporary resident permit. Temporary, since as a traveling minstrel he wouldn't be here permanently.

"I will stay until winter," he'd said during his questioning; and that was how long the permit was good for.

He was surprised things had gone so easily, surprised that the Felk had the necessary bureaucracy in place to handle his peculiar status as a troubadour. He was certainly being allowed freedoms not enjoyed by others. Callah's residents, for instance, were required to stay inside the city limits. Those that worked the outlying farmlands were restricted to those areas, under penalty of arrest or even summary execution.

As to what was happening elsewhere on the Isthmus . . . who knew? People were hungry for news, and when they couldn't find it, they invented it.

There was a mist on the autumn air this afternoon that was fast on its way to becoming rain. Were he still in U'delph, some distance south, this rain would be light. Here it promised to be unseasonably heavy.

The street was already wet, and the soldiers' boots left behind a neat pattern of prints, each foot falling cleanly atop the last.

Bryck moved. His thick greying hair was getting damp. He turned up his coat's collar and kept near the buildings, under their ornamental eaves.

He had learned the details of Callah's conquest since arriving. He didn't need to interrogate anyone; most wouldn't shut up about it once they got started, particularly in the taverns. Everybody had a personal tale of woe.

Did the Felk annihilate *your* city, slaughter *your* people? Bryck always asked silently, darkly. But that sort of bitterness was as useless as it was reflexive. He should feel a kinship with these Callahans. Shouldn't he? The Felk had conquered them. Felk was the enemy of Callah. Therefore . . .

Wars had sides. If one was a participant in a war, one chose one side or the other.

Or, perhaps, a sole individual could be his *own* side. A lone front. A singular army. Yes. Perhaps.

Muck oozed up around his boots as he made for a particular alley.

Callah's conquest, he had learned, was orchestrated by a Lord Weisel, who was said to still be heading the Felk forces. That the Felk were using magic as an instrument of war was disquieting. Where, Bryck wondered, had all those potent magicians appeared from so suddenly? Rumor had it that a small contingent of the wizards was here in Callah, as part of the garrison, though nobody seemed to have actually seen any of these magicians. It might be they were secluded somewhere in the Registry building. Or they might not exist at all.

Bryck rapped his knuckles on the doorjamb. The tight alleyway smelled of spoiling meat. A drape of woven fiber hung across the doorway, allowing glimpses into the dim chamber beyond.

There was no response for some while, but he didn't knock again; instead, waited blandly as the rain started in earnest.

Finally feet scraped the floor beyond the doorway. A hand reached up to whisk aside the drapery. "You don't know enough to come in out of the rain?"

"I know enough not to enter uninvited."

"Then you're summoned. Come in." The little man moved back, and Bryck entered. Inside, things smelled much more pleasant—a scent like berries and milk, but mixed with a gentle wood smoke. Bryck inhaled the incense gratefully.

Slydis's workshop was designed to accommodate its

master. That Slydis, three tenwinters old, stood no taller than a child meant that Bryck fairly towered above the furnishings. The scribe wasn't merely short, but stunted; limbs ill-proportioned to his somewhat stumpy trunk.

Bryck had once penned a play about little people. A comedy, naturally. In it the "all-dwarf" cast—normal-sized players—acted out their scenes amidst oversized backdrops and props.

Slydis's repute as a copyist was a good one. Bryck had made inquiries at several city market stalls that sold reading matter. He had visited this shop two days ago, offering half of what would add up to a handsome fee—in silver—for the completion of a special job. Slydis had accepted. People still preferred to transact in coin, despite the prohibition.

Beneath the incense was a rich odor of ink and paper. The workshop shelves were heavy with materials. Slydis settled at a desk that stood only as high as Bryck's knee. The scribe's wispy hair and grey stubble made him look impossibly old as he set a lamp on a hook over the desk, the light cutting shadows from his features.

Bryck had taken a risk with this man. Transacting in coin was a crime in Callah. What he had asked this copyist to duplicate surely constituted a worse offense.

Slydis's permanently ink-black fingers carefully laid out the vellum under the lamplight. "Here we are. What do you think?"

Bryck crouched down for a look. This was a costly purchase, but it was immediately apparent that he'd paid for quality. Studying the imprint in the yellow wax closer only deepened his appreciation of the product. He pinched a corner of the paper. Even the texture felt correct.

"It's a fine job," Bryck said, straightening up. When he dropped a small bundle of Felk-issued colored scrip on the desk, the dwarf's eyes went narrow and his hand slapped down atop the forged civilian travel pass.

"*Not* paper. That wasn't our contract." He seemed on the verge of crumpling the vellum then and there.

But Bryck had already dug out the proper number of silver coins. He stooped and put the neat stack on the desk. "That's your payment. And here's another—a goldie. Prepayment for another job, if you're interested."

"Make me interested." The silvers were already in Slydis's tunic pocket. He was eyeing the gold coin lustfully.

Bryck pointed to the notes. "That. The paper money."

"If you want quality, paying with coin is—"

"I *am* paying in coin. What I want copied is that money."

Slydis stared up at Bryck a long time. At last he said, "By the sanity of the gods . . . that is a diabolical notion."

Bryck told the little man he wanted to see a convincing facsimile of each denomination. If the work was as good as that which had gone into the travel pass, he would pay for more notes. Many more.

Bryck left the shop with the pass tucked away in his coat. The Felk had confiscated the one he'd been issued earlier. He had decided that having a replacement pass of his own would be prudent, in the event he wanted to leave Callah before the start of winter.

He permitted himself a small smile as he walked. One of the very first theatricals he had ever written was *The Deceitful Doings and Derring-do of Dabran Del.* (Back then he had thought alliteration inherently funny.) It was the sort of unremarkable early effort every artist cringed over, he imagined. Weak, forced, demonstrating more potential for talent than actual skill. Fortunately the play hadn't been performed in years and was by now probably mercifully lost. Bryck himself could remember few of its particulars.

In truth, all he really recollected was that the lead character had forged some crucial document—a certificate of marriage, he suddenly recalled—and that that simple

piece of paper had by the play's end brought about the fall
of an entire kingdom.

HE STILL MISSED Aaysue. Still missed his children.
Their glaring absences were the central source of his internal pain, which was considerable . . . which was excruciating at times. But he could temper his agony. He could
alleviate its worst heat by applying cooling thoughts of
vengeance to it.

The Felk occupiers were handling their captured city
shrewdly, he judged. Women weren't being raped; people
weren't being killed arbitrarily. Callah's citizens still had
their livelihoods, still earned money—albeit the loathed
paper variety. There were some food shortages, but not serious ones. The Felk, then, weren't behaving as barbarians.

It seemed improbable that these were the same people
that had slaughtered and incinerated his home. U'delph's
destruction was an act of evil mindless savagery. Bryck
didn't relent an iota in his hatred of his enemy, but the
strange dichotomy in the behavior of the Felk was curious.

He was letting his beard grow. He'd felt only a slight
alarm when he found it coming in almost entirely grey. It
made him appear older than his—nearly—four tenwinters. Once vanity would have made him shave it, in an effort to still look young and vigorous, no matter that his
years might say otherwise.

Actually, he thought as he approached a tavern, vox-
mellie on his back, he was more physically fit now than he
had been in a long time. He had lost a considerable amount
of weight. In fact, he had initially decided to grow the
beard to cover the recent gauntness of his once round face.

He wasn't living a coddled noble's life anymore. No
rich foods, a minimum of drinking. Once he had been soft.
Now he was toughened.

Bryck had scouted out the tavern and made his arrange-
ments with the proprietor. He entered through the rear,

stepping over a rivulet of slops and presenting himself to the one-eyed landlady whose remaining eye held a flinty intensity.

"Need a meal?" Animal blood flecked her apron.

"Not now. Later perhaps."

"Play good as y'did before, and there'll be a later. Y'can have a drink now, if you want."

"Hot wine."

"I'll bring it to your corner. Go there now. Play."

He wended his way through the tables. A fair number of people were gathered. It was a good venue for what he intended. The place was spacious enough to accommodate a crowd but still felt intimate. Bryck sat and, ignoring a tingling of stage nerves, started playing.

He deliberately sang songs he knew to be unfamiliar this far north. It was best that these people understand he was a foreigner.

He drank his wine in cooling stages between bawdy ballads and mawkish verses. The tavern's patrons drank likewise, and ordered and ate their suppers, thereby bringing a satisfied glint to the proprietress's intact eye.

His fingers moved with a nimbleness they hadn't possessed even a half-lune ago. He had become, in his own humble estimation, a reasonably respectable musician—certainly a finer one than he'd been before this adventure. Back in U'delph, back during his lighthearted days of carousing and gambling and penning the occasional theatrical, music-making had been merely a hobby, a stunt to make himself the life of the party. And so many parties there had been, so carefree and uncomplicated was his life, what with his nobility, wealth, fame, a loving wife, a cheerful passel of children.

He had played past his allotted time. It would be curfew in another watch. He now picked out the doleful melody of "Lament for the Unnamed Dead," moving the winder with dirge-like slowness, intoning the sad simple words, feeling nothing more than a vague melancholy. It had been some while now since he had actually wept, for Aaysue and the children, for all he'd lost. His tears had gone cold.

The last notes played to a nearly silent room. Bryck blinked, having almost forgotten about his audience. Dimly lit faces regarded him. Here and there in the crowd he saw the shine of tears.

He lifted off the stringbox and waved over the landlady. Money had accumulated over time in the empty jar he'd set on the floor at his feet. Paper only, he saw, no coins. He recalled the Felk soldier, a conscripted Callahan, who at the city's border checkpoint had offered a coin (itself an illegal act!) for the music Bryck had played.

He counted out the notes from the jar where the landlady could see.

"Y'might've ended with something a mite more jolly," she muttered, but still seemed pleased with her take. She'd brought him his meal. He ate.

He waited, and they came to him slowly, the patrons. First, a few congratulators; then, the ones with questions.

"You're a real bard, then? A . . . traveler?"

"Yes." He finished his food. Someone bought him a fresh mug of wine without asking if he wanted another. They pulled chairs near him. They leaned in. He was in a semicircle of ten, twelve, more. The vox-mellifluous stood propped beside him. Some had left the tavern when he'd finished playing. Everybody else was now gathered near.

"Have you any . . . news?"

It was a man with the soot of a forge embedded in the age-lines of his face who asked. None in Bryck's audience was young. All were roughly his age or older. In Callah there were only such semi-elders, and children, and the infirm and crippled. All able bodies had been drafted into the military.

The man's question touched off many others, all at once. All wanted word about this place or that, cities and hamlets both nearby Callah and far away. They went so far as to ask urgently after specific individuals who lived in these places, some of which Bryck had never heard of. He lifted a hand and waited.

When he had quiet, he darted his eyes right and left, adding to the sense of secretiveness that had come over the scene. His questioners huddled closer.

"I've come from the south," he said, and they hung on his syllables. These Callahans were the first of the Felk conquests. They effectively knew nothing about the current state of the war. Or little enough that Bryck's inventions wouldn't immediately be decried as lies.

So he told them of the uprising against the Felk in the captured city of Windal, not far to the southeast.

The one-eyed landlady quietly took a seat to hear. Everyone behaved as he'd hoped, much like the gullible ensemble of *Chicanery by Moonlight* behaved when Gleed the wandering fortune-teller declared that their village had been built atop the belly of a slumbering giant. It was one of his more popular plays.

Bryck left while there was still time to get indoors before curfew.

DARDAS

(3)

DARDAS FELT THE cold. It was Weisel's body he was wearing, yes, but this chill came from deep within, and it had nothing to do with the cooling autumn weather of the Isthmus.

"Hurry with it," he said, intending the command to be stony but hearing a tiny thread of unease in it. That was nothing, of course, to the unease he actually did feel, and justifiably so.

He was, after all, dying. Or rather being returned to the death from which he'd been resurrected.

It was unavoidable, inevitable. So Matokin had explained it, some while ago. Matokin, naturally, was the first person Dardas had seen upon waking from his own death inside the fleshy vessel of Lord Weisel.

Resurrection magic was powerful, fantastically so. But it needed to be maintained, with rejuvenation spells. Without these, death would return, like a chronic disease.

It had started early in the night. Dardas had been informed as to what symptoms would present themselves, and had sent word directly to Matokin in Felk, via Berkant and his Far Speak abilities. The message was coded. Matokin had acknowledged.

A short while later, as Dardas felt his condition worsening, a mage came through a portal and reported immediately to Weisel's tent.

The army, which was marching and riding south by conventional means, was already camped for the night. Dardas hadn't yet opted to use the Far Movement magic to transport his forces instantly to the city-state of Trael, which was their next logical target.

This mage had identified himself as Kumbat. Like all the wizards Dardas had encountered, he looked no different from anyone else. Just a man. But he was more than that. He had powers that most men and women didn't possess.

"Hurry," Dardas repeated, barely able to hold back the fear now.

Death was coming for him . . . death that had been cheated once, and now wanted its property back. It was like a great cold mouth was opening beneath him, rising swiftly now, meaning to swallow him whole.

Kumbat shed his dark robe and suddenly launched into a whirl of gestures and gyrations. Words croaked from his lips, fast and unrecognizable. His face contorted and reddened. Sweat stood out on his forehead. There was no one in the tent but the two of them. Dardas lay on his bunk, no longer able to keep to his feet.

It was a mighty display. Dardas watched, transfixed, still feeling the cold death-mouth rising to consume him, but distracted in these last moments of life by the uproar of the mage's movements and the atonal chanting.

Dardas remembered his original death. His heart had seized, and he had died a few days later, in bed, fading in and out of consciousness. This death, now, was much more intense, immediate, and personal. Death itself was coming for him specifically and the nonsensical actions of this so-called mage were doing nothing to stave it off.

Matokin had cheated him. The godsdamned Felk bleeder!

Kumbat, sweat streaming off his half-naked body now, lunged forward and laid his hands on Dardas's chest.

A great shock erupted through Dardas's body. Incredibly, he felt his hair actually standing on end. His body jumped, and it felt like his blood was suddenly boiling in his veins. He tried to cry out, but his tongue locked.

Kumbat removed his hands.

Death was no longer near. Dardas blinked wildly. He vaulted off the bunk, his heart racing.

"By the madness of the gods!" he exclaimed. It was one of those Isthmus sayings he had picked up in this new life.

New life, he thought, a grin cutting his features. That new life, it seemed, was going to continue awhile longer.

Kumbat, himself recovering, was putting his robe back on.

"That," Dardas heaved, "was fine work."

"I only obey my Lord's orders," the mage said.

That was Matokin, of course, not Lord Weisel he was referring to.

Dardas's grin cooled a bit. "Well, I'm glad for your efforts. Tell me, Kumbat, how did you accomplish it? It felt to me as if you were pouring, I don't know, naked *energy* into my body."

Kumbat's face went still. He looked levelly at Dardas. "I must apologize, General Weisel, for I cannot speak of such matters."

Dardas's grin had vanished entirely now. He was drawing steady breaths.

"General, I am to report immediately to Lord Matokin upon completion of this assignment. May I have your leave to go?"

Asking permission, Dardas thought sarcastically. As if these damned mages needed his consent to do anything.

They were all Matokin's instruments. He must never forget that.

"Dismissed," Dardas said quietly. Kumbat had arrived at the camp by Far Movement, and by Far Movement magic he would return to Matokin to report that Dardas remained alive.

Kumbat had even addressed him as "General Weisel," though this mage certainly knew the truth . . . that another lived inside the host body of Lord Weisel. It was another subtle affront, a reminder as to who was really in charge here.

Suddenly, there was an intrusion.

What happened? That was the strangest experience I've ever had. Do I understand right, that the resurrection magic was wearing off—

With what was now a reflexive mental motion, Dardas suppressed Weisel's thoughts till they could no longer be heard. He didn't need the distraction or the annoyance right now. Offhandedly he wondered if Weisel would have died along with him if Kumbat hadn't intervened. Maybe not. Death had been coming for Dardas. The host body, including Weisel's consciousness, probably would have survived.

It was past the midnight watch, but Dardas felt charged with strength and vigor, despite the long ride today and the one he and his army would undertake tomorrow. He paced around his tent, flexing his limbs. Death had been close enough that he'd felt its icy breath on him. Now, he was restored, just as Matokin had promised the rejuvenation spells would do.

He ought to call for one of the female playthings that his aides always seemed able to produce for him. Why, he would cork her brains out.

No. That student he had requisitioned. He had arrived today. No, *she* had. Sent by portal from the Academy at Felk, fresh, hopefully uncontaminated by the strictures Matokin had imposed on all the other mages in Dardas's army. Perhaps this student, if she was naive enough, could be manipulated to divulge the information he wanted.

He called for his aide. Just about every one of his junior officers had been rotated through the post by now. Dardas had learned a good deal about his army this way. These were good troops, for the most part. Dardas would lead them to victories, and their loyalty would grow.

While he waited for the student, he poured a glass of the liquor he had shared with Berkant. It tasted wonderful. His senses were preternaturally alive.

"General Weisel."

He had heard her being ushered inside and deliberately kept his back to the flap. He let a small smile move his lips now. She hadn't addressed him as "Lord Weisel."

He turned, taking his time. What he found was a rather stout young woman, her hair uncared for, her dour features indicating that she did not consider herself in any way physically attractive—and what's more she never had. There was a great purpose in her eyes, though. She was dedicated. She meant to perform well, to please.

But, Dardas mused, sipping more of his drink, *who did she mean to please?*

He let himself chuckle aloud. Judging character was a talent every commander needed.

"If I have amused," she said, carefully, "I hope I have not also offended."

He shook his head. "No. Neither." He slung himself into a seat, putting his bare feet up, taking a deliberately relaxed posture. "It's . . . Raven. Right?"

"Yes, General."

"They got you here quick enough."

"Traveling by portal is definitely expedient, sir."

Dardas nodded. "A bit unnerving, though, didn't you think? Or maybe you've got guts made of metal."

"It doesn't take nerve to go through a portal, General," Raven said. "It only takes the willingness to obey one's orders. My orders said to go through, sir."

Dedicated, indeed.

"How good a wizard are you?" he asked, bluntly.

At last a look of hesitation crossed her otherwise stoic face. "My training is incomplete."

"That I know. Answer my question." But he didn't say it too sharply.

"I can perform, successfully and consistently, only the simplest spells we were being taught at the Academy." Her eyes flickered downward. "I . . . I am not of the caliber of those who serve you here in the field."

Dardas took another swallow from his glass. "What is your favorite spell?"

"Sir?"

He waved. "Not the one you were best at, or tried the hardest to master. Which one did you like to do the very most?"

Raven, a bit taken aback, nonetheless considered. She was about to answer.

Dardas cut her off. "No. Don't tell me. *Show* me."

She frowned, deepening the normal dour look on her chubby face. If she could learn to smile, he judged, she might just be on her way to being passably attractive.

He watched, interested, as she looked about the tent. He had a lamp burning, but there was a candle stub on the small table on which he was resting his feet. He had been examining maps earlier.

Raven drew a long, deep breath. Dardas eyed her young breasts as they pushed outward. She was concentrating, gathering herself, much as Kumbat had in this same tent only a short while ago.

Dardas's eyes moved to the unlit candle, which Raven's own gaze was now fastened to.

Suddenly, a large curl of flame erupted around the wick. A spark leapt off, touching Dardas's bare foot.

"Sorry, General!" she said, suddenly fearful.

Dardas chuckled again, slapping casually at his foot. "What for, girl? That was good. I've witnessed acts of magic in this army that I never in all my years expected to see. Amazing feats. But, I tell you now, it's the little things that impress me most."

She looked perplexed.

Dardas continued. "I've seen this entire army, every last man, woman, wagon, and spear, moved through those portals. It's incredible. Mind-boggling, in fact. But, somehow, you can't really *believe* in it. It just seems too impossible to be happening, even with the evidence right before your eyes."

He nodded toward the candle. The flame had steadied. "Now, that is something I can believe in. You made it happen. I saw you do it. And even though I don't understand how you accomplished it, I can believe. Understand?"

He watched her carefully. He saw her digesting his words. When he saw the faintest tickle of a smile pull at her mouth, he knew he had his first victory.

"Yes, General. I think I see."

He smiled back.

"That's all for now, Raven. We'll talk again, when I have time. Get some sleep."

She exited the tent. He called his aide again as he reexamined the maps. Trael was still some days of marching away, if he didn't order the portals to be used. Naturally, he had advance scouts, mages among them, who were reporting directly to him (and probably to Matokin as well) by Far Speak about any signs of organized resistance ahead.

There was nothing to speak of, just small local militaries desperately and futilely preparing against the coming onslaught. No great army rising in the path of his forces.

It offended Dardas's sensibilities. What was he going to have to do, *create* an enemy worthy of standing against him?

"Damned Isthmusers," he muttered.

"General?" The aide was still waiting.

Dardas waved it off. He gave his instructions. The

newly arrived fledgling wizard, Raven, was to be groomed and given something flattering to wear. Mages weren't required to dress in uniforms, but they all seemed to opt for those dreary dark robes. The next time Dardas saw her, he wanted Raven to look more presentable.

The aide didn't even blink, simply acknowledging the orders. Weisel had proven himself to be an able military commander; he'd earned the respect of his officers.

His eyes fell again to the maps. Trael. There he was going to have to take drastic actions once more, as he had at U'delph. This time it would be even worse, though. U'delph had merely been obliterated.

But, as Dardas knew from a lifetime of warfare, there were worse things than death.

AQUINT

(3)

AQUINT DIDN'T LIKE the portals. He hadn't liked stepping into one when the Felk army had attacked U'delph, and he didn't like how frequently they were used here at the warehouse.

But Far Movement was a great way to move goods. If he'd had access to this kind of magic for his freight business in Callah, he would have been rich enough to get by as a strictly legitimate business owner.

He chuckled to himself at the thought. No, probably not. He just wasn't the legitimate type, not as a civilian, and not as a soldier.

He double-checked a manifest for a shipment that was going out to a village where the Felk had a small garrison. Occupying the conquered territories of the Isthmus was quite a drain on military personnel, but General Weisel was no doubt on his way to capturing yet another city-state, from which fresh conscripts would help fill out the ranks.

Aquint didn't follow the war news much. He was glad,

certainly, to be out of the fighting. Here in the warehouse, he was back in his rightful element.

That element, of course, was crime. Within the first days of his assignment here, he had successfully "cracked" the theft ring plaguing this warehouse. The officer who was the quartermaster was very pleased, and had given Aquint a citation, which he accepted with humility.

Immediately afterward, Aquint implemented a new, much more efficient theft ring, using Vahnka's agents. They were now smuggling out of the warehouse only those choicest items that could turn the best and fastest profit. Everybody was happy, even the quartermaster, who accepted these small losses as inevitable, but who was well pleased with the overall reduction in pilferage.

Aquint even found being an officer tolerable. Once he'd completed his undercover assignment, he had assumed his new rank openly. Officers enjoyed privileges he hadn't known during his time as a simple soldier. He had good food, good wine. He kept the warehouse running smoothly, and nobody bothered him much.

It seemed like a stable situation. Let the rest of the Isthmus worry about the war. He had carved himself a cozy little niche here.

Suddenly, a patch of wavy air appeared in the middle of the warehouse. Aquint automatically retreated a step. It was a portal opening. He frowned. This was unscheduled.

The man who stepped out of the Far Movement portal was tall, lean, and dressed importantly. The wizards who were assigned to the warehouse all bowed respectfully, including the Far Movement and Far Speak mages who had handled this end of the portal—all without prior clearance from Aquint. That boded ill. He didn't like the idea of anyone dropping in unannounced.

Aquint suppressed his anxiety and annoyance and strode forward to greet the noble. Probably he was a wizard. Most of the top Felk politicos were.

"Welcome to Sook, Lord," Aquint said.

The man's flat eyes fell on him. "I do believe you are Aquint. Is that correct?"

Aquint felt his throat tighten a bit. Was this some bit of magic? And why would a Felk lord know *his* name?

Unless his smuggling operation had been found out . . .

"I am Aquint, Lord," he said, keeping his voice steady. "Shall I fetch the quartermaster? He's in his office just over there—"

The man waved a long-fingered hand. "No. I wish to see you. My name is Abraxis."

Aquint's eyes widened involuntarily. He recognized the name, and an instant later, he realized why. Abraxis was Matokin's second in command.

He was also supposedly in charge of the internal security throughout the empire. Dread closed its fingers completely around Aquint's throat now. Where had he slipped up? Had Vahnka betrayed him? It didn't matter. What was done was done.

"Take me somewhere private. I wish to speak to you."

Aquint led the way. His mind raced, but he could see no way out. Up in the rafters he noticed a quick darting movement. Cat was up there, watching. He would miss the boy, Aquint thought. Wherever he was going, Cat would not be following.

Aquint closed the door of the small, empty storage chamber behind him. It had held grain that they had shipped out to the general's troops yesterday.

Abraxis faced him.

"You are originally from Callah?"

Aquint blinked at the unexpected question. "That's correct, Lord."

"The reports I have read credit you with reducing the theft and pilferage from this warehouse," Abraxis said. "Very impressive. In fact, it borders on the unbelievable."

Aquint said nothing. There was nothing to say. It really was over.

"I am the chief of the Internal Security Corps," Abraxis

went on, almost conversationally. "It is my job to root out traitors and malcontents throughout the empire."

"That must keep you busy," Aquint was shocked to hear himself suddenly say. It was his nerves. He was probably on the verge of breaking down, right here.

Abraxis, unsurprisingly, didn't smile.

"And what is that supposed to mean?" he said. "Are you implying that discontent is so rampant in the empire?"

"Not at all," Aquint said, groping desperately for the right words. "It just strikes me that, with the empire growing as fast as it has, it's quite a job for one person to be in charge of security."

Abraxis actually appeared to consider that for a moment, then gave a deep sigh.

"It is," he said. "This is a relatively new post, despite its importance. When Lord Matokin first rose to power in Felk, he discussed it. His plans for expanding his dominion were, well, *ambitious*. I'm not sure any of us who backed him from the first expected things to turn out so successfully."

Aquint kept the frown off his face. What was this man saying? Maybe he wasn't here to arrest Aquint after all.

"Now, however," Abraxis said, "the Felk Empire is an ever-growing reality. And it must be policed from within."

"I see," Aquint said slowly.

"Do you?" Abraxis fixed him with those flat eyes.

Aquint waited.

"Effective immediately, you are relieved of your duties with the army," Abraxis said, holding out a scroll. "Instead, you will work for me as one of my agents."

Aquint was flabbergasted. This was so far from what he had been expecting, his brain reeled, unable to cope with the new situation.

"Me?" he managed to sputter. "But what use can I possibly be?"

"For your first assignment, quite a lot," Abraxis said, still holding out the scroll. "There are reports of potential unrest in Callah. You know the place and the people. I want you to look into it. If it is more than general grumbling, find out who is behind it, so they can be dealt with."

"But I know nothing of that kind of work," Aquint protested.

"You know enough to have broken, almost overnight, a pilferage operation that the quartermaster could do nothing to stop." A smile at last came to his nearly expressionless face. It wasn't a pleasant smile. "And you've had the wiliness and guile to substitute it with your own smuggling operation."

Aquint almost denied it, reflexively. He was immediately glad he hadn't. Plainly this Abraxis knew what he was talking about. Aquint didn't even wonder how he'd come by the information. Apparently this Internal Security Corps was effective.

"Besides," the chief of the corps said, "I don't recall saying you had a choice."

"Yes, Lord."

"I need agents, Aquint. This is important enough that I recruit my people personally whenever possible. This is a new world we are building. A better one. Matokin will unite the entire Isthmus, and when that's done, there will be no more war. We will have one rule, and it will be up to my corps to see that it stands. Understood?"

"Yes, Lord."

Abraxis thrust the scroll into Aquint's hand.

"This scroll will give you all the authority you need to deal with the military and even the mages. I'll give you a brief time to set your personal affairs in order locally, then have yourself Far Moved directly to Callah."

"Yes, Lord," Aquint repeated, numbly. He could barely believe what was happening. So much for his cozy niche.

"I think you'll like the work, really, once you get accustomed. You'll have a free hand to operate as you see fit. All I ask for is results."

"Thank you, Lord," Aquint said.

WARTORN: RESURRECTION 149

"Oh, yes. One more thing. Give me your hand a moment."

Puzzled, Aquint held out his hand. Abraxis turned it palm up, then produced a small knife and made a small, fast cut on his thumb. He dabbed at the cut with a small piece of white cloth.

"There," he said. "That makes it binding."

"What was that?" Aquint said. "A blood oath?"

"Rather more than that," Abraxis said, placing the cloth in a small red carrying bag. "It's standard procedure for students at the Academy. Also for anyone of high rank or power in the empire. Should you prove to be untrustworthy or lax in your duties, that sample of your blood will mean that we won't have to hunt you down to administer discipline."

"I see," Aquint said, feeling suddenly queasy.

"It was my idea," Abraxis said with a note of pride. "It was one of the first measures I implemented as chief of Internal Security. It's proven very effective."

"I imagine it has, Lord. May I ask where that sample will be kept?"

"What do you want to know that for?" Abraxis said.

"Merely self-preservation," Aquint said. "If my well-being is tied to that sample of blood, I would like to be assured that it won't fall into the wrong hands. Though you haven't said specifically, I imagine that our work will make us unpopular in certain quarters."

"That's reasonable," Abraxis nodded, after a moment's consideration. "I keep such samples with me at all times. Under the circumstances, I feel it's the safest place for them to be."

He nodded to the scroll in Aquint's hand.

"The procedural details of your assignment are in there as well. You'll contact Colonel Jesile, Callah's governor. He will give you full cooperation."

"Does it also detail . . . my new rate of payment, Lord?"

Abraxis's smile was a bit more sincere this time. "It does. And you'll be pleased with it."

"Yes, Lord."

The corps chief exited the room.

Alone with his thoughts, Aquint reflected on the sudden remarkable turn his life had taken. He tried to imagine Cat's reaction to the news. He would, of course, take the boy along to Callah. They would both be going home. If Abraxis was right about his new authority as an agent, there wasn't anybody who could stop him.

Even as Aquint sorted out his reactions, though, a part of his mind was starting to piece together a plan. There must be some way to switch the sample of his blood that Abraxis carried for another, harmless substitute.

PRAULTH
(3)

•

CLOSING HER EYES without first coupling with Xink would mean seeing lines and arrows and text maddeningly crisscrossing the backs of her eyelids. It would mean restlessness and uneasiness and a poor sleep. Fortunately she and Xink had sexual intercourse—though she was learning to call the act by less formal, more lively names—each night without fail, oftentimes more than once. He indulged her tirelessly, never seeming sated, always hungry for her body, which she had always thought, if she thought of it at all, as sadly commonplace. He assured her she wore the shape of a passion goddess.

She had discovered that her appetites, too, were boundless, and nightly she was still learning the apparently endless variations of physical love. Xink was a marvelous instructor.

Amusing . . . *instructor* had once meant something quite different to her, back when she'd been a mere *student*. Now what was she? She didn't rightly know. Her work for Master Honnis consumed her intellectually, while

Xink absorbed her emotionally and physically. Her life of late was a very full thing, indeed.

Tonight she slept her usual, sublimely exhausted sleep. They did not wear any clothing in the bed they shared, the big bed with the soft mattress. They held each other, squirmed against each other, nuzzled, and nestled together even as they slumbered. Sometimes, waking a bit, she would feel Xink's rigidness pressing her—his manhood firm and warm, and he still asleep . . . at least until she touched him there, and he woke—never complaining, always eager—and they chose from among the dizzying array of options just *where* inside her that fine fleshy pillar should be placed.

It was not desire for further intercourse that woke her tonight. It was a hand, shaking her shoulder firmly.

She went from dark dreamlessness to the brightness of their chamber in the University's Blue Annex. There was a window set into one wall, but the light wasn't coming from there; and besides, she could feel immediately that she hadn't had a sufficient amount of sleep—two watches at most. It was the dead of night . . . but the lamp hanging from its bronze hook burned overhead, blinding.

"Praulth—beauty, you must, you *must*—"

She touched Xink's shaking hand to stop it. She blinked painfully. Despite their intimate relationship, she was secretly still vastly intimidated by him, as though with a few words of criticism or disapproval he could undo everything, every change that had occurred in her, reduce her to the nothingness of . . . of *before*. That he had never said any harsh word to her or made any sign that he meant her the least hurt didn't quell the fear.

"I'm sorry to wake you," he was saying. She could make out his face now, gorgeous as usual and framed by dark cascading hair. "No choice, though, beauty. Come now."

She pushed herself up. He was in his robe and holding hers out to her.

"What's . . . going on?"

He looked oddly embarrassed, as if caught at something illicit. He shook his head. "I am to take you somewhere."

"Where?" She felt alarm now. What was this? Everything had been so stable, so steady for almost half a lune now, a seemingly interminable time, just her doing her work for Master Honnis and Xink seeing to his duties with Mistress Cestrello of the sociology council, and the two of them together every night. Why, why, why was something going wrong now? Did he mean to abandon her? Her young heart shook beneath the breasts that he and he alone had ever touched. "Where?" she said again, but Xink looked away.

Praulth took her robe and put it on. She was quivering slightly, already feeling herself reducing, her newfound womanhood shrinking away. She gazed after him, as he led the way from the chamber into the Blue Annex corridor. Her feet felt numb as she moved, staying several steps behind him, arms folded around her chest, huddling into herself.

She *loved* him! How could anything possibly go wrong between two people in love?

Did he still love her? He said so often enough, but . . .

Desperate for other, less fatal thoughts to fill her head, she pictured maps of battle, projecting military movements as she'd been doing quite some while now.

Making Master Honnis proud. Yes, that was still important. Not as important, though, as wanting to make Xink happy—happy so that they would remain together always. Yes, do old Honnis's tasks to the exclusion of all other academic work, so that she could maintain this situation forever, living with Xink in their wonderful quarters, her days belonging to the Felk war, her nights to . . . to . . .

They had crossed out of the corridor, descended stairs, were walking some faintly lit underground stretch she didn't recognize; only now she had stopped. Her vision had smeared over with tears. Xink was beside her, laying his strong manly arm across her stiff shoulders and saying, softly, "Please, beauty . . . please, Praulth, you've been summoned. Honnis will be there. Come. Come."

His breath warmed her cheek. She allowed herself to be guided onward, not looking up any longer. Everything was ending. She knew it. But she would go with him, toward whatever conclusion was waiting.

THE FLOOR WAS earth and chilly. The chamber was a dome, with arched entrances all around. It all looked extremely old. The stone was pocked and crumbling. The bowl of the dome overhead was made of shaped sheets of deeply tarnished brass. It was a wide area, without any furnishings of any kind. Many of the archways were sloppily bricked up, and even those constructions appeared ancient.

Praulth had heard that the University here at Febretree was constructed atop the ruins of some antediluvian stronghold, but she had never seen any supporting documentation and so discounted it.

They had come some distance, and her tears had dried. Xink was still at her side but was stepping back now, bowing, flourishing her way forward with his arm as if to present her to someone.

They were not alone in this large underground space that smelled of old soil and rat droppings. There were others. She saw cloaks, armor, sheathed weapons, a dozen figures, more, a few holding the torches that lit this space. And there—Master Honnis, someone familiar but standing at a distance, nearby a tall sturdy figure with red and gold hair.

"Praulth."

Her name, spoken and echoing, Master Honnis's voice—but announcing her, not addressing her. She blinked, looking about, as confused now as when Xink had first woken her.

"What's wrong with her?"

This voice was stronger, richer than Honnis's. It wasn't loud but carried itself confidently through the circular chamber. It had come from the big man. He wore . . . some sort of military apparel, Praulth saw, squinting his way. But it looked more like the uniform of a royal court than that of an army.

Master Honnis looked urgently her way. His manner was intense, even excited, and perhaps afraid? No. Not possible. Honnis evoked fear. He did not experience it.

"She is nervous," the old, dark-fleshed instructor said.

"Does she have cause to be?"

Xink had vanished somewhere behind her. There was no one else wearing a University robe to be seen but Honnis. Just these . . . soldiers. And the one with the red-gold hair who was surely their leader.

He took a single step her way now, his gait as assured as his voice. She guessed him to be some five tenwinters old, though he was still too far away for a good look. He seemed to exude a robust poise. Yes, a leader surely.

"Maybe she's got a right to her nervousness at that," he said, answering his own question, staring at her a moment across the intervening distance. "You claim she knows nothing?"

"Only the movements and maneuvers of the war that she has successfully predicted for some time now," Master Honnis said with a tinge of his normal peevish self.

A stirring went through the soldiers ranked behind the two older men.

A deep chuckle echoed through the dome briefly. Above, torchlight rebounded among tarnished brass.

"I daresay, elder Master, if I hadn't gone on from this place to truly make something of my life, I imagine you would now be raking me apart for ever daring to leave before achieving Thinker. As I recall, our farewell was . . . I'm not sure how to quite put it."

"Enthusiastic?" Honnis ventured.

"Yes. Mutually so. Couldn't wait to get apart from each other."

Praulth watched the exchange, waiting for it—waiting for this night, for everything—to make sense. She wished only that she were still asleep in bed, in the glow of Xink's warmth.

Now the two men were crossing toward her. Master Honnis did indeed appear somewhat flustered, bony fingers tugging at each other. Praulth's gaze was drawn to the other, though. Tall, broad across the shoulders and chest, but some of that size seemed to come strictly from his commanding presence. His face was cut by crags and dressed in a beard of red and gold—and grey too, she saw—but it was a face of authority, even supremacy. Eyes of harsh blue burned from surrounding pouches of flesh. His hair was a mane, thicker and wilder even than Xink's tumbling locks. Five tenwinters old? Yes. At least. Likely more. But still a hardy figure.

He and Honnis came to a halt at arm's length.

"Thinker Praulth," said Master Honnis in a formal tone, "this is Premier Nâ Niroki Cultat of the Noble State of Petgrad—"

"Cultat of Petgrad should, I think, suffice." Those blue eyes—full of command and ruthlessness—measured her. His wasn't a kind face, but looking back into it, Praulth felt some inkling that this man might be honorable.

She uncrossed the arms that she still had folded about her chest. She bowed toward him. "Premier," she said, the first word she'd uttered since leaving her and Xink's quarters. It was chilly enough in here to raise gooseflesh beneath her robe. One or the other of those unbricked archways must lead up to the outside and the open night. Probably they were on the periphery of the campus . . . some secret place.

Cultat continued to scrutinize her. "You had no expectation of my arrival. You have no idea at all why I am here."

Honnis made a sharp furtive gesture at her to respond. She merely shook her head at the premier.

Cultat gave Honnis a full look, then said, "Master Honnis is quite correct. You have been predicting the movements of the Felk since the atrocity at U'delph. You still believe Weisel is leading his forces toward the city-state of Trael?"

The field intelligence that Honnis provided her now definitely indicated as much, though she had made her forecast much earlier. Apparently this premier knew that. Praulth still didn't know how Master Honnis was so miraculously coming by his facts.

"Taking Trael, as opposed to attacking Grat or Ompellus Prime—both also within striking distance—will drive the Felk deepest into the South. It will effectively open the second half of this war." She spoke almost numbly. She didn't understand what was happening here, and she didn't have the mental energy to try to puzzle it out. Something on a grand scale was occurring, but it was too big for her to see.

The premier's fierce blue eyes studied her. "Why doesn't General Weisel use that transport magic he has at his disposal—attack Trael right now? Why march his army at all?"

"I don't know." This was some sort of test.

Cultat shot another look at Honnis, this one dire.

"Perhaps because Dardas didn't have such magics," Praulth added.

"Dardas?" Cultat spoke the name slowly.

"Weisel *is* Dardas. His tactics are a flawless match. I could cite numerous examples—"

"That won't be necessary," Honnis interrupted. "The premier was a passable enough student in his day to recall the Northlander's name."

Cultat's eyes burned Praulth once more. He had traveled here to meet her, she realized. Somehow the war predictions she had been making for Honnis—the great

assignment he had entrusted to her—had been finding
their way to this premier. Petgrad, if the Felk went
unchecked, would soon enough stand in the path of
Weisel's forces.

Cultat meant to stop him; but the army of Petgrad, relatively large though it was, couldn't hope to meet the Felk.
Cultat had to have an edge, an advantage.

He turned slightly, lifting a hand gloved in leather. Immediately one of the torch-bearing soldiers jogged over.
Out of a cloak he produced a small sheaf of papers. Cultat
took them, then held the papers toward Praulth.

"Look at these, young Thinker. They are our current intelligence of the Felk advancement, collected by an elite
Petgrad scouting force. We've had them in the field some
while now. Tell me"—his teeth glinted briefly in that red-
gold beard—"does Weisel truly intend to conquer the entire Isthmus?"

Her hand accepted the papers, familiar-looking lines
and arrows.

"Premier," she said, "I find it difficult to believe that
anyone with the least inkling of a military sensibility could
see it otherwise."

Cultat nodded, and in that moment some hint of his true
age shone through. "Unfortunately, Thinker Praulth, military minds are in scarce supply . . . now that we need them
most."

"I believe that Weisel is intentionally trying to provoke
resistance," she said. "That was the true purpose of the destruction of U'delph."

"So you concluded to Master Honnis. I would agree
with you, though it's not the most sensible act on Weisel's
part."

"But Dardas was known to commit such actions."

"Dardas," Cultat breathed grimly. His eyes flickered to
the papers he'd passed her. "You can read that well
enough?"

Praulth looked at the sheets, which showed the Felk,

Trael, and that city-state's outer environs. The torch-bearer remained nearby, throwing more than enough light on the pages.

"Study this here. Now." Cultat's deep voice brooked no protest.

Master Honnis was tugging his fingers once more. She looked first to him, then to the premier.

"I will wait here while you do this," said Cultat. "Tell me, how can we engage Weisel successfully in battle?"

TIME HAD LOST easy definition, but she was done. Had a watch passed or only a few moments? She stood rooted where she'd been standing. The others were still there—Honnis, the premier and his entourage. Xink? She didn't look behind to see if he was still in the domed chamber. She hoped vaguely he was.

Praulth felt herself swaying on her feet. The ground's earthy chill had bled upward to her knees. This was a new task. This wasn't analytical prophecy. She had been told to devise the countermeasures against the Felk. Against Weisel. Against *Dardas*. This new task was engrossing, challenging, thoroughly satisfying. Without her knowing it, she had been aching for just this sort of work.

She lifted her head, and Cultat was still there, waiting.

"Battle of Torran Flats," she said; then she explained.

"WHAT HAVE YOU to do with it?"

She was sitting on the bed, at its foot, still robed, holding herself rigidly. Xink had put his hand gently to her shoulder after leading her back here; but she hadn't responded, and he'd withdrawn it.

He was standing now in a far corner of the chamber, eyes downcast. He had heard her question.

"I . . . don't know what it means. Beauty—" He cut himself off.

Petgrad. It was the largest and most powerful of the
southern city-states, located not too far from Febretree.
However, no single state of the Isthmus could, at this stage,
muster a force to stand against the Felk. Cultat was trying
to gather an alliance of the remaining free states. It was a
formidable task. But he needed more than an army to meet
Weisel and the Felk.

Cultat, Petgrad's premier, had visited *her*. Specifically.
She had known some while now that Trael was the next
logical step for the Felk. Devising a plan of counterattack,
however . . . that had been a categorically different task for
her—far more difficult, far more rewarding. But she had
succeeded. She was certain. The Battle of Torran Flats.
Use the tactics of Dardas against the Felk military leader;
turn the tables.

Afterward Cultat, that great fierce man, had gone with
his entourage. Obviously the entire meeting was meant to
be secret. Honnis had directed Xink—who'd waited all
the while inside one of the archways into the dome—to return her to their quarters.

Xink was doubtlessly a part of this . . . though she still
didn't know exactly what *this* was.

"You're working with Honnis, too," she said. Her san-
daled feet still felt cold from that old underground chamber.

"Working . . . with . . . ?"

She was staring directly at him now, but he was still
watching the floor.

"How conveniently you appeared," she said, a quiver
tugging at her voice. "And with you these comfortable
quarters. And so I neglected my other studies. Honnis
means for me to work exclusively on his war project—
means to squeeze every possible effort from me. And so I
am kept . . . k-k-kept *happy*. By you. You . . ."

He was awash in blurs now, as if the lamplight overhead
had turned to liquid. Through the haze, she saw him take a
few steps toward her, hesitate.

"B— Praulth. Please. I beg you to believe. If it's a machination, I've only played the slightest role in it. Surely if you're being used, so am I."

"You?" It was a sob.

"And I don't care. I'm grateful for the time we've had together . . . the times I hope we'll still have. I don't care if—why—Honnis—"

"He put you on to me," she said; then stopped and choked down the tears, fiercely. She would not whimper like a child. "He . . . what? Offered a reward, perhaps, to you? Payment?"

Wiping her eyes, she saw him clearer, his handsome face etched with pain, tears of his own in his limpid blue eyes, the flecks of gold in them sparkling.

"I have loved you, Praulth. I *have*. I wish to go on doing so."

"What are you getting?"

"You're beautiful to me. When I first saw you, you were like a radiant child—"

"I'm not a child."

It was the first sharp thing she'd ever said to him, the first she had dared to say. But now she dared. In among the churning confusion and fear, she most certainly felt anger.

He hastily licked his lips. "I—I know you are not—"

"What reward are you getting from Honnis for . . . for being with me?" Hateful, so hateful to say the words, to even think the thoughts.

Xink drew a breath, drew himself erect. He shook his head once, as if to clear it. His features became composed. "Master Honnis has promised me an eventual seat on the sociology council. He has the means to leverage it."

It was a confession. Praulth stared at her lover, her beautiful lover, feeling the hotness in her throat, feeling emotions tearing and ripping.

But Xink wasn't done. "I have also fallen genuinely in love with you during the course of this. My heart belongs to you—whether you choose to reject it or not, it's yours. Now and forever. In this . . . I'm helpless."

He spoke it in the same level divulging tone, even as the tears continued to ooze from his eyes.

Believe? Disbelieve? It seemed impossible. So much to sort through. Her very existence had been upended tonight; but perhaps it hadn't been utterly destroyed after all.

Xink remained where he was. Waiting. Waiting for her judgment, her pronouncement of sentence.

She gazed at him, and, yes, he was still beautiful, and, yes, her heart soared even as it desperately ached. Her mind whirled.

Evidently Cultat was in cahoots with Honnis—the war studies master using her, Praulth, to predict Weisel's movements . . . and now Cultat using her to formulate the winning plan of battle.

It was overwhelming.

Praulth lifted a trembling hand toward Xink. A look of hope flowed over his face.

"Come to me," she said. "We must talk. We have . . . so much to talk about."

RADSTAC
(3)

SHE ROCKED UP and forward, standing on the stirrups, and took the arrow just above her right breast.

Do the thing that'll most confuse your enemies.

It had carried over a substantial distance. She'd seen the startled bird wing and squawk into the sky, far back in the brush—the creature's movement too sudden, its cry too alarmed. Whoever was back there was a terrifically skilled—or lucky—archer.

The arrow had lost some of its momentum. Still, it hit more than hard enough to punch her off the saddle. She went with the movement, rolling her body at the hips, reaching out and seizing Deo's heavy buckled belt as she tumbled toward the ground. He came off his saddle with a half-yelp of surprise. She managed not to pull his full weight down on top of herself.

The shaft had bit into her weathered leather armor, the flanged head lodged there. If it had gone past her, struck her employer, her charge . . . well, she would have failed in this her first job as a bodyguard/escort. That wouldn't have sat well with her. Actually it was possible the arrow had been meant to go past their noses, a warning, but the archer was either off the mark or so talented he or she could cut it just that finely; either way, Radstac hadn't felt inclined to risk it.

Their horses fussed, but neither reared. They had landed between the beasts, just a few paces from the riverbank where they'd been heading. Water the horses, fill the waterskins. A brief rest. Deo talking, telling one of an apparently limitless store of anecdotes about the topsy-turvy travails of growing up as a noble in Petgrad. Then she'd seen the bird. Instinct sprang like a coiled trap.

He was scrambling for his feet. Radstac, still gripping his belt, kept him on the ground. She rolled, stayed low, getting her scabbard out from under her but not yet drawing the combat sword. Her head swiveled. She checked every bearing. They were on a northward road, a minor one. Brush on one side, thick; trees over there. There the river.

They weren't alone. More than just the archer. She saw the telltales—the bushes stirring in the breezeless midday, the small swirls of dust. There—and *there*. She heard, over the river's disinterested gurgle, the crackle of the brush. Closing from three different points. It was a good ambush.

She turned, still on her elbows, and had a throwing knife in her right hand. Deo had loosed his sword. He remained on the ground. Rugged face set—primed, not panicky. His eyes were picking out the more obvious signs of their waylayers.

"Stay," she said and, in a ball, rolled herself under the strong black-bodied horse she'd been allocated. She came out, up onto her feet, the sword flashing into her left hand—the hand that wore the weighted leather glove, its hooks still retracted.

The startled face looked up at her, a body prowling through the tall yellow grass on its belly. Her metal-toed boot struck the brow above the shock-wide left eye. Then she performed another pivot, hearing the arrow's whistle going through the air she no longer occupied. Not as good a shot. Different archer, this one.

Back to the horses. Deo up on one knee but holding there, sword in a two-fisted grip at the ready. She went past. Three figures were racing up the road, charging. They wore mismatched bits of armor. One carried a shield, also a cudgel. The other two, swords.

She flung the throwing knife—hard, accurate trajectory, into the shield with a resounding *thump*. Her heavy sword came up for the other two assailants, both of whom were chopping their swords for her, downward strokes, side by side. She caught both blades against her sword, her sinewy left shoulder absorbing the impacts. Neither of their weapons was going to break her blade.

The one with the club had had his shield jammed violently back against his body by the force of the throwing knife, whose tip had spiked through the shield's metal mantle and into the wood beneath. He was still blundering forward.

Radstac reached, tore the knife free, kicked the clubber's knee out from under him; down he went.

The scarred bracer on her right wrist caught the blow as one of the swords tried another chop. She stepped out— seeing two more here, two more *here,* figures coming out of the trees and scrub.

The finely balanced throwing knife launched again. Her combat sword jumped nimbly from her left to her right hand. Out from her glove came the paired prongs, her left leathered fist a fighting weight. She swung, hearing and feeling hooks catch a too-slow limb as she turned the other way with her sword. Deo still behind her. Herself between him and these ambushers, quite a few of them. Another arrow now, this one picking off a bit of her left earlobe; she'd barely moved in time. Spinning, parrying, chopping, dancing just outside of the blows, but they were closing.

They were good, but she was better. But they had numbers. They weren't going to have an easy time of it, though. They—

"Stop it! *Stop.*"

She hopped back, cut a hard slice out of the air to keep anyone from immediately following.

"Stop it! We lay down."

Deo's sword hit the ground. He had called the surrender.

She waited, stance firm, head swiveling once more, meeting the ambushers' eyes, seeing that the words were heard. Waited until all movement stopped. Then she let her sword fall to the ground—a step away, still in reach for her. She wiped her hooks on her black leggings, gave the hand a fast snap, and retracted the prongs into their glove. The pain from her ear was at once intense and remote. Blood was pouring warmly down her neck.

Twelve, she counted, including the initial archer who was now approaching from farthest away. She'd hurt a few; none were dead.

Bandits, obviously. Their interests, traditionally, were merchant caravans, the ones that moved in the high summer, on larger roads. No doubt, however, the Felk war had seriously disrupted trade. By now those caravans that had ventured forth had returned to the Southsoil or their home city-states.

One among the bandits strode forward, waving down everyone's weapons, an air of command about her. "Desist!" The group held their places. "That means you, too!" She threw this last back over her shoulder at the archer, tall and young, coming up the road.

Radstac slid a glance at Deo. He was watching the woman, measuring, studying. His posture was confident. A look of calm about him.

The woman was short and exaggeratedly muscled. She halted several paces off, her body seeming to plant itself.

"If you've killed any of my people, you die." She said it to Radstac like someone explaining a dice game's rules.

"She's in my employ," Deo said to the muscular woman. "If you intend to kill her, after we have laid down arms, she'll hear it through me. Not from you."

Radstac heard the resolute tone in his smooth, eloquent voice. Hard wood beneath attractive varnish.

"Then for your sake," the woman said, "I hope you've been worth the trouble of ambushing."

"Worth it? Monetarily?" Deo asked, tone becoming almost droll. He put a hand into his coat pocket. He wore traveler's clothes of purely functional cut; but of course he wore them particularly well. The man would look suave dressed in a sack. "I should think so." His hand came out smoothly, then shook, rattling the coins.

A very distinct sound, Radstac thought, the sound of money.

That focused everyone's attention, keenly. When Deo opened the hand and let the midday sun gleam lovingly all over that gold, the group was mesmerized.

At that Deo turned. His hand swept behind him, and the goldies went flashing into the river just a few steps away. A lively current, foam around the rock outcroppings. It wasn't a wide river—they hadn't been concerned about fording it—but it was no streamlet either.

No less than five of the bandits raced for the bank, including—incredibly—the one that Radstac had ripped with her hooks.

The short woman shouted, "Godsdamn you fools! Leave it!"

They hit the water anyway. Radstac's sword was still only a step away.

Deo put back his head and laughed. He had a laugh as fine as his smile, as sincere and rich. The archer who'd shot away a part of Radstac's ear was now standing behind the woman who was spitting more exasperated orders.

The archer had meant that second arrow to kill her. The

head of his first arrow, which she'd put herself in the way of purposely, was still jammed into her armor above her right breast, though the shaft had snapped off when she hit the ground.

"You're laughing yourself toward a slit throat."

Deo's chuckling trailed off, but he only smiled back at the woman's glare.

"A demonstration." He slapped the same pocket, made the contents jingle. "There is more. But everything I carry, every scrap of money, is a bent copper compared to what I can offer. To the wealth I can tap. I can make you rich. Every single one of you. I can write a promissory note, to be redeemed in the Noble State of Petgrad . . . if you will do what I say."

"Let you go?" sneered the woman.

Deo took an easy step forward, still showing no fear. "Take me north. To the Felk. To their army. I wish to intercept it. I will assassinate the individual who leads that army. Get me to him, and I'll glut you with more money than you'd want to spend in your lifetimes."

THEY WERE IN the bandits' tent for negotiations, though there was nothing to negotiate, really. Deo had made his offer, his *very* generous offer, and it had plainly already been accepted, despite the perfunctory dickering on the part of the bandit leader. She had introduced herself as Anzal.

They sat on the canvas floor, Radstac behind Deo. She was wearing her weapons once more. The bandit leader didn't like her, though none in the gang had died of the wounds she'd inflicted. Radstac herself had smeared a bit of plaster on her ear, using the small aid kit that she carried. The chunk that had been torn from her lobe was gone; she didn't give it any more thought than she did her body's scars.

Anzal named a staggering sum of money. Deo nodded. She doubled the sum. He nodded still.

He shook a page of paper from a sheaf he removed from his coat pocket. It bore a dark border and much official-looking print, stamped here and there.

"Promissory note," he said.

"To be filled in . . . ?" Anzal was trying to hide the hunger in her eyes.

"When you've gotten me to the Felk war commander, of course. Or"—he grunted a tiny chuckle—"just *before,* I suppose. Or," he said, a sober crease appearing between his red brows, "you could murder my bodyguard, hold a blade to my throat, and force me to sign now. And when you got to Petgrad and the Municipal Funds Office, they would read the name I had written. It would be a code word. You would never leave that city. You would never see daylight for the remainder of your lives, which wouldn't last long."

He had not given his name to these people, Radstac realized, her scarred face remaining bland.

Shortly after the negotations, she and Deo left the tent, picked through the small camp, past the campfire, and went to where their own tent was pitched. The archer who had nicked Radstac's ear was scowling at her. So were most of the others. A guard or guards would stand outside their tent through the night.

No one would come in, though. She laid her sword alongside their blankets, leaving the glove on her hand. The tent's interior was dark. She would probably chew a bit of *mansìd* later.

They lay together, heads touching, blankets across their legs, breathing words at each other that nobody would overhear.

"What of your ambassadorial mission to Trael?" She had been waiting some while to ask. "Your uncle's plan to gather an alliance."

"It's too late for Trael. The Felk are already making for it. Cultat knows so."

"So why send you there?"

"I'm expendable." Deo's voice was steady. "I don't imply that Cultat wants me dead. I know he cares for me, for all of his family. But he cares—*must* care—for his people more. And so we of that family must make the first sacrifices as Petgradites in this war, which is why I volunteered. He is right to have made the judgment."

"But you won't obey it?" Radstac's voice was equally level.

"The Felk are not stoppable. I don't believe that even the alliance my uncle is hoping for will stand against their strength. They are led by a man named Weisel. He is the key. Our field intelligence indicates that he is a master war commander. If I eliminate *that* one . . ."

She heard the eagerness now. He wanted to do this. Badly.

"The Felk will still have their mighty army and their wizards and—"

"No one to lead."

She allowed him to cut her off. It was what she'd expected him to say.

"Cultat has sent emissaries to all the major states. To Q'ang, Ebzo, Grat, Ompellus Prime. To the smaller cities as well. Dral Blidst. Hingo. Places you've never heard of. Insane. Impossible. Petgrad has fought wars with just about every place I've mentioned. Well . . . not *us*. Not in our lifetime. But in generations past. And the rivalries persist, culturally embedded. If he waits until he's sealed an accord with all those disparate states . . ." He grunted a laugh. "By that time the Felk will possess the Isthmus."

"Your war's hopeless, then." Not her war. No. She wasn't even borrowing this one. She hadn't been hired as a soldier to go against the Felk, which was what she envisioned when she'd come north from the Southsoil. Instead, she was serving a single client.

"Cultat has other means," Deo said. "He's in highly secret contact with someone at Febretree, at the University there."

"Highly secret. Are you your uncle's confidant?"

"Hardly." Something dark moved behind the word. "But his elder daughter is."

"A pretty child."

"Not a child," Deo said. "But attractive."

Radstac sniffed a laugh. They told jokes back home about the intimacies of Isthmuser cousins.

"It's purely a flirtation. I'm *her* confidant. She pities me because I was so thoroughly overlooked for the post of premier—but she keeps her sympathies private from her father. I tell her I'm glad I was overlooked. I tell Uncle the same. His daughter tells me secrets."

"Why is Cultat in contact with the University?"

"I don't know entirely. Some sort of . . . strategist there. He won't speak directly about it. But I suspect the intelligence he's receiving from his scouts is also going there. Maybe there's more to his plans than I know. Uncle likes decent odds."

"Most people do."

"Yes. Most."

She felt the warmth of him, lying alongside her. They remained clothed. She wondered when they might be lovers again; maybe never.

"But not you," Radstac breathed.

"Oh, I like favorable odds. That's why I've hired these bandits. They'll know this territory, know how to move through it quickly and stealthily. They're a tough bunch, I'd say."

"I agree." Though, she added silently, she would be surprised if any of them lived to redeem that priceless promissory note. Probably Deo'd had that in mind when he wrote it.

"I like the idea of winning," Deo said. "It's a fine abstract desire. Unluckily the odds have stood against me all my life. I wish to do something more than my circumstances would likely have ever allowed me to. Something worthwhile."

"Assassinate the head of the Felk military? You won't succeed." Flat words—not opinion; judgment. She was a mercenary of many years. She'd earned the right to judge. She would point this out if he argued.

He didn't. "My own life hasn't succeeded. My mother chose to exclude herself—and me—from the hardships of being premier. It went to Cultat. My uncle . . . who, when he was a tenwinter younger than I am now, was utterly unfit for the post. I remember his ascendancy ceremony. I was young, but I understood what was happening. I knew what was out of my reach, forever."

Their heads were still together. She felt the tear—quite warm—sliding off his cheek onto her scarred one.

"I won't succeed. I won't manage to kill Weisel. I also won't waste any more of my life. But for this . . . I think I may be remembered for trying. For making the effort, the sacrifice. If it's not a purely selfless or spotlessly noble act, it may at least seem so to those who hear of my deed. I would be satisfied with that."

She drew the blanket up from their legs, spread it farther onto their bodies.

"You'll stay with me?" It was a tone of voice she had never heard from him—small, nearly defenseless; speaking for someone deep inside.

"I'll stay." She kept it simple. "Until I am told to go."

RAVEN

(3)

SHE BARELY RECOGNIZED herself, which, apparently, was the whole point.

It was a female soldier from the mess corps who was sent to remake Raven. She was very matter-of-fact about things. She had gotten a basin and some soap, boiled some water, and scrubbed Raven's stringy dark hair, untangling knots that had been there some long time.

She winced as the woman's tough fingers scoured her scalp, but Raven knew that General Weisel had ordered this, so she went along.

The soldier dried her hair with a cloth, then quickly and neatly braided it. Raven had never been able to learn the knack of that, and so had ignored her hair, just as she had ignored her plump, short, and disappointing body all her life. That disappointment had been shared by her mother, who herself had been beautiful enough in her youth to attract the attentions of Lord Matokin.

Raven shook herself. It was difficult sometimes not to spend every waking moment dwelling on her father . . .

dwelling as well on the terrible secret fear she harbored, that her mother might somehow be mistaken in the identity of her father.

No. She wouldn't consider it. She had met Matokin. She had felt their connection. They were father and daughter. She would serve him with the full loyalty of a daughter.

The mess soldier dressed her in new clothes, not a uniform but also not like the drab robes that most of the army's wizards wore. These clothes had some style. The tunic was cut so as to deliberately expose the tops of her admittedly full breasts. She had never dressed in anything like this before.

The clothes were, nonetheless, functional enough to be worn in the field.

"Where did you get these?" Raven had asked, after changing inside a tent.

"I was given leave to requisition anything I wanted from the best shops in Felk."

A portal had been opened just to fetch Raven's *clothes*? It was incredible.

"But they fit so well," Raven said, looking down at herself. The clothes didn't hide the thickness of her body, but they emphasized her natural curves in a pleasing way.

"I used to be a seamstress in Windal," the soldier said dully. With the transformation completed, she left Raven to admire herself.

Raven, on arriving in the field, had quickly noted the simmering hostility that existed between the regular troops and the squads of military mages. It was an irrational prejudice, one that had a long history. The Great Upheavals had brought low the mighty cultures of the Northern and Southern Continents. Magic, stupidly, had been blamed for the vast calamities.

But that was how people behaved when things went wrong. They blamed whoever was the oddest among themselves. Gods knew the children she'd grown up with in that horrid village had used her as the object of blame whenever it was convenient.

How much more they would have despised her, she thought, if they had known about her latent magical abilities.

At the moment the army was on the move. They marched and rode every day, during the daylight watches, pausing for carefully timed food and rest periods.

It was strenuous, even though Raven had been assigned a horse to ride. The animal frightened her a bit at first, but she had gotten used to it. She rode among a small company of mages, a mixed bag of Far Speak wizards and healers. They showed her camaraderie, despite the fact that she hadn't even properly graduated from the Academy and was thus a novice in the magical arts.

Apparently, they were just happy to have another magician in the ranks. The regular troops far outnumbered the wizards in Weisel's army.

They were heading for Trael, so went the scuttlebutt. It was another of the Isthmus's city-states. Raven, despite herself, felt a little giddy at the thought that she might be witness to an actual battle. Somehow during her two years at the Academy, she had never successfully imagined herself in combat conditions.

Not that she expected to *fight*. Of course not. So she could use her minor magics to light a candle or two, so what? It wasn't going to help much in battle.

She was here because Weisel wanted her here. And because Matokin wanted to give Weisel what he wanted.

But she knew damned well there was more to it than that. Those years at the Academy had taught her duplicity as much as magic. Matokin wanted her to spy on Weisel. Very well. But she had no idea what, exactly, she was supposed to be looking for. Was the Felk general suspected of disloyalty, of treason? It seemed unlikely, considering the victories he'd won for the empire.

But, one never knew where a traitor was going to spring up.

That night, after the long day's riding, she was summoned to Weisel's tent a second time.

The Felk general's eyes widened. "Well, I honestly don't believe I'd have recognized you if you had not been announced."

"General?" Raven was nonplussed, and suddenly, terribly self-conscious.

"I mean to say," Weisel went on, chuckling at her confusion, "that there was a pretty girl underneath that dreary robe and untidy hair. Just like I suspected."

Raven felt heat rush to her cheeks, but it wasn't shame making her blush. That she was used to. Being complimented, though, was almost an entirely new experience.

It spread an adolescent smile across her face, a face that wasn't at all used to the expression.

Weisel laughed harder. "Prettier still! You look infinitely less mopy with a smile. You might want to practice it." He was at his table, where a plate of what looked like regular soldier's rations sat beside a set of maps.

"Thank you, General Weisel."

He waved it off. "But enough. I do enjoy your company, Raven, but we are closing fast on our next target, and my senior staff will soon want their orders. I want a word or two with you before that."

She couldn't help but feel special that the general was making this time for her.

"It's time I told you why I requisitioned you directly out of the Academy," Weisel said. He sounded frank. "I wanted to know about Far Movement magic."

Raven blinked. "Far Movement?" It suddenly flashed in her mind—that bully girl Hert at the Academy jamming her face against the corridor wall, telling her to open a portal and walk through it.

"Yes. Portals. Fascinating stuff." Weisel picked up a fork. "I employed Far Movement magic during the Battle of U'delph. It was of inestimable value for a surprise attack. But I wanted to learn all I could about how the portals operated." He ate a bite of his dinner, showing a little less apathy for the food than the mages in her unit had at supper tonight.

"Portals, General?" Obviously a mistake had occurred. How would Weisel react when he discovered it? A feeling of dread stole over her. What, exactly, had Matokin set her up for?

But she was loyal. She was obedient. She would point out the mistake now, to Weisel, before things went too far. Then she would no doubt be returned to Felk, to face whatever consequences might await there.

"I am afraid, General Weisel, that I am not at all sufficiently versed in the complex particulars of Far Movement spells to be of—"

He set down his fork somewhat sharply. Raven managed not to wince.

"I *know* that, girl. I may not be a wizard like the rest of Matokin's political cadre back there in Felk, but I'm still of noble blood." His face had darkened a bit.

"Of course, General," she said, pleased with the steadiness of her voice. Panic was only the result of a lack of discipline.

Weisel had hunched forward slightly. Now his body relaxed. "I know that *now,* I should say. About the relative magical abilities of someone who hasn't yet graduated from the Academy. I've made some inquiries, something I should've done in the first place I realize in hindsight. I've learned how exceptional a wizard must be to master the opening of portals."

"It is perhaps the most difficult of all magics, General Weisel."

"That I'm not sure about," he said, solemnly.

"Sir?"

"Have you ever heard of resurrection magic?" There was now an odd glint in his eyes.

"No, General," she said honestly.

"Rejuvenation spells?"

"Yes. I have heard of those. They are practiced by healers, but only by the most advanced ones. I am afraid I wouldn't—"

"—know anything about it," he shrugged. "No matter. But about the Far Movement magic, yes, I wanted to know more about it. As a war commander, I felt it incumbent on me to know everything I could about the weapons and resources at my disposal. Far Movement is, make no mistake, a very new weapon of war."

He let out a bitter-sounding sigh. "But these mages Matokin has appointed to my army, every last one of them, have been instructed to keep their lips locked about magic around me. Can you imagine? I am to know *nothing* about the wizardry I might employ in battle. Ludicrous, isn't it?"

Raven herself had certainly been surprised when she'd learned about the standing order there in Matokin's office at the palace.

Suddenly, Weisel erupted into laughter, much longer and louder than before. "Then, of course, I realized," he finally said, as Raven looked on, perplexed.

"General?"

He stood up, looking directly into her eyes. "Matokin," Weisel said slowly, "doesn't want to win this war."

Raven frowned mightily. Then Weisel waved her into a seat, and explained.

SHE HAD RETURNED to her unit, peripherally aware that here and there a male soldier was looking her way, a leer on his face. Being the object of a man's lust—again, an almost entirely new experience—should have been more interesting to her. But she was quite preoccupied.

She went numbly into the small tent that was hers and lay down, still in her new clothes, on the bedroll. She could still feel the hard ground underneath, but she ignored it.

Weisel's allegation about her father was the single most treasonous thing she'd ever heard anyone say! If any student at the Academy had spoken such a thing aloud, he would be reported by a dozen fellow students before he could take his next breath.

Matokin, Weisel claimed, was deliberately sabotaging the efforts of his own military to conquer the entire Isthmus. Weisel's explanation for such an unbelievable, outrageous course of action was simple.

Lord Matokin, supreme master of the expanding Felk Empire, wanted to perpetuate a state of war. While the Isthmus was at war, while lands and city-states remained unconquered, the Felk leader was indispensable. The people looked to him for guidance, for authority, for assurance. He was at the very heart of things.

But without a war, without the urgency and fanaticism that accompanied it . . . he would, inevitably, diminish. He was a brilliant political leader. His rise to power alone proved that. But, without war, he would become an administrator. A caretaker of the lands he had sent his army of wizards and soldiers out to subdue.

Matokin, according to General Weisel, feared such a future for himself. So, he meant to sustain the present.

Thus, again according to Weisel, he was preventing the Felk war commander from fully using the magical potential supposedly at his disposal. If the general was kept ignorant, he would be less inclined to use such resources; and so the war would continue. The free states of the south might even rise up against the Felk advance.

Treason. Purest treason.

Raven must, of course, find that Far Speak mage mentioned in her orders. Berkant. Yes, find Berkant and inform Matokin immediately of Weisel's disloyalty. Here obviously was why they wanted her to act as a spy. Matokin and Abraxis had suspected Weisel's treachery.

Well, she could confirm it.

She rolled off her bedroll, groping for the tent flap. Why

hadn't she gone straight to Berkant after being dismissed from Weisel's tent? Shock, probably.

Her hand, somehow, did not reach the flap.

Weisel wanted to know about magic. He himself wasn't a wizard, but he was plainly a cunning military strategist. Why was all knowledge of magic being denied him? What sense did that make?

Did that lack of knowledge actually impair his ability to operate this army? It . . . might. It certainly couldn't *help* him, what with this huge force of mixed mages and regular troops, each hostile to the other.

Is *that* what it was? Raven wondered in sudden dismay. Did this all come down to the basic enmity between magic-users and non-magic-users?

Was there a similar irrational bigotry between Matokin and Weisel?

It seemed impossible. Or maybe she just didn't want to give the thought any space in her head. There was so much at stake. The fate of the entire Isthmus hung in the balance. So did the future of the mighty Felk Empire, which would stand for hundredwinters and more . . . unless foolish men undermined this great war of unification.

She had to find Berkant and inform Matokin. Weisel was a traitor. Or he was at least harboring treasonous views.

Yet, even now, her hand would not part the tent's flap. After a long time she dropped it, and laid back down on her bedroll. She didn't sleep that night, so full was her head with doubts and distress.

BRYCK
(4)

THE FIRST ATTEMPT squeezed his skull sharply and briefly, while a cold sweat broke out across his body. That was distinctly uncomfortable in the chilly morning.

Despite this, he persisted. The first attempt would naturally be the most difficult.

He had dedicated himself to this vengeance. Hardships would come with that. U'delph had suffered. U'delph had met its end brutally, ferociously. He could at least endure a throbbing head and short fever chill.

Nonetheless, he stopped for a hot breakfast before trying the second one. The first had succeeded. So did this. It was also less taxing. As with the vox-mellifluous, Bryck had practiced this. It too was a talent that needed honing, but since the death of his old life he had found himself more disciplined in this one.

It was a sizzling kabob he'd eaten, the meat braised and the flavor startling but good. The same vendor was hawking cups of *stife,* a sharp-smelling green wine.

"Wouldn't be Lacfoddalmendowl without it." This was

said with an ingratiating semitoothless grin. It didn't entice
Bryck into buying the drink.

He wended the streets. If by now every avenue and
alley of Callah wasn't intimately familiar to him, then he
had a more than rough idea of the city's layout. He had
planned today's route carefully.

Today he meant to see a great deal of Callah.

Today the very air crackled. There was a palpable sense
of jubilee—heard in every voice, seen in virtually every
face, felt as he made his way among the milling, churning
people. Songs whipped through the crowds. Felk occupation or not, evidently Lacfoddalmendowl *would* be celebrated.

It was of course the city's Felk conquerors that were
permitting this festival. Without official approval, this
mighty hullabaloo would have already been suppressed
by the armed patrols. But the Felk governor of Callah—
a colonel named Jesile, who resided at the Registry—
had sent out the criers with the decree. A limited form of
the old traditional Callahan holiday was to be allowed,
though the curfew would remain in effect and some of
the more boisterous customary events would be cur-
tailed.

Bryck thought it a very wise move. This Jesile was no
fool, surely. Let the Callahans—those that hadn't been
conscripted into the Felk army—have their idiotic Lacfoddalmendowl. They would be joyous at being permitted
to publicly observe the holiday. They would perhaps even
be *grateful* to the Felk governor for his generosity.

And so the Callahans might sink a little further into
their conquered complacency, which would make them
easier to manage and of better value as assets to the growing Felk Empire.

Few adults were without their cups of *stife*. Bryck wondered what the streets would be like later in the day. No
doubt, though, all these activities were being monitored.
Even as he thought this, he saw two soldiers standing by a

stone wall in armor and helmets, weapons sheathed, observing. If anything got out of hand, it wouldn't remain so for long.

Lacfoddalmendowl . . . the word sounded like some ancient bastardization. He had heard it was Callah's oldest festival.

To blend, he had purchased the pink and red streamers, had tied the strips of cloth appropriately about his left wrist, leaving the ends to dangle. One was supposed to wave one's arm, trailing the colorful ribbons, and this he did now and then. Others were wrapped neck to ankle in the streamers and dancing mad whirling jigs.

Lacfoddalmendowl would serve Bryck well, of course. So far, two successful sigils. No one had seen, no alarm raised. He kept a wary eye out for soldiers. It was time for another sigil. Over the course of what promised to be a busy chaotic day, he hoped to leave quite a few of these emblems on walls and posts and doors throughout the city.

"YOU'RE THE STRINGBOX player. I saw you play."

He was holding out two green bronze notes, buying another kabob, apparently the traditional meal of this holiday.

The vendor's eyes seemed to fill with pointed unsaid words. She looked roughly his own age, maybe a winter or two younger. Her cart was parked nearby the mouth of a narrow side street. Revelers poured and staggered past.

She still did not take his money, "It was good playing."

"Thank you." He stood tense.

"Where will you appear next?"

He didn't like the intensity of her stare. "Appear?"

"To play your 'box . . . and to speak."

"I play when I need money," he said, now forcing the notes into her hand. "I am a troubadour."

"Yes." She was nodding. "Yes. Why trust me? Of

course. Correct. You don't remember me from the evening when I heard you. There was a fair-sized crowd. Still, you changed my life that night."

Suddenly she was holding out a cup of *stife*.

"Joyous Lacfoddalmendowl."

It would be wisest, of course, to simply scurry away. But Bryck found himself taking the drink. It was his first taste of the tart, green wine. It was at first quite awful, almost stinging; but as the aftertaste came, the richness of the flavor took hold.

"I've a niece in Windal, you see," the vendor continued. "I asked you of her that night by name, but you didn't know her—and, of course, why would you? I couldn't but hope, though."

"I'm sure she's well," he found himself saying.

"The uprising," she said.

He took another swallow of *stife*. It was helping the general ache in his head.

"Violence in the streets, you said. Windal in chaos."

"So I've heard on my travels." He bit into the kabob now. It was well past midday. He was tired, already nearly spent. And still there were several sigils to go.

"You've not seen Windal yourself?" she pressed.

"I never said I had." It was true. He had been careful never to claim that; had maintained he was only circulating prevalent rumors from the outside world. It was a way of not getting pinned to the "facts." It was delicate . . . all of it, what he was trying to do, the machinations of his revenge.

"I must go," he said. He drained the cup and handed it back to her.

Her hand touched his elbow—lightly, but with tense fingers. "Please . . . where will I see you again?"

He knew he should flee—*now.* "Why?"

"Because there are others, others I've told of your news from Windal. They want to hear the tales themselves."

"They're not tales," Bryck lied.

"I know. Yes, I know. But . . . all of us who heard that night, we carried the news, passed it onward. Now others want to hear it firsthand. From you. Where will you be that they can come to listen?"

He blinked. It had *worked*. Worked better than he'd imagined. He had played half a dozen times in the city, at various taverns; and after each evening's playing, his audience had implored him for news of the lands outside Callah. And so he told them about the "uprising" in the Felk-occupied city of Windal.

"What is your name?" he asked impulsively.

"Quentis."

Her eyes were a soft amber, Bryck noted. Then he turned and fled down a side street.

IT WAS NOISY in the marketplace. Private industries were still doing business in Callah. Ceramicists, toolmakers, leather goods manufacturers. Bryck wondered about their raw materials, though. Eventually, it seemed, they would run out of local supplies. If the Felk wanted the city's enterprises to survive, they would have to allow goods to be brought in once more from outside the city limits. Some travel restrictions would have to be lifted.

Restrictions that didn't apply to him, he thought with more than a little satisfaction. It had been damned clever of him to have that copyist, Slydis, falsify a new civilian travel pass for him. Now Bryck could take up his stringbox and light out of Callah as a verifiable traveling minstrel whenever he wanted. He kept the paper on him at all times.

The large whitewashed stones of the Registry loomed over the stalls and tents. The building was a natural hub, located as it was in the city's center, and now serving as the seat of the occupying Felk bureaucracy. Callah's largest marketplace abutted it.

Bryck wandered through the haphazard rows. Lacfod-dalmendowl hadn't slowed business much. He desperately wanted to return to his rented room, there to collapse into sleep. But there was still a watch of daylight left. He had work to do.

He had collected a huge sheaf of bogus Felk scrip from Slydis's workshop two days ago. The dwarf copyist had done outstanding work. Bryck had studied the notes. The Felk evidently used an inked stamp on the differently colored bits of paper. Slydis had reproduced that stamp flawlessly. He had also scrounged up from gods knew where the precise stock of paper the Felk were using.

Citizens hadn't liked trading their coin for paper. Merchants didn't like accepting it for goods and services. But the Felk decreed their scrip to be lawful currency.

So be it.

Bryck made continuous purchases in the marketplace. He looked for items that were easily portable and expensive. He bought things for which he had no need whatever—gaudy jewelry, ornate eating utensils, overpriced vials of exotic spices, a necklace of shells belonging to creatures that lived in the Bane Sea to the east (which apparently didn't mind swimming poisoned waters), if the dealer was to be believed.

He haggled as little as possible, trying to pay as near to the full scandalous amounts as he could. He unloaded handfuls of the paper money Slydis had manufactured. He made many merchants very happy.

Finally he headed for his lodgings. He would dispose of his purchases before he reached his room, though he thought he might keep the utensils, strictly as an indulgent luxury. It had been quite satisfying to commit his crimes in plain view of the Registry, beneath the very noses of the Felk. He had even passed a few soldiers among the stalls. No one had questioned the authenticity of his money, though more than one vendor had furtively hinted that coin would get him a more economical price.

Meanwhile his counterfeit scrip, which was truly worth nothing more than ink and the paper it imprinted, now circulated among dozens of trading hands.

HE FELL ONTO his bed. He had truly driven himself today.

Bryck had already commissioned Slydis to create another large batch of notes, which he was due to collect tomorrow. Slydis, of course, was no doubt using the forged imprinting stamps for his own use. That served Bryck's purposes just fine. It didn't matter who was moving the crooked money, just as long as it got into circulation. Slydis could manufacture wealth that had no theoretical limits. He could make a thousand of the blue-colored goldie notes. Two thousand—or twenty. He needed only paper, ink, and time.

Falsifying coins wasn't a practical business. Perhaps that was why coins had remained the Isthmus's standard currency so many hundredwinters.

This Felk system of paper money, however, was something else entirely. Bryck likened it to those "I-owe-unto" notes that desperate gamblers sometimes tried to pass. Like cheaters, those players usually found out quickly that games could become very serious, indeed.

Criers were announcing the curfew in the street below. Lacfoddalmendowl had run its course.

He'd had fun inventing the sigil. That was odd—enjoying himself, even just a little bit. He had become a creature of cold hate and little else. He was seeing to his vengeance against his enemy with cold-blooded callousness.

Yet, crafting that emblem had engaged him. It wasn't of great importance what he settled on; he knew that. He needed only some distinct—preferably simple—symbol that people would readily recognize. It need only be original.

Nevertheless, the former artist in him insisted the sigil be just right.

Bryck had finally settled on a circle cut through by a vertical line. Simple. Easily memorized. It satisfied him. The circle, in old myths, was regarded as a symbol of evil. Its closed loop represented the eternalness of what was wicked in life, since bad times never went away entirely.

That was still true today, he thought ruefully.

The vertical line, of course, cut the cycle. Bryck was pleased with the sigil's underlying message, even if no one else ever grasped it. After he had first conceived of the slashed circle, he had practiced awhile here in his room scorching it onto a scrap of cloth he'd found in the street.

That emblem was now burned onto twenty-eight wood surfaces in twenty-eight different places in the city.

He found his weary eyes unfocusing as they turned up toward the ceiling. His left wrist was still trailing the pink and red streamers. He had used more wizardry today than on any other single day in his life. It had been costly, and now he was paying. He felt feverish.

It had gone so well, though, so successfully. He was proud.

Searing that slashed circle onto the surface of a wall or door was a different order of magnitude from influencing dice. He'd had to keep the sigil's shape clearly in mind as he cooperated with those energies that allowed the wood to heat and char. He had also been performing these feats at some minor distance—standing, say, across a street, focusing his will, burning the emblem onto a temporarily unnoticed wall, while all about, the Lacfoddalmendowl celebrants capered and raised their distracting tumult.

It wouldn't have done, for instance, to go wandering about Callah physically branding that design onto surfaces here and there. His way was safer, subtler, more insidious. It appealed to the style of vengeance he'd embraced.

Tomorrow and the days that followed he would give

meaning to the sigil, which he'd gone to such lengths to make appear all about the city.

He had no accurate means of determining what effect his efforts were having. That was frustrating. But he had resigned himself to the fact. Surely flooding the market with counterfeit money was going to have a detrimental impact on Callah's economy. Just as surely, his tales of violent resistance against the Felk in Windal were stirring up these Callahans. Of that at least he now had some proof—and was grateful for it.

He was pleased he'd met that female vendor Quentis. He could see her amber eyes now, even as his were drifting shut.

Bryck at last untied the streamers and removed his boots. He felt even hotter now. Weaker. No. He couldn't afford a fever. He needed rest urgently. It had been a long Lacfoddalmendowl.

He collapsed into deep sleep.

DARDAS
(4)

"HALT!"

Dardas reined his horse. It was a fine beast, strong and robust. It tossed its head as it came to a stop.

He held a gloved hand high in the air. It was well past midday, and the air was cooler than it had been yesterday. Of course, this weather was nothing compared to an average autumn day on the Northern Continent. As for a Northland winter, well, he wondered if snow even fell here on this Isthmus.

As general, he naturally rode toward the rear of his army. So it was that he had an excellent view of its many units as they, too, gradually came to a halt, as word of his order spread. It was by now quite a vast army, swollen with troops from Felk, Callah, Windal, and Sook. They were all under his command. With a word and a raised hand, he had halted this vast military force here in its tracks.

A rush of exhilaration surged through him. What power he had!

His senior staff was automatically gathering. Dardas remained atop his horse, surveying his mighty military apparatus. Matokin might think this was *his* army. He was wrong. Armies belonged to their generals.

This was not a scheduled food or rest break. Dardas's officers were curious as to why he had ordered the halt. They were only two more days of traveling from Trael.

Berkant, too, was lingering on the edge of the gathering. The Far Speak specialist no doubt imagined the general would want to make an immediate report to Matokin in Felk.

"Bivouac!" Dardas called in the same thunderous voice of command.

His senior officers looked bewildered, but they relayed the order. When it became plain that the general had no further commands, they dispersed. Dardas watched, pleased, as his army set about making camp. They were becoming very efficient troops.

Eventually, he dismounted. His groom took the horse. Berkant, Dardas saw, was still loitering nearby. He called the mage over with a wave.

"Yes, General?" the young wizard asked.

"Are we in contact with the advance scouts? Those Far Movement mages?"

"Uh . . . of course, General. But it's Mage Limmel that is in charge of field operations—"

"I know," Dardas nodded.

Those scouting parties, by necessity, included both Far Movement and Far Speak wizards. How else could the opening of a portal be coordinated between two distant points? Naturally, a squad of regular soldiers accompanied these parties.

"I want to know their exact positions around Trael," Dardas went on. "Report to my aide personally within the watch."

"Yes, General Weisel."

"And, Berkant."

"General?"

"I will be reporting to Lord Matokin later in the day," Dardas said, almost casually. "He'll no doubt want to know what we're up to here."

"I am at your disposal, sir," Berkant bowed, his guileless face unable to hide an expression of relief. Off he went.

Dardas allowed himself a small, private smile. Naturally he had no intention of letting Matokin in on his real plans. He already resented having to report to the Felk leader.

His latest aide was also hovering nearby. Dardas called her over.

"General Weisel?"

"I've made a special requisition from the food storehouses in Windal," he said. "A shipment will be arriving from there by portal very soon. I've ordered some cured meats set aside for our troops. Choice cuts. Should be a welcome change from the rations *they* have been eating."

Again, he smiled, this time letting his aide see. She couldn't quite repress an answering smile of her own. It was common knowledge among the ranks by now that General Weisel ate the same food as his troops.

Off she went as well.

Dardas saw that his pavilion had been erected. Instead of entering, however, he turned and strode off, snatching up an anonymous-looking cloak as he went.

IF ONE KNEW what one was doing, it was easy to move unnoticed through the camp.

Dardas avoided officers or anyone of rank who looked like they were in the mood to bark orders. His cloak hid his insignias. He looked like a nameless soldier, which suited his purposes perfectly.

This was something he had done from time to time in the old days, when he was leading his brave, ferocious troops across the Northland. It hadn't all been battles, of course, despite what history seemed to have recorded about Dardas the Butcher. Like this army, his former one had encamped regularly, pausing to eat, drink, rest, and tell ribald tales around their campfires.

Dusk was settling in. It made him even more of a vague shadow.

"Why're we stopped? Do y'think we got orders from Felk?"

"I'm just grateful for the rest."

"Me too. Cavalry and officers ride horses. We infantry go it *on foot*."

The men and women were sprawled around the campfire. A bottle of something was being passed around. Dardas lingered within earshot.

"But what about Trael?"

"What about it?"

"Aren't we supposed to be invading it? I mean, why stop here, a day or two away?"

It was the oldest among the circle who answered, a jowly sergeant. "The general has his reasons."

"What makes you think Weisel ordered this?" a younger soldier with a wispy mustache retorted with a sneer. "Everyone knows that spook Matokin is pulling the strings from all the way up there in Felk."

The sergeant looked flatly at him. "Kid, do you really think a mage could command an army as good as the general has?"

The younger soldier shrugged, making it look insolent. "Why not?"

"Because, ass, Matokin isn't even here in the field with us. You can't just receive reports by Far Speak and study maps and know what move to make. Not unless you're some kind of incredible war theory genius. And Matokin's not that. He's a godsdamned clever wizard, and he'll make a great emperor when we're done conquering his empire, but it's General Weisel who is leading us here. Don't you forget that!"

The bottle was passed to the sergeant. He took a generous swallow, while the soldier with the wispy mustache sulked.

Dardas furtively studied the other faces around the fire. They seemed to be on the sergeant's side. That was good. He moved on silently.

Similar conversations were taking place throughout the camp. He paused to sample them, covertly. The majority of his troops supported him, he found. Certainly there were some malcontents, but that couldn't be avoided. Dardas took note of only the most vitriolic ones. He could have them dealt with later, if he chose.

Berkant had probably already delivered his report about the scouts' positions around Trael. Dardas should get back to his tent soon.

But he had one more task.

Still hidden in his cloak, he skulked into an area of the camp where a mixed unit of wizards had their tents. It was not the same company to which Raven was attached.

Here Dardas felt a palpable tension among the encamped mages. It was the same tightly wound stress that was evident in most of the army's wizards. The general hostility between magicians and the regular troops couldn't entirely account for the anxiety and strain.

That Academy in Felk, whatever it was, was apparently turning out accomplished wizards. But it was also producing personnel who felt persecuted and paranoid.

Dardas ducked low now, moving fast. Magic was an incredible tool, and these practitioners probably deserved more respect than they got. But they were also cooperating with Matokin in that conspiracy of silence that kept any useful knowledge of magic from Dardas.

He was glad once again that Weisel kept his body fit. Weisel's consciousness hadn't made a peep in some while now, and Dardas didn't miss those mental conversations with his host.

He rolled silently on the ground, drawing a knife and

slicing cleanly through the side of a small tent. He rolled right on through the rent, onto the individual lying alone inside.

The Far Movement mage tried to make a startled squawk, but Dardas jammed a hand over his mouth. He also pinned the wizard's body with his own, and touched the very sharp point of his knife to the tip of the mage's nose.

Dardas had seen the mages open portals. He knew— without understanding the meaning of the actions—that complex chants and gyrations were involved in Far Movement magic, much like that rejuvenation spell that Kumbat had performed.

This mage wasn't going to get the chance to work his magic and escape this tent. After a few moments he stopped struggling beneath Dardas. Now he began to tremble in fear.

Dardas grinned in the tent's darkness.

"Now," he whispered, "you're going to answer some questions, earnestly and wholeheartedly."

BERKANT WAS CLUTCHING a shred of fabric in one hand. It looked like it had come from a piece of clothing. Dardas had noticed this before, whenever the mage was communicating directly with Matokin.

They were in Dardas's tent. Berkant had brought maps that indicated the locations of the scout parties. Dardas would make a few adjustments, place them just so around the city-state of Trael.

At the moment, he was explaining himself to Lord Matokin. The indignity of reporting to a "superior" chafed him.

"I am making preparations to use the portals," Dardas said. "That's why I've halted the army."

Berkant's face was vacant. His eyes stared forward at nothing. But he was still hearing Dardas's words and relaying them magically north to distant Felk. In turn, Matokin was able to send his own messages here. It was, admittedly, an amazing feat.

Someday maybe Dardas would educate himself about the methods of Far Speak, just as he now knew much more about Far Movement magic than he had before.

"Why have you waited until you are so close to Trael to do so?" Berkant asked, in a voice that barely sounded like his own. "It seems to me that the greater the distance you cross, the more effective the portals are for a surprise attack. The people of Trael no doubt know you intend to invade there by now."

"But what defenses can they raise?" Dardas countered. "My scouts tell me it is a typical Isthmus city-state. Their army is no match for . . . yours."

He had nearly said "mine." He silently chided himself.

"That does not answer my question, General," Berkant/Matokin said. "Why have you waited?"

Dardas lowered his eyes. It took a great effort to make himself look humble, but he didn't know if Matokin could see through Berkant's eyes as well as hear with his ears.

"I . . ." he said hesitantly. "I . . . am not comfortable going through those portals."

"What?" The Far Speak mage conveyed Matokin's surprise.

Dardas shifted uncomfortably on his seat. "I don't entirely trust that particular magic, Lord Matokin. I must admit that stepping into one of those portals, I don't know if I'll step out the other side again."

There was silence. Berkant's eyes stared dully.

Then he said, "General Weisel, that is ridiculous. Whatever fears you have, you must overcome them. I am disappointed that you have allowed this bias to affect your battle strategies in any way. I have provided you with the best mages possible to aid you in this war. You *will* make use of them. Is that clear?"

Contritely, Dardas said, "Yes, Lord."

A few moments later the communication ended. Dardas watched Berkant recover himself, blinking as if he were waking from a dream. The mage immediately stuffed the shred of cloth back into his robe.

"Are you all right?" Dardas asked.

"Yes, General Weisel. I—"

"You're dismissed."

Berkant exited the pavilion. Dardas didn't know if the Far Speak mage could overhear the messages he relayed, but it was shameful the way Dardas had had to abase himself before Matokin . . . even if it was all a ruse.

Dardas told his aide to fetch Raven to his tent. He was informed that the special foodstuffs had arrived via Far Movement from Windal and were being distributed among the troops. He acknowledged this with a nod.

When Raven entered, Dardas's gaze lingered candidly over her. It really was a vast improvement. Groomed and decently clothed, she was decidedly attractive. Raven didn't shy from his stare, either.

"You called for me, General?" Her voice was exaggeratedly husky.

He was careful not to laugh. Let her enjoy her new-found sensuality. It was all part of the plan to attach her more firmly to him. He needed allies among his army's mages. He thought it best to start with her.

He wondered, briefly, if she would struggle under him like that Far Movement mage had. Dardas liked his bed partners to put up a bit of a fight.

Of course, that mage hadn't been a lover. Dardas had questioned the wizard, who was very forthcoming with that knife against his nose. Then, when Dardas had what he wanted, he had flicked the sharp tip of the blade across the mage's upper right arm, just a tiny cut. The poison on the blade acted fast. Dardas escaped the tent the way he'd come in, and flitted invisibly away through the falling night.

The mage, whenever he was discovered, would appear to have died from a seizure of some sort.

"Sir?" Raven was still waiting, looking a little nervous now.

Dardas favored her with a smile. "Now, don't frown, girl. I've told you how pretty your smile is. There, that's it."

She didn't blush this time, but proudly displayed her smile, even instinctively thrusting out her breasts for added effect.

"Raven," he said, quietly now, "I have need of you."

Her face went still, expectantly.

He took a step toward her, laying his hands on her shoulders and squeezing slightly. He stooped so that he could peer directly into her eyes.

"How can I serve you, General?" she asked.

"I know the secret of Far Movement," he said. "I know which world it is the portals lead into. I intend to use those portals in a way your wizards haven't yet thought of."

Raven was listening very solemnly and intently.

"And I want you to help me."

AQUINT

(4)

THEY HAD MISSED the joyous festival of Lacfoddal-mendowl, which was disappointing. But Aquint and Cat were both glad to be back in Callah, even if they were now serving the enemy that had captured the city-state.

Aquint presented his credentials to Colonel Jesile at the Registry. The Felk governor of Callah had cropped hair the color of metal and a face equally hard. Nonetheless, his manner was polite, if somewhat cold.

"I trust you had a pleasant . . . journey," Jesile said, looking at the scroll Lord Abraxis had given Aquint.

"As pleasant as it could be, I suppose," Aquint said rue-fully.

It was the second time he had passed through that weird, milky other-reality, crossing the distance from Sook in a matter of a few dozen steps. The world those portals opened into was so strange and disorienting. He and Cat had been instructed to walk a perfectly straight line, not to dawdle or deviate in any way.

They had done just that, eyes straight ahead. And

yet . . . all the while Aquint had the awful, uneasy feeling that someone or something in that place was *watching* him and Cat pass.

He shuddered, thinking about it.

Jesile grunted. "Yes. I feel the same way about being Far Moved. I supposed we'll have to get used to it. Once the Isthmus belongs entirely to Felk, we might all be moving around like that."

"You think the wizards will be running everything when the war's over?" Aquint asked.

Jesile was suddenly leery. Aquint didn't understand; it had just been a casual question.

"What can we here in Callah do for Internal Security?" the Felk military governor finally said.

"I've been ordered to investigate local unrest." Next to Aquint, Cat stood silently, eyes moving. "This is my assistant."

"Very well. How can my garrison assist you?"

Aquint had visited the Registry before, to file the licenses for his old freight hauling business. The building was large.

"I wish to see all your recent reports of arrests and disturbances," Aquint said, adopting a businesslike tone. "Tell me, do your soldiers arrest people for speaking treason against the empire?"

Jesile pursed his lips a moment, considering. He didn't want to say the wrong thing in front of an agent of the Internal Security Corps, Aquint realized.

"My garrison," Jesile said, carefully, "is instructed to exercise a degree of latitude when dealing with these locals. The aim, I believe, is to win them over as functional citizens of the empire . . . not to terrorize them into useless submission."

Aquint nodded. "That's good, Colonel. I agree." He was glad Callah was being governed by someone with some sense.

He requested a set of Callahan clothing for himself and

Cat. He also procured a sling for his left arm. That way, if anyone asked why he, someone of qualified age, wasn't with the army, he could say he was on furlough after having been wounded.

He hit the streets eagerly, Cat alongside. He sucked in lungfuls of sweet, cool Callahan air, soaking up the familiar sights around him. There was evidence of the Felk occupation just about everywhere, from the patrols to the fact that there were no civilians of eligible military age around, but it didn't dampen his spirits.

"Wonderful to be home, isn't it?" he said, as they crossed through the marketplace and turned down a street.

"I was getting used to Sook, actually," Cat said.

"*That* place? Well, I admit I was enjoying that sweet operation we had at that army warehouse. I don't doubt Tyber's cousin Vahnka will keep it running at a profit."

"Do you plan on looking up Tyber while we're here?" Cat said.

Aquint raised his hand. "One racket at a time. Right now, I'm an Internal Security agent. You saw what pull that had just now, with our esteemed governor."

"I saw," Cat said.

"I think the possibilities of lining our pockets with this job are damned near limitless. But first, we've got to prove ourselves. Abraxis is going to want a report."

"Why not just make one up?" Cat suggested blandly.

Aquint wasn't sure if the boy was being facetious or not. "Too risky at the start. I want you to do what you do best, haunt the shadows and hear what people are saying."

"That's not what I do best," Cat said, his hand opening to reveal the brooch he'd snatched off a table in the marketplace.

"Call it one of your many talents, then, lad," Aquint said. "Jesile says people haven't been very happy about the new paper currency they've issued here. We'll start with that. Let's hope there's somebody committing treasonous crimes somewhere here. Otherwise, this Internal Security agent is going to find himself out of a job."

AS PLEASING AS it was to be home again, Aquint was hardly totally relaxed. Thoughts of Abraxis hung over him like a dark cloud. He recalled vividly the sample of his blood the mage had taken in Sook. Abraxis kept those samples on his person at all times, he had said. That meant, if he appeared here in Callah to make a snap inspection, Aquint's sample would be with him, in that small red bag.

Aquint definitely didn't like the idea of Abraxis having the power of life and death over him, which was what possession of his blood sample implied.

Damned wizards.

He avoided revisiting his old warehouse, thinking the sight would probably depress him, but he did reacquaint himself with much of the city.

Inevitably he bumped into people he knew. His "wounded" arm was effective in explaining his presence. It was good to see these old acquaintances, though many had a tired, beaten look about them. Every one of them asked him for news of the outside world. He sidestepped this by claiming he had been wounded shortly after being inducted into the Felk army, the injury serious enough to leave him virtually senseless for the past few lunes.

Jesile had provided him with an apartment in one of Callah's better neighborhoods. Aquint would draw pay from Jesile's coffers of proper coin. However, for walking around money, the Governor's Office had issued him some of the new paper scrip, so he could blend in with the locals.

It was funny-looking stuff, Aquint thought. Green notes, red notes, all stamped with odd designs. The system hadn't yet been introduced in Windal or Sook. Callah, he was told, was the test case.

An anonymous messenger brought Aquint the arrest reports he'd asked for. He studied them in his new rooms. Cat was still out.

There were the expected incidents of drunken behavior. Actually, as far as Lacfoddalmendowl went, there were far fewer than normal. Of course Jesile had only allowed a toned down version of the holiday to be celebrated. But it was better that than nothing, Aquint thought.

Mixed in among the pages, he found several accounts of vandalism. He culled these, curious.

Eventually Cat reappeared, having picked the apartment's lock.

"Well," the boy said, "there's a lot of under-the-counter transactions still being made in coin. I guess when the Felk confiscated everybody's jingle, they didn't get every single coin. You're right about people not liking the paper money. But they're getting used to it anyway."

Aquint nodded. He tossed a scrap of paper to Cat. "What do you make of that?"

The lad's eyes flicked over the paper. After a moment, he said, "I've seen this."

"Where?" Aquint asked, interested.

"Around," Cat said. "On walls and doors . . . branded there. Just here and there around the city. None of it really registered, until now."

Aquint allowed himself a tight smile. "The Felk police patrols didn't make much of it either. But I think it means something."

Cat handed him back the scrap of paper. "What?"

Aquint looked at the design he had drawn, as described in the reports. A circle cut through with a vertical slash.

"I don't know," he said. "But Internal Security is supposed to investigate unrest in Callah. This looks like it might lead somewhere."

"And if it doesn't?"

"Then," Aquint smiled wider, "we'll lead it somewhere ourselves."

IT WAS INDEED a luxurious apartment, with kitchens below that served the building's various units. Aquint ordered up hot dinners for him and Cat, plus a bottle of the best wine available. Everything was going to be billed to the Governor's Office, after all.

The next day Aquint prowled Callah's streets once more. Cat was a good eavesdropper, but Aquint was a very capable socializer. He dropped in at various taverns and cafés over the course of the day, being careful not to drink too much. Again he chanced upon old acquaintances and spent some time in casual conversation. Some at first were leery about speaking to a member of the Felk military.

Usually, without much effort, Aquint was able to convince them that despite being conscripted into the army, he was the same old Aquint and, most importantly, a Callahan above all else.

So it was that they divulged to him, often after he'd bought a round or two with the scrip that had been issued to him. It was a surer way to gather information than by simply spying.

Later, he met with Cat at a prearranged site. From there they went to the Registry.

Aquint brought the intelligence he'd garnered to Governor Jesile. Despite his important status as an agent of the Internal Security Corps, Aquint still got nervous in the presence of authority. It was probably left over from his days of smuggling and black marketeering.

"It's nonsense," the governor said, resolutely. "Windal is secure. Those Far Speak mages pass messages back and forth all the time. We received one only this morning, relayed from Colonel Palo, the governor. It's business as usual in Windal."

Aquint shrugged.

"I can only tell you what people are mumbling about," he said. "Everybody in Callah is starving for news about the war, about the outside. Without it, people will simply make stories up, and pass them on as fact."

"Then this talk of an uprising in Windal," Jesile said, "the people *know* it's just a rumor?"

"Some. Maybe. But some believe it. Of that I'm sure."

Colonel Jesile turned his eyes toward Cat. "And you? You've heard the same?"

Cat stood mute.

"My associate is working on other matters," Aquint said.

The governor sighed.

Aquint didn't offer up news of the slashed circle brands that had appeared around Callah, evidently during the Lacfoddalmendowl celebrations. Those had already been reported by the Felk patrols. If the governor didn't understand how widespread they were, or what the brands might indicate, Aquint saw no need to play the hand now.

"Well," Jesile said, "I will not publicly deny the rumors."

"I think that's wise," Aquint said. Callah's citizens had been kept purposely isolated. A lack of knowledge about the Isthmus at large helped keep the people controlled. It would only weaken the Felk hold on the city if Jesile acknowledged the rumor's existence.

The governor gave Aquint a look that made it clear he didn't particularly care what the Internal Security agent thought about the matter.

"There's something else," Jesile continued grudgingly. "Something much more urgent."

The governor produced two notes of Felk scrip. They were the blue ones that represented gold coins. Jesile held them up, side by side.

"One of my off-duty soldiers noticed that an inordinate

amount of money seemed to be changing hands in the marketplace right next to this building," Jesile said grimly. "Trade has been suspended for the duration among the city-states. Therefore, Callah is a closed economy. It was odd, then, that simple vendors should be in possession of so much money."

Aquint, confused, was peering at the blue notes the governor was still dangling.

"*This* is a legitimate gold note, printed by a special mint in Felk." He raised his other hand. "*This* is an incredibly skillful forgery."

Aquint's eyes widened. "How can you tell?" The notes looked exactly alike to him.

Jesile sighed again. "I almost hate to admit it, but it was one of the magicians in my garrison who discovered it. She cast some sort of divining spell. Apparently it's very specialized magic."

"So," Aquint said, "if this wizard of yours can weed out the fake notes from the real—"

The governor favored him with a stony glare. "She can't very well examine every single scrip note in Callah to determine its authenticity."

Jesile suddenly crumbled both notes into a blue wad.

"Gods know how much counterfeit money is circulating out there right now," the Felk governor spat. "But I want whoever is responsible."

Aquint managed to contain his glee until he and Cat were out of the building. It was nearing curfew.

"Well," he said to his young companion, slapping the boy's shoulders, "it looks like there's serious unrest in Callah after all."

"That sounds like work for us," Cat grumbled.

"Yes. It also means *job security.*" Aquint chuckled as they headed along the street. Though he wasn't in the habit of praying, he paused to silently thank the gods for whoever was stirring things up here in his old home city.

PRAULTH
(4)

IT WAS A large campus, but news, when it was compelling enough, could travel at impressive speed.

There was, of course, gossip; but gossip meant tawdry murmurings about romantic trysts, the exaggeratedly strange personal habits of instructors, and news—factual and otherwise—about academic advancements and demotions. The lowest-phase students, those most susceptible to dismissal from the University, existed in a kind of perpetual fear. Many were desperate to stay at Febretree, escaping unpleasant lives back home or zealously devoted to achieving the higher rankings of Thinker or even Attaché. Gossip was a cheap form of entertainment to take one's mind off one's troubles, particularly when jammed into some airless dormitory.

So, when Praulth at last irritably pushed herself from her desk to answer the hammering at her door and found the lowly first-phase pupil there, she wasn't inclined to take much heed.

The student, a boy a few years her junior, was jabbering

excitedly—and not a little bit enjoying the supposedly dire news he was imparting. Among the rush of words, she heard Master Honnis's name. The watch was late. Xink was off attending Mistress Cestrello.

"Speak clearly. You're addressing a Thinker."

It was almost comical to hear herself invoking her academic rank. She rarely thought of herself as a student anymore. Her role was more active than that, she had learned. She wasn't studying the history of war any longer; she was helping *create* it.

The Battle of Torran Flats . . .

The boy continued his breathless babbling.

It smelled of a prank, though she had not been subjected to such torments since her first-phase days. Patience, however, hadn't been with her lately, and she finally slammed shut the door, locking it.

Maps were spread over the desk. Honnis was still feeding her field reports, and she was still playing along, continuing their project of studying the Felk war. Just as she was continuing her relationship with Xink, though she knew that Honnis had arranged it, knew that the old . . . old *devil* had manipulated her. That heartless sack of bones.

She sat, examining the maps, as she had done most of the day. The Felk had abruptly halted a short distance from Trael. What was Weisel up to? She wanted to know. So did Honnis. And so doubtlessly did Premier Cultat, with whom Honnis was in contact.

A moment later Praulth heard the sound of a latchkey finding the lock that she'd insisted be installed. She wanted privacy here in the Blue Annex. She didn't shy from making demands these days. Xink entered the chamber.

He did not meet her eyes. That, too, wasn't unusual these days. Things had changed between the two of them, drastically. But something more seemed amiss now.

"What's wrong?"

"You haven't heard?" Those blue eyes of his, flecked with gold, showed white all around. His complexion tended toward the pale, but now his face looked almost bloodless.

"Let's presume I haven't," she snapped. Until recently she wouldn't have dared speak to him in such a tone. That stage of their relationship was over.

"I sent a messenger to tell you. A first-phase student. It's Master Honnis—"

That got her up from her comfortable chair a second time. She grabbed her robe from its hook by the door, twirling it onto herself. Whatever this was, it wasn't a prank.

"Tell me on the way," she said.

THE UNIVERSITY'S FACULTY was housed at the center of the campus, within a separate complex of structures dating back to the institution's founding. These interconnected and quaintly aging buildings were encircled by shrubbery and overgrowing trees that had supposedly been manicured gardens once. The semi-wild growths served to isolate the compound.

Praulth hesitated on the path that bridged its way onto this island. The autumn night was cool, and a rising and falling wind rolled through the turning leaves. The way ahead looked ominous.

With Xink at her side, she crossed the path and entered the complex. Inside, they hurried through passageways. The interior was much shabbier than she would have guessed, but the antique buildings had a charm that the rest of the University's structures lacked. There was a warm penetrating scent of age here, and of paper, ink, knowledge, perhaps even wisdom.

She had never visited this place, but she knew where Honnis's quarters were. An upper level—she'd had the circular window pointed out to her once. Praulth found stairs and bustled upward, her heart pounding hard in her chest.

A trio of instructors passed murmurs among themselves before a door. The door was ajar, and from within a sharp unpleasant voice barked.

At last Praulth checked her headlong dash. Master Honnis was alive. So Xink had assured her.

The three instructors turned with deliberate slowness to regard her. It was likely she wasn't terribly popular among the faculty nowadays. She had been an exemplary pupil once, blazing a diligent trail toward a rare kind of academic excellence. Now she was . . . what? Someone else.

Only a small part of her—the younger, innocent Praulth—still cared about pleasing the University's faculty. That individual seemed to disintegrate a bit more with every passing watch.

She pushed through the robed instructors, hearing Honnis's snarl beyond the door. It was usual for the elderly man to be disagreeable; it wasn't normal for him to be so energetic about it. He had always been one to favor the icy glower over the shrill reprimand.

His quarters were, in their way, as austere as the student's cell she had occupied before relocating to the Blue Annex. It was a small space, the ceiling quite low. There was a lamp, cot, stool, a simple square table. Dense pebbled glass in the circle of the window.

The room was also *thick* with paper. Parchments were everywhere, in stacks, in drifts, obliterating every corner. Some were pages, some were in the form of the scrolls that were favored in the north. Not a single sheet of any of it could possibly be organized, it was so scattered.

Xink waited outside. Praulth saw Master Honnis on the cot. He was arguing with the campus surgeon, a man named Chiegel. Chiegel, with perfect aplomb, was lecturing Honnis on the value of bed rest, and the University's war studies head was telling him what practical methods the Skrall No't tribe of barbarians in the Northland used to dispose of their wounded. Chiegel responded to nothing Honnis said. That made the exchange equal.

Finally it was done. Chiegel exited the chamber, and Honnis's eyes fell on Praulth.

"I see now what is required to merit a visit from you."

Honnis's dark features settled into a cast she didn't quite recognize. Now that Chiegel was gone, the ire had gone out of him. Something had happened, obviously. Something dire.

She had not seen or spoken directly to him since the night of Premier Cultat's secret visit. That night Praulth had learned those awful truths about how Honnis had exploited her.

"Are you well?" The cliché was out before she was aware of speaking it.

It was a display of vast uncharacteristic politeness that he ignored it. "I have things to tell you, if you'll hear them. They are important. Some perhaps only to myself."

Xink had told her that Master Honnis had collapsed suddenly in a corridor. It had happened only a watch ago.

"I'll hear." She closed the door and came to the foot of the cot, being careful where she stepped. The quantity of paper in the room truly was astounding, more than most individuals of wealth could comfortably afford.

Honnis's inner irascible fire had always lent him figurative size. Lying on the cot now, though, he seemed to inhabit only the meek bodily dimensions that his great age had left him.

"I am at least as old as you imagine I am," he said, cutting into her thoughts. "Likely I'm much older than what you'd guess. I have, for several years now, been sustaining my existence with the aid of rejuvenation magic."

Praulth blinked. Obviously Honnis had been laid low by some attack or seizure. But . . . had his mind been affected as well? It was a deeply disturbing thought.

"Who has been practicing this . . . magic . . . on you?" she asked.

"I have been doing it myself."

She drew her lower lip softly between her teeth.

"Your next question is, am I a wizard? Perhaps. I have some knowing, a knowledge that once, long ago in other lands, would have been fairly commonplace. But we live in a fearful age here on our sad little Isthmus."

There was sorrow in that gaunt, aged face. How sad he looked, how pitiful. Praulth felt something wrench in her chest.

"But I am past a fixed point. Rejuvenation magic is dangerous, and I've cheated that danger some while now. It's fair and right that it should be satisfied soon. Don't grieve me!"

The twin tracks of Praulth's sudden tears seemed to freeze on her cheeks at his command.

"I didn't waste my life," he explained, his voice now assuming an unfamiliar gentleness. "I have lived long, and I have done many things. Accomplishments that preceded my arrival here at Febretree. I've known pity and arrogance and anger and love. I have grown concerned these past few years over the rise of magic in the north. I . . . secretly feared what has come to pass."

"The Felk war?"

"A war of *magic*." His white-fringed head shook once, sharply. "I made Cultat aware of these doings some time ago. Of Matokin, a powerful mage, rising to power in Felk. Of the founding of the Academy, where wizards were trained to be part of an army. All the indicators were there. This war has been inevitable for several years."

Praulth furtively wiped her eyes.

Honnis's hand moved beneath his bedclothes. He was now holding a single glove in his lap.

"I am still in contact with the premier. And with the scouts I convinced Cultat to deploy into the field to observe the Felk advancements. Those scouts come from a particular noble house in Petgrad, traditionally and clandestinely trained in arts that have, with time, fallen out of favor."

Praulth gazed at the glove.

"You don't believe me," Honnis said.

"Master—"

"Why should you?" Some of his normal vehemence returned. "You know nothing of magic. You're as ignorant as everyone else on this miserable Isthmus of ours. Everyone, that is, except one wily wizard in the north, who tapped into a power that has gone witlessly neglected and nearly forgotten for hundredwinters and more."

Praulth chose her words carefully. "It is true that I don't know much regarding magic. But I accept that the Felk military is employing it." She had seen detailed maps of what had happened at U'delph, how General Weisel used the transport portals to move his forces.

"Then," Honnis said, a bit out of breath, drained by his outburst, "you have faith in something that most people turn away from in prejudicial fear. Magic is natural. And like most natural things, it is also dangerous."

He lifted the glove. Praulth saw, with some alarm, that Honnis's hand could not hold it steady.

"You have wondered from the start how I have been providing you with current intelligence of the Felk movements occurring so far away."

"Yes," Praulth said honestly. "I have wondered."

"Far Speak."

"Master?"

"Communication magic. This glove belongs to one of the elite scouts dispatched by Cultat. That scout, in turn, possesses an item of mine, something I've handled often, that has essentially taken on something of my . . . spirit, if you will."

"Spirit?" Praulth retreated from the word. It had no place in her world of cool logic and deductive insight.

Honnis gritted his teeth. "By the sanity of the gods, Thinker Praulth, don't close your mind now."

"My apologies, Master Honnis." How strange. Only a watch ago she had been silently cursing this man. Now she was affording him all the courtesies of his academic status. Not to mention the respect she owed him as her mentor.

Yet Honnis had betrayed her. How could she forgive that . . . even if this was his deathbed?

"Everyone," Honnis pronounced, "has the capacity to work magic. But the facility for it is another matter. It is a penchant, no different from the distinct ability to, say, understand at a fundamental level the strategies and cunning of a war commander who has been dead two and a half hundredwinters."

"I see," said Praulth.

"I don't believe you do." But he said it gently.

"Tell me then."

Honnis closed his eyes, drew a breath that rattled slightly. "Magic has a source. People commonly believe— if they believe at all—that practitioners draw on energies that are locked away inside themselves. Some even who use magic in a minor capacity believe this themselves. They don't know better, and they've not been formally taught otherwise. But magic doesn't come from within."

She was curious. "Where then?"

"Elsewhere. The source has as many names as the gods have faces. The Wellspring. The First Divinity. The Glorious Birth."

She puzzled over the names. They sounded archaic, superstitious.

"It is the place from which we come," said Honnis, "and to where we are all restored. It is a reality of great energy, of vast power."

"*A* reality?" Praulth felt herself frowning as her logical mind instinctively picked apart Honnis's words. "Are you implying that there is a reality *other* than this one?"

"It is self-evident."

"How so?"

"This reality is life. What is life's opposite?"

"I am not Master Turogo's pupil," she said. Turogo headed the philosophy council. "I am yours." This last came out somewhat hoarsely.

"Life's opposite is . . . ?" pressed Honnis.

"Death," Praulth said, with a small shrug.

"That is yet another name. The oldest."

She wasn't following. She wasn't even convinced this was leading anywhere. But she had promised to hear this man's words. Then, what he had said registered.

"Are you saying," Praulth whispered, "that magic taps into a reality beyond this one . . . beyond *life*? Its source is—death? That makes no sense." In truth, all this was greatly offensive to her rational mind. She accepted the authenticity of magic. The Felk had used it in their war, and war was a reality not to be denied. But this babble about the Wellspring or whatever Honnis had said—

"From which we come and to where we are restored," the elderly instructor repeated. His eyes had remained closed. Now he opened them, peering up at Praulth.

She felt the impulse to go to him, to kneel by the cot, take his hand. But she didn't know if such actions would be welcome. She remained standing.

"I am dying because the rejuvenation spells are failing," said Honnis. "Also because I have strained myself by exercising the Far Speak magic. Death is not evil. Life is not good. Both are potent forces, as all opposites are. Both draw great power from the other."

He needed to pause again, for another labored breath.

"Matokin has reawakened magic in this reality to a degree it has not known for many, many years," he continued. "He has produced many practitioners. He has schooled his mages in magic's methods, but he has taught nothing of the ethics of the art. They don't grasp the consequences of what they do. Only the most powerful—the Far Movement mages, I would say—would know anything of the Wellspring. Most would only know that with enough training, with the proper incantations and gestures and discipline, they can achieve spectacular feats."

Praulth absorbed this. "But what are the consequences?"

The thinnest of smiles touched Honnis's lips. It was startling nonetheless to see any sort of smile on his face.

"They are using Far Movement magic," he said. "Opening doorways, portals. They are *entering* the reality beyond this. They are flirting with dangers that perhaps Matokin himself doesn't even understand."

It was Praulth's turn to press. "Yes—but what are those dangers?" A coldness spread through her.

Honnis abruptly gathered himself. His face became the severe disagreeable mask she had seen so often before. He fixed her with his withering stare.

"Why did the mighty empires of the Northern and Southern Continents crumble so many hundredwinters ago?" he asked as if she was some pathetic first-phase student.

"The Great Upheavals," she answered.

"And they were?"

"Internal strife. If you require a detailed accounting, I can recite what historians have cobbled together from that chaotic period—"

"Since the time of the Upheavals," Honnis said, trampling her words heedlessly, "what has been the prevalent attitude toward wizards?"

It was a broad question, yet it was still answerable. "Practitioners of magic have been feared by most cultures."

"Why?" Honnis asked.

"They were made to blame for the Upheavals. They . . ."

Honnis's gaze fairly drilled into her now. She halted. His bald head moved slightly in a significant nod. "Yes," he said, voice gone breathy and weak once more. "It was the misuse of magic that caused the Great Upheavals. Magicians were shunned because they *were* to blame. Those mighty empires were no wiser, in the end, than Matokin and his followers."

She needed to sit. She groped behind herself, found the stool, spilled a pile of pages off of it, and sat. She could say nothing. Shock gripped her.

"There is something else I wish to say."

Praulth blinked. Some moments had passed. Honnis was watching her, barely able to lift his head. She moved the stool nearer, though she didn't take his hand.

"I cannot be proud of you," he said, measuring out the words. "I don't have the right. Actually no one can properly take pride in another's accomplishments. It's a sickening practice. But—your work has been exceptional. You do not know how gifted you are. I labored over each and every field report I received from Cultat's scouts. Yes, I recognized Dardas's patterns. But I could not—not with nearly the degree of accuracy you have demonstrated— predict his movements. You *know* Dardas." That fragile smile came once more. "Your tactic—using the Battle of Torran Flats . . . brilliant."

Praulth felt tears threaten her eyes a second time. Whatever Honnis had done, it was for a greater good. For the alliance Cultat was hoping to build. For the defeat of the Felk.

"Thank you, Master Honnis," she said.

"It's Dardas. You know that."

"Of course, Master Honnis."

"No . . . Praulth. It *is* Dardas."

She stared.

"Let me," he said, "tell you about resurrection magic . . ."

THE BATTLE OF Torran Flats. Brilliant? Perhaps. To Praulth it seemed the obvious tactic. She had simply approached the problem logically. She knew Dardas's style.

She could predict his movements. How to engage him in the field was merely a matter of analysis and deduction.

How to engage *Dardas*. Not Weisel. No, Weisel was no imitator after all.

Incredible . . . this war of magic. How historically significant it all was.

Torran Flats was the site of one of Dardas's greatest victories some two hundred and fifty years ago. An army had stood against his forces. The leader was a rival Northland warlord who had some knowledge of battle tactics. He had arrayed his troops to draw Dardas's warriors into a trap. It was a fairly cunning ambush, relying on flanking units that remained out of sight until the crucial moment.

Dardas of course didn't take the bait. He outflanked the flankers and cut a butchering swath through the enemy army, the remains of which he absorbed into his own forces.

Praulth's counsel to Cultat was to reconstruct this very same battle scenario. Cultat should array his forces (whatever forces he could or had managed to raise) to duplicate the placement of that ancient warlord's troops. Weisel—*Dardas*—would recognize the "trap" and enact the same outflanking maneuver.

It was an artifice, of course. The Felk, when they moved to outflank, would be spread out, separated. There was unavoidable vulnerability there. A decisive forward thrust at the right time and place could not be successfully defended against. The Felk could be slashed in two.

Praulth knew this. She had previously studied the Battle of Torran Flats. She had debated it exhaustively with other war studies students. She had reenacted it, on paper. Dardas was a dazzling war commander, likely the best that history had to offer. But he wasn't infallible—particularly when his enemy was armed with such intimate knowledge of his strategies and techniques.

She found the door to their chamber unlocked, Xink still awake inside.

"I told you," she said, hearing how inert her voice sounded, "I like that door locked, always."

"Sorry."

She removed her robe. Leaving the faculty compound, she had seen first light in the sky. The coming day would be overcast.

"How is Master Honnis?" Xink asked.

She dropped herself onto the bed. "He died. Come to bed with me."

He stood hesitantly from the chair where he was sitting. This time it was Praulth who didn't meet his eyes. She merely waited to feel the comfort of his body. She needed that solace now. Her role in the Felk war was done.

RADSTAC
(4)

THE BANDITS HAD fast horses that had the memories of secret trails through the scrub and woods. Here and there they crossed a road, empty, the merchant caravans that were the bandits' prey long gone. The summer, Radstac had learned, had been a poor one for this professional band. The short, heavily muscled bandit chief Anzal opined that this buggering Felk war had ruined business for her and her kind, perhaps permanently.

It was possible, Radstac mused. This was no simple Isthmus tussle between feuding city-states. If the Felk remade this entire land in their image, they would have no more enemies. *All* would be Felk. And so the Isthmus would no longer be a reliable source of petty wars in which she could fight.

A mercenary needed wars. And she needed her *mansìd* leaves.

She peeled one away from its wax paper and bit off half. She was, inevitably, building up a tolerance to the painstakingly cultivated narcotic. Fortunately the batch that Deo had procured for her was particularly potent. The fearsome ache that sang through her teeth now was evidence enough of that.

She had not dismounted her horse to take her dose. It was done in the saddle, her black mount and those of the twelve bandits keeping up a pounding pace through the wilderness.

Deo rode at her side. He made no complaints about the punishing speed at which they were moving. Barely a meal break in the day, scarcely two watches of sleep in the night. Northward. To the Felk. As fast as possible.

For Radstac this was decidedly different from being loosed on a battlefield to hack at some arbitrary enemy. A new role. Bodyguard. Escort. Protector. It was truly a shame, then, that her charge was doomed.

She neatly ducked the gnarled elbow of a branch as the trail suddenly narrowed. The bandits rode both ahead and behind.

"How far from Trael are we, do you suppose?" the Petgrad noble grunted, obviously feeling the soreness and cramped muscles of their prolonged riding.

"Are we going there after all?" Radstac asked drolly.

"No."

Simple, toneless. Yet she heard the regret there, the finality. The *mansìd* was rapidly sharpening her perceptions. Deo was still waiting for an answer.

She said, "I believe we are passing or past the city already." The bandits, by her calculations, had been taking their group just east of Trael.

"Another day or two, in that case, until we reach the Felk."

Then what? But Radstac left the retort unsaid. She hadn't been hired to dissuade this man from his goal. His scheme to infiltrate the vast mass of the Felk army and murder its commander, however, was probably just a vague fantasy in his mind.

Of course, he might change his plans at the last mo-

ment. When he saw the naked reality of what he was facing. When his death was there waiting for his next forward
step.

Radstac, despite years of seeing men and women lose
their lives in battle, hoped Deo would recant. This was
senseless. A waste.

She eyed Deo sidelong, his handsome rugged profile. A
face of heavy bones. Fatigue in those blue eyes. Being
born into the vast privileges of the nobility hadn't ruined
his honor, his sense of responsibility. She wondered—the
thought sharp and *mansìd*-inspired—if he would have in
fact made a better premier of Petgrad than Cultat.

Now he had recast himself as an assassin, a ready-made
folk hero who would be remembered for a failed, but
valiant, deed.

And she—would she be remembered by these Isthmusers? If so, it could only be as the one who had allowed
the hero to meet his fate.

She didn't want it. She wanted Deo alive.

Ahead, a hand flew into the air among the trees and
bramble. Anzal, on the lead horse. She was a very able
leader, Radstac judged. Her band was loyal. Yet the full
dozen had been purchased with Deo's promissory note.

Radstac lunged for Deo's reins, even as she nimbly
drew her own mount to a halt. But Deo had seen the signal, too. The whole band was stopping, hooves clambering, dust roiling through the trees.

Her hand fell to her sword. If there was to be a fight, it
wouldn't be the first one she had fought while under the in-
fluence of *mansìd*. It wouldn't be the tenth. Her eyes
darted all around, ears tuned sharply. Nothing came out of
the dust.

The bandits were silent, weapons at the ready. At the
front of the pack, Anzal was standing in her stirrups, peering at something through the trees that Radstac—maddeningly—couldn't see. Not even the leaf half she'd chewed
helped. But this territory belonged to these bandits; they

knew it intimately, and they knew when something wasn't right. Or so it seemed.

Deo sat calmly in the saddle.

Finally Anzal came down from hers. Murmuring softly to the others in the band, she walked back down the line. On foot she barely came up to Radstac's kidskin boot.

"Someone's encamped," the bandit chief said quietly. Her eyes indicated the direction through the woods.

"An army?" Radstac asked. Had they reached the Felk faster than expected? She didn't like the thought.

"Smaller. A lot smaller." Anzal went to tell the rest.

Scouts, thought Radstac, though the camp might be anything, including a band of rival bandits. But instinct, when it was honed by so many hard-bitten years, was to be trusted.

They all dismounted.

"Why don't we go around?" Deo asked, but he spoke the question mildly. Anzal had returned.

"Turf's ours," the chief said, shrugging her muscular shoulders. "If somebody's on it, we need to know who. They might have friends."

Which meant this wasn't simply a matter of animal territoriality, Radstac noted. True professionals then. That was good.

"I'll go with you," Deo said to Anzal, who was gathering up a small party.

"No need."

"If I decide I go, I go."

The chief frowned a moment, but Deo's words were certainly true. She moved off to the tall lad who was the expert archer.

"Why should you go?" Radstac wanted to know. It meant, of course, that she would go with him.

"Do these waylayers know the Felk?" A glimmer of his familiar charming smile crossed his features.

"Do you?" she countered. "Have you ever laid eyes on one in your life?"

"No. I never cared for the Isthmus's less gentle northerly climes. But from what I've gathered from the intelligence reports Uncle has received, I believe I can recognize a uniformed soldier. Or a wizard."

Radstac didn't fear wizards or wizardry. She was of the Southsoil, and she gave no quarter to baseless dreads. Nonetheless, she didn't know the extent of the powers these Felk mages might possess, or how she could successfully protect her client against such talents.

Regardless of what magic could do, she told herself as they prepared to move out, a blade could always cut flesh.

She had her heavy combat sword in hand as they fanned out quietly through the trees. Anzal, the archer, one other bandit, herself, and Deo. Deo still at her side. He hadn't drawn his sword, but he was tensed, ready, as they stalked through the woods.

It was late morning. There were birds making song and flitting among the wide canopy of branches overhead, small animals rustling through the brush. Good. Cover noise. Radstac let a glint of teeth show in her doubly scarred face. She felt the dark powerful current of combat readiness moving her blood through her veins.

They crept along low, in the direction Anzal had indicated. The three bandits demonstrated admirable stealth. Radstac peered ahead, picking out the movements of individual leaves, careful not to let her growing frustration throw her off. What exactly had Anzal seen?

Then she picked out the figures. They were glimpses among the trees. A camp. Yes. They were in a clearing. Radstac smelled meat cooked over a fire.

Anzal was gesturing sharply at her. She had missed the first signal. The bandit chief glared; Radstac still was not popular with this band. She put a hand to Deo's arm, and they both halted, crouched in the brush.

They were six. Two in dark robes, four in military uni-

forms. They lolled about the small camp. Deo studied the
figures intently. Radstac had already plotted out the best
way to raid the camp and slay its occupants—not that she
saw any need for such an action. Deo's original idea was
surely best. Just go around this camp.

Anzal signaled the retreat.

When they returned to the horses, it was Deo who
spoke first. "They're Felk. They've got to be scouting out
Trael."

"Shouldn't we take them, just for the sake of good manners?" ventured the archer with a smirk.

"Shut up, Frog." Anzal shot the boy a glare. To Deo she
said, "I agree. Scouts. That army's not going to be far away
now."

Deo nodded. "But we need to capture one of those soldiers. I've got questions I want to ask."

"No way to pick off one," Radstac said. "Have to raid
the whole camp."

Anzal's ready glare turned her way once more. "We can
handle that. But what about those two in the robes? Are
they soldiers, too?"

Deo pursed his lips a moment. "I believe those two are
wizards," he finally said.

Radstac watched the shock ripple through the band.
Fearful faces turned toward one another. It was comical—
and so typical of these Isthmusers. This was still a young
land, and these were young peoples, with juvenile cultures.
They were unsettled by fears that adults learned to manage.

Protesting voices were rising, some quivering. Anzal si-
lenced everyone harshly, clouting the archer—Frog—
who had lost his smirk the instant Deo had said *wizards.*

"Actually," Deo continued, unperturbed by the hub-
bub, "it's one of those wizards I want to talk to." Again
he allowed a glimpse of his smile. He owned these bandits. They were bought and paid for, and what he said
stood.

Radstac saw that realization reach the entire group. Comical indeed. But she didn't laugh. Instead she set about explaining how they could take the camp.

THEY HAD TO kill one to prove they were serious. Likely they'd have to kill all these Felk in the end, Radstac figured. What were they going to do—take prisoners?

The bandits prowled silently into their positions, ringing the little clearing. None of the Felk had a weapon in hand. A crossbow leaned against a tumbled log, but no one was near it. Frog shot an arrow into the embers of the cooking fire, sending up a cloud of sparks.

"Surrender yourselves—now!" Radstac called. She was behind a thick tree trunk, observing the camp through one eye.

For soldiers—for *Felk* soldiers, who had supposedly conquered the north half of this Isthmus—they did not respond professionally. The four in uniforms and the two robed figures all leaped to their feet, looking desperately around, seeing nothing but the surrounding woods. No one even seemed to know from which direction the arrow had come.

Radstac called again for their surrender. This gave one of the soldiers the idea of grabbing up his sword and chopping it through the air.

"Come and fight us, you dogs!"

It was the sort of heroic drivel Radstac had heard on many battlefields in her time. It was most often cried out by simpletons who had never before lifted a blade against an enemy, but who had heard exotic tales of war all their lives.

And like many of those, these were the last words ever said by the Felk soldier. Frog was as well camouflaged among the trees as the rest of the band, but he had taken up a blind that gave him clear sight lines into the camp. He put a shaft into the soldier's face. Radstac knew how taut the lad could draw that bow, and the force of the blow lifted the soldier off his feet. Blood sprayed. The sword thumped the ground.

Most persuasively of all, it took a long, grueling moment for the man to die, and he was not quiet about it. His fellow Felk agreed to surrender the next time Radstac called for it.

The bandits took the camp.

Deo asked questions, first of the soldiers. They replied readily. Yes, they were scouting ahead of the main body of the army. Yes, Trael was the next target of the Felk, so far as they knew. The city-state possessed no adequate defenses that they had observed. It would fall.

The bandits helped themselves to what rations they found. They divvied up the Felk weapons, eyeing the blades critically, debating the virtues of balance and heft. Deo confiscated the crossbow for himself.

When Deo motioned for the two wizards to be brought forward, the bandits quieted. They were uneasy about the two robed specters in their midst, despite the fact that they wore perfectly ordinary faces and had the same number of limbs as everyone else present. Even the Felk soldiers, remarkably enough, appeared to share in the uneasiness.

Radstac remained at Deo's side. The wizards' hands were bound, but she didn't know how well this would hinder their powers—if at all. Though magic was practiced and relatively accepted on the Southern Continent, she had never actually encountered a practitioner. They tended to live remote, cloistered lives.

One of the robed figures was male, the other female. Both looked very frightened. Deo studied the pair, intrigued. Not wary and apprehensive like the bandits.

After a time he said, "You serve the Felk. Why?"

The female blinked and said, "We *are* Felk."

"You don't consider yourselves wizards above all? Interesting. I would've thought that would come first."

The male wizard chewed at his lower lip. "We are, of course . . . loyal . . . to our arts as well."

Deo nodded. "And that doesn't conflict with your loyalty to your state? Well, I suppose it needn't necessarily. Forgive me. I've never met a magician, outside of carnival hucksters. You are, frankly, fascinating."

He was using his charm, Radstac noted. How effortlessly the Petgrad noble could put another at ease, even under conditions like this. It was impressive.

"I imagine you're valuable assets to your military," he went on. "From the stories we've heard about what the Felk have done in the north"—he grunted a wry laugh— "I wish we had a company of wizards for ourselves."

The female wizard glanced shyly around. "You're not . . . bandits?" she asked softly.

Deo laughed aloud now, the sound rich and infectious.

"*Some* of us are," he said. "But others among us have other purposes. Toward those purposes I must now ask you questions."

Radstac's palm rested on her sword's scratched pommel. Her colorless eyes watched the pair carefully. It was unnerving, though, not knowing what telltales to look for, not knowing what magic the two mages might furtively enact.

At the first sign of anything untoward, she would naturally lop off their heads.

"Tell me," Deo said gently, "what sort of magic is it that you work?"

He simply waited for their answers. And after a moment's reluctance they divulged. Deo nodded, listening. A polite, attentive audience.

"Now, what exactly is Far Speak and Far Movement magic?" the nephew of the premier of Petgrad asked.

RAVEN
(4)

LOYALTY, SHE HAD found, was a complicated thing.

She had sworn allegiance routinely to Matokin while at the Academy. It sometimes seemed like a daily exercise, like the spells she and her fellow students had practiced so repetitiously. But she had also privately dedicated herself to the Felk emperor, not least because he was, she continued to believe, her father.

Raven had also sworn to carry out her duties when she personally received this assignment from Lord Matokin himself. That meeting had been the single greatest thrill of her young life. She had been charged with, among other responsibilities, spying on the Felk war commander.

But, now that she was here at General Weisel's side, didn't she also owe *him* some measure of loyalty? He had, after all, taken her into his confidence and shown as much faith in her talents as Matokin had demonstrated. Maybe more.

But Weisel had talked treason, hadn't he? She had to report to Matokin. When she at last resolved to do so, she was ashamed that she had hesitated so long.

Weisel had given her new orders. She would carry those orders out. But first, she would find Berkant, the Far Speak mage.

She was getting used to traveling with the army, though the sight of so many troops and so much mobile equipment was still very impressive. She found her way through the camp to the mage's tent. Scuttlebutt had it that the army would mobilize tomorrow, once the portals had been arranged. The soldiers would be Far Moved the remaining distance to Trael, and they would invade and capture the city.

Raven knew the real plan, though. Weisel had entrusted her with the knowledge. He had even recruited her to play a key role in the incredible scheme. She couldn't help but glow a little from that.

Nevertheless, she *had* to speak to Lord Matokin.

"Mage Berkant," she said, presenting herself, "I am Raven, newly arrived from the Academy, and I—"

"I know who you are," the wizard said. "Come inside."

His tent was small but private.

"I must communicate with Lord Matokin." She had brought along the scroll that contained her orders, just for good measure.

"Very well. It will take a moment to arrange."

Berkant seated himself on a folding chair, taking up a piece of fabric and squeezing it tightly in his hand. Raven understood. Though she certainly couldn't perform anything as complex as a Far Speak spell, she at least grasped the principles. That cloth no doubt came from an item of clothing that belonged to the wizard who Berkant was communicating with.

Raven wondered when she would be able to resume her studies of magic. She had so much left to learn. But . . . wasn't *this* much more exciting than being at the Academy? Here she was participating actively, not just passively absorbing. She was caught up in a fascinating intrigue that involved the two most powerful men in the whole empire, Lord Matokin and General Weisel. Her life certainly wasn't boring these days.

Berkant's face gradually lost all expression. His eyes stared dully forward. When he spoke, it was as if with another voice.

"Raven, I have been expecting your report."

She felt a fierce stab of guilt. She should have done this days ago. "I-I am sorry, Lord. I—"

"What have you to tell us?" Matokin, speaking through Berkant, cut her off.

Raven scrambled to get her thoughts together, realizing she should have rehearsed this ahead of time. "General Weisel first questioned me about Far Movement magic. But he had already deduced that my knowledge of such powerful spells was very limited."

"Raven, Lord Abraxis is here with me. He wishes to know why the general was interested in Far Movement."

So, she was in the "presence" of both the emperor and the chief of imperial security once again.

"The general seemed to want some firsthand knowledge of that particular magic," she said carefully. "He seemed to think it would aid him in employing it in the field." Which, she silently added, still made sense to her.

"I see." It was as if someone else were moving Berkant's lips. The effect was eerie.

"Also, Lord," Raven said, her hands bunching into little fists, "General Weisel has made some unusual comments."

"Regarding what?"

"Regarding . . . you." Why did it feel like she was betraying the general? She was only doing her duty.

Unexpectedly, Berkant's face twisted with laughter. His chortles filled the tent. Raven stared, confused.

Finally he said, "I doubt very much, young Raven, that anything the good general might say about myself would surprise me. Let us just put it down to hasty words, shall we?"

"As you wish, sir," she said.

"Is there anything else?"

Raven caught herself just before she spoke. If her news wasn't important enough for Matokin to even listen to, she didn't see why she should say anything further.

"Nothing, Lord," she heard herself say.

"Carry on, then." Berkant's hand opened and the piece of cloth fell into his lap. He blinked, recovering himself.

"My thanks, Mage Berkant," Raven said.

"Only doing my job," he said, waving her off.

Yes, she thought, exiting the tent. So was she.

SHE HAD PLANNED to inform Matokin about Weisel's unorthodox scheme involving the Far Movement portals. She had even meant to tell the emperor about her part in the plan. But Lord Matokin seemed uninterested in what she had to say. She felt silly now for having fretted so much about making the report.

Why wasn't her father showing her more attention? She had certainly thought this assignment was an important one. Maybe Matokin had plans for her that she couldn't even guess at. Maybe. But why not tell her *now?*

Raven realized with a start that she was virtually pouting. That was an adolescent pursuit. It was beneath her. She was nearly two tenwinters old, an adult.

As an adult she had adult responsibilities. That meant serving Weisel as much as it meant serving Lord Matokin. It was time she got on with her duties to the general.

She sought out the unit of Far Movement mages. Weisel had written her an order that gave her the authority to use these powerful wizards' abilities. Moments later a portal was being opened for her.

Knowing what Weisel planned to use these portals for made stepping into this one a particularly unnerving experience. But she needed only to tap her strong sense of discipline to make herself put one foot in front of the other.

The air rippled before her. She walked directly into the distortion, finding herself suddenly swallowed by a new reality. This new world was a milky white, and her eye could not fix on any single feature. The landscape rolled and roiled, as if it were made of mist. She had no sense of the dimensions of the place, which was especially disturbing. Distances might be infinite or tiny. There was no horizon line, no sky, not even any evidence of ground, other than the fact that her feet didn't plunge into nothingness beneath her.

She had passed through a portal when Lord Matokin dispatched her from Felk. She had experienced this before. She followed the instructions she had been given, keeping her eyes ahead and carefully walking a perfectly straight line. Ahead, she could just make out the second portal, which appeared as another ripple.

Despite the cautions, she couldn't help but let her eyes stray a bit. At the Academy, she had never learned anything about the nature of portal magic. It simply wasn't part of the curriculum to explain the underlying principles of the arts. Instructors only showed the students how to perform feats. Knowing *how* something was done was different from being privy to the technique that allowed one to do something.

But the Academy, which Matokin had founded, was interested only in producing functional magicians. Nothing else mattered. Raven, as she neared the second portal, allowed herself to silently question the wisdom of that.

As disorienting as this place was, there was something that was even more disturbing about it. Raven's steps slowed involuntarily. She looked slowly around. Something, she was almost certain, was watching her!

Her heart was beating fast. She peered into the eerie, misty surroundings, expecting at any instant to see eyes staring back at her. She realized she had stopped walking. That was a mistake. She wasn't supposed to dally.

The sense of being observed only got stronger. Panic was trying to overtake her, but she wouldn't let it. Her ears suddenly pricked up. She thought she heard something, but it was as distorted as everything else here.

Her head whipped around, trying to pin the source. Every impulse told her to get moving, to make for the exit portal. This was dangerous. Back at the Academy, the students told stories to each other about how some people disappeared when they stepped into a portal, never coming out the far side.

The sounds were growing closer, it seemed. It sounded like . . . like . . . *voices*. A whole horde of voices. Closing in around her.

She turned suddenly and hurled herself toward the second portal, hands outstretched, a cry of fear just behind her lips. She expected a thousand hands to seize her before she reached it.

Instead, she broke through into a clearing in the woods. There were trees, sunlight, solid ground, all the comforts of reality that she had always taken for granted. Panting, she staggered, nearly collapsing to the ground.

Hands did catch her now, and for a moment she felt true terror, but she shook it off. She straightened both herself and her new clothes. A wizard in a robe was peering at her.

"Had a bad journey?" he asked.

She blinked back at him.

"It happens sometimes," he said philosophically, shrugging. "What was it—voices, or did you actually see something?"

Another mage stood with him, no doubt the Far Speak wizard who helped coordinate the portal opening. A small party of soldiers sat around a cooking fire, one or two of them eyeing Raven curiously, but none coming forward.

"*See* something?" Raven asked.

The Far Movement mage shrugged. "It happens. Strange shapes, sounds."

"I . . . thought I heard voices," she admitted.

"Maybe you did," the Far Speak mage said, sounding just as casual about it.

"Who knows what goes on in that other place?" the first mage continued. "Most of the time, you walk through a portal, ten steps, and you've crossed a huge distance. No problems. Sometimes, though, you'll hear or see something. We're not supposed to talk about it, of course. Don't want to scare the troops." He glanced sourly at the soldiers by the fire. "Scary, wasn't it?"

"I'm perfectly all right," Raven said, a bit icily.

The Far Speak wizard was now ogling her. "I don't suppose you're here to *entertain* us, are you? It's lonely being a scout."

Raven sighed, disgustedly. If this was what being attractive did for a woman, maybe Weisel hadn't done her a favor by having her made over.

"I am General Weisel's personal liaison to the magic-using units of this army," she said, proudly announcing her new title for the first time. Weisel had appointed her to the post last night. The soldiers all looked her way now.

The Far Movement mage shrugged again. It seemed to be a habitual gesture. "What does that mean exactly?" he asked.

"It means this army is dangerously divided. Magic-users and non-magic-using troops are indulging in a useless bigotry that will only undermine our glorious cause. I have been appointed by the general himself to act as an intermediary, a first step toward repairing an ancient, stupid prejudice. I expect the full cooperation of every person in this army."

She spoke with impressive authority. She felt, at that moment, that she radiated the air of the officer she now was.

The ranking soldier stood and approached. "Do you

have orders to back that up?" She asked it neutrally, careful not to make it a challenge.

Raven produced the document Weisel had drawn up. The mages and the soldier all studied it.

The soldier saluted. "How can we serve you?"

Raven liked the reaction. "I have orders for this squad. And for the other scouting parties that have been sent ahead to observe Trael's defenses."

The soldier snorted. "Defenses? They've got maybe a few dozen troops. This place'll tumble easier than U'delph did."

"The general has heard your reports," Raven said. She turned her eyes on the mages. "He has decided to use the portals."

The Far Movement mage nodded this time, instead of shrugging. "We've been waiting for that order," he said.

"But why didn't the general just relay it?" asked the Far Speak wizard. "Why send you?"

"Because General Weisel isn't planning to Far Move the army," Raven said.

"Then . . . what does he want to use the portals for?" The Far Movement mage suddenly looked uneasy.

Raven explained the plan in the simple terms that Weisel had spelled out. By now the rest of the soldiers had gathered around, listening intently. One or two gasped as she spoke.

"That's . . . *risky,*" said one mage.

"That's not how the magic is meant to be used," said the other.

Raven alone kept her composure. "Those are the general's orders. He guessed there might be some reluctance, which is why he sent me. I will be visiting the three other scouting parties. You will all take up new positions just on the outskirts of Trael. When you've received the signal through your Far Speak mage, you will obey those orders. Any questions?"

They had none.

Raven ordered the mages to arrange her transport to the next scout camp. She hid her uneasiness about passing through the portals again so soon after that last disquieting episode. She could still hear those voices, in her head.

But she squashed her fear, and stepped through when the portal opened. Loyalty could serve as well as bravery.

BRYCK
(5)

HE LOOKED AWAY from the naked backs that the soldiers were methodically flogging. The sounds of hide whips impacting flesh and bone, and the attending cries for mercy and shrieks of agony, echoed across the plaza even as his eyes furtively roved the crowd. Bryck was vaguely repelled by the violence of the punishments being meted out; but these were, after all, only *whippings*. No one was being butchered. Acts of inhumanity were inevitably measured against the annihilation of U'delph. That was his standard.

Nonetheless, it was difficult not to feel a little pity.

The turnout was sizable, though attendance wasn't mandatory. Everybody liked a show though, Bryck thought with a callous cynicism that would have once shocked him. In bygone days when he was a husband, father, noble, playwright, he had somehow always managed to see the better side of people.

No. No point in taking a revisionist view of his past. He had almost always been able to find the *comical* side—of people, of events. But humor had such amazing scope. Humor had the capacity to contain horror, sadness, murder, epic tragedy. Some of his most beloved theatricals embraced such subjects but did so in that special way that permitted laughter. That had been his gift.

Still, he was hard-pressed to imagine what sort of slant would make humorous this row of ten stripped bodies being beaten bloody by whips. The Felk soldiers had erected a long horizontal crosspiece and shackled each of the criminals with his or her hands well above the head, backs exposed to the two floggers that were working their way inward from either end. They were professionals, not sadists. Bryck had counted them delivering equal numbers of blows to each offender. It was a high count, but it was equal.

He blended easily enough in the crowd. He no longer radiated a forceful presence, no longer drew attention automatically. The extrovert in him had gone grey and numb.

So, almost invisibly, he slipped away through the grimly watching faces. He could still hear the blows as he left the plaza behind. The Callahans under those whips had all committed various offensives against the Felk laws of occupation. The charges had been read by an officer of the garrison at the start of the proceedings. Most of the people had been caught transacting illegally in coin. No doubt displays like this would deter other potential offenders.

Lately the Felk had stepped up their enforcement efforts. The patrols through the city weren't strictly for show anymore. Bryck wondered if these Callahans were stirring up trouble, causing the Felk to clamp down. But, as it had been from the start, he had no way to accurately gauge what effect his efforts to sabotage the Felk occupation were having.

He passed the door of a shop where, during that Lacfoddalmendowl festival, he had branded a sigil onto the wood. The door was gone now, replaced with boards. He had discovered that at virtually every site where he had left it, the brand had been defaced or removed completely. Apparently the Felk had taken note.

He had pushed himself too far that day, and he had paid. He was no wizard. The magic had drained him, and he had lain in bed, burning with fever and unable to eat, for two days. Once he had recuperated, however, he had set about spreading word of the Broken Circle, the name of the cell of rebels here in Callah who were planning to overthrow the Felk occupiers. As before, he used his capacity as a stringbox-playing minstrel to deliver the news.

The market nearby the Registry was doing its normal business. He entered it.

Moments later Bryck was handing over two blue-colored goldie notes and carrying away an ornate candlestick from a stall. It was heavy and, looking at it closely for the first time, also quite handsome. He had of course purchased it merely to put yet more of Slydis's ingeniously false currency into circulation. The stall's keeper was certainly pleased Bryck had agreed without undue dickering to pay nearly the full asking price. Nothing was said about coin fetching a better price. Perhaps those public floggings were already having effect.

The candlestick was finely molded to resemble the stalk of a plant; around the empty socket the metal flared out like petals.

Normally he would dispose of something like this. He regularly bought expensive items only to discard them in waste barrels. Once, he had collected and taken pleasure in objects—pieces of art, items of decor. Pointless, frivolous things. But that was a different life.

Still, he might keep this candlestick, take it back to his room. It might brighten up his modest lodgings . . . not that he cared anything about his own comfort any longer.

He moved through the streets. Rain had fallen earlier, enough to make a thick paste of mud for everyone to trudge through. Those rains were coming more frequently and turning colder. Autumn came sooner in this northern city than in U'delph.

He wondered about the mild pity he'd felt for those Callahans who were being lashed. It was odd he should feel *anything*. Since his initial shock-horror at U'delph's destruction had worn off, since he had turned grief and hate into grim, focused vengeance, he hadn't felt much in the way of real emotion. Even deliberate thoughts of Aaysue and his children didn't provoke fits of sorrow anymore.

So why should these Callahans matter to him? They were foreigners, a conquered people. They were merely players in the revenge that he was orchestrating.

They were giving substance to his fiction of the Broken Circle by believing in it. They were, in a way, his audience. After all it had been his audiences flocking to see the likes of *Glad of Nothing* and *Possibly I Misheard* who made those farces almost real. Without performers to play the roles and without viewers to accept those characters as true, Bryck's works would have been only absurd fantasies scribbled on paper.

This new "theatrical," however, was definitely a departure from his past works. The fabrication of the Broken Circle was so obvious a wish-fulfillment for these people of Callah. At the taverns where he quietly introduced the story, people were wildly excited. He'd claimed it was merely a rumor, but his talent for storytelling served well. With a few earnest whispers, reenforced by the curious sigils that had sprung up around the city recently, he created the Broken Circle from the air.

Hopefully they were spreading the word themselves now, probably inventing "news" of the local uprising, the plans being made, the arms being gathered, the men and women preparing to usurp the Felk rule.

It was a fine fantasy. A pity for these Callahans that it had no reality but what they gave it. Yet if it provoked *one* of these people to raise a hand against the Felk, it was an accomplishment.

Bryck of course wanted more. He wanted these people to truly rise up. To annihilate the Felk. To slaughter them in the streets like diseased dogs. But until he actually saw that, he wouldn't know if his fabricated Broken Circle had inspired anyone.

He was taking a roundabout route back to the building where he had his room. He consciously avoided falling into patterns. He didn't walk the same streets every day or eat at the same places. He was doing his best to stay anonymous.

Nevertheless, as he rounded a corner, squelching through mud, an elderly but still burly blacksmith at the entrance to his shop lifted a hand and called a greeting. Bryck returned it and strode quickly onward. The man hadn't called him by name; that was good. He must have seen Bryck often enough in the neighborhood to recognize him, or perhaps he'd been at one of the taverns where Bryck played. He was careful never to perform at the same place twice.

Maybe it was time to relocate, he thought. With the ridiculous amount of counterfeit money he still had, he could secure lodgings just about anywhere. Callah was a large city. Lots of places to hide.

The candlestick swung at his side. Above, the overcast sky was darkening again. More rain, likely. Bryck pulled his coat tighter about himself as he turned another corner. There he hitched to a sharp halt. His heart suddenly thumped hard in his chest.

Soldiers.

It wasn't a patrol. That was evident at a glance. Four armed and armored soldiers were standing outside the entry into the ramshackle building that housed his room on its third floor. They were scrutinizing passersby. People were seized, their faces examined, then shoved away. The soldiers were only inspecting males.

Bryck felt eyes looking his way. Even at a distance of half the street's length his abrupt halt may have drawn notice. Another helmeted head turned. Now wasn't the time to try to deduce how this might have come about, who might have given his description and whereabouts to the Felk authorities. All that could most certainly wait. He moved, turning, striding back the way he had come, doing what he could to make the move appear natural, casual. His boot heels slid over the mud.

From the corner of his eye he saw two of the soldiers start in his direction. A voice rose. A command was snapped. The sound of armor rattling as they fell into a jog.

Bryck let go the pretense and bolted. Fear was boiling through his veins, lending him speed. He pounded along the street, while behind the commanding voice barked once more—ordering him to halt, raising the alarm. No doubt now; they were after *him* . . . or his fleeing had just singled him out. Maybe they were making some kind of random search. Maybe they were after some petty criminal that looked something like him. Maybe any number of things, and it could wait, he reminded himself fiercely.

He had covered a full street by now, limbs pumping. Ahead, people, hearing the commotion, were shying back against the buildings.

Risking a fast peek behind, he saw that three of the four were pursuing him. Their drawn short swords swung rhythmically at their sides, honed edges gleaming even in the dull daylight. One of the soldiers appeared older and somewhat hefty. He was at the rear and already lagging. The other two were youths, in their primes, legs flashing. The nearer was only half a street behind Bryck.

He knew this quarter of Callah well. Being a poorer district, it had been built in rather slapdash manner, without the pleasing symmetry of more affluent quarters. This made for numerous alleyways, cul-de-sacs and some narrow, crooked streets that went nowhere.

The burly old blacksmith was still in his doorway.

Where sweat didn't run freely, his flesh was thick with soot. He lifted his hand again, seeing Bryck, then frowning, seeing his pursuers.

Bryck thought frantically of dashing into the smithy, then discarded the impulse. He had a better plan—a grim and dangerous one.

The hefty soldier was no longer in view as Bryck peeled off the main thoroughfare, dashing narrowly between a cart and a heavily loaded beast of burden. The two younger soldiers remained on him, gaining. Bryck was leaner and tougher than he had been in many a winter, but that couldn't erase the years he'd lived.

Even so, he didn't flag, didn't break stride. His lungs burned, and the hand grasping the candlestick was starting to ache, but all physical discomforts had to be ignored for the time being. Whatever happened, he must not be captured.

Cries of surprise and fear rose as people saw the rushing soldiers and drawn swords. The mud here wasn't so churned up, but was no easier to navigate. Bryck had already nearly spilled twice.

Bryck changed direction yet again, ducking this time into a stinking alley. He chanced another glance behind, just in time to see one of the soldiers lose her footing completely in the mud, short sword flinging from her grip, face plowing into the muck. The other soldier didn't glance back at his tumbled comrade.

The alley had many sharp twists and jogs. There were moldering crates and debris scattered throughout it, also a few side entrances into dark little shops. Places to hide and places to burrow into.

Bryck pulled up sharply just beyond the first corner. He braced his stance, listened intently, heart hammering. Coming . . . coming . . .

When the soldier, still with all the momentum of the chase behind him, crashed around the corner, Bryck used the candlestick to club him across the face with every iota of muscle he could muster. The soldier quite simply never saw it coming. If a fleeing man ducked into an alleyway, he must mean to hide or must know some special escape from it or, even if he meant to waylay his pursuer, he would surely go *deeper* into the alley to do so, into thicker shadows and better cover, not make an ambush around the very first bend.

The molded metal petals around the candlestick's socket dug into the soldier's cheek and jaw, tearing, spraying blood and teeth, snapping bone. The head whipped wildly about. The chin strap of his helmet wasn't secured, and that helmet flew off his head, clanging against a crumbling wall. His skull hit that same wall as his feet tangled.

His sword dropped, as his body, following his head, smashed the wall. Then he crumpled to the ground. The head was now turned at a very peculiar angle.

Bryck was ready—mentally and physically—to swing the candlestick again. It was not necessary. Instead, he tossed it down beside the soldier where he lay, ruined face turned upward.

Then Bryck scrambled away.

HE STILL HAD his cache of coins in the lining of his coat, as well as a small sheaf of counterfeit money, minus the two gold notes he'd spent on the candlestick. His vox-mellifluous, however, was back in his room, gone. That caused an unexpected pang. His pretense of being a troubadour had carried him far. He had grown comfortable playing his music . . . as if he really were a minstrel.

Dangerous to start believing one's own fictions, he thought, chopping and scraping at his bristly grey beard as fast as he dared with the razor. Beneath, he was finding a gaunt face, bones prominent—the reason he'd let the beard grow in the first place. There was no looking glass in the room. He waited for the water in the basin to settle and took another look at his reflection on the surface. It was a startling change. He looked a tenwinter younger. Or at least it took away a few years.

. He shook his head and attacked the last of the whiskers. It mattered only that he appear *different*. This shave was a start, but he would have to do more.

A board gave a creak just beyond the door. Bryck turned sharply, then heard the two sharp knocks, a pause, repeated.

"These," Quentis said, entering. "My father's."

She laid out the clothes. The room was small and used for storage. Quentis shared these lodgings with her older cousin, Ondak. He was currently posted out in front of the house, watching, ready to raise the alert if soldiers came.

Unlikely, thought Bryck, despite his own anxiety. If he had been followed here, the Felk wouldn't be delaying. They would storm the place for him, maybe kill him on the spot.

"My thanks," he said to Quentis, eyeing the clothes. Typically Callahan in style. That was good.

He realized he had been thanking this woman almost constantly since arriving at this house with her. He could not, of course, express the fullness of his gratitude. Not for lack of trying, but because it simply wasn't possible. He had fled the district where he'd killed the soldier and made his way as swiftly and invisibly as he could, expecting capture at every step, until he found the street where he had first met Quentis during that Lacfoddalmendowl holiday.

Hers was a mobile vendor cart, not a stationary shop, but he had searched the area until he saw her. He approached, she recognized him, and he asked for refuge.

It had seemed so suddenly and impossibly absurd at that moment. He had no right at all to ask such a thing; she had no reason to aid him. Yet, here he was. She had saved him.

She was looking at him now, studying his face. At last she nodded. "It looks good." Her tone was businesslike. He knew virtually nothing about this woman, but he was certain she didn't easily panic.

He patted a damp cloth over his face.

He hadn't had time to examine the impulse—the sure instinct—that had caused him to seek her out. Surely he could have hidden somewhere else. Callah was indeed a large city. He couldn't go to an inn, however. Callah received no travelers these days, and such places were virtually deserted or shut up. Besides, surely the Felk would look for him there.

Quentis's presence with him in this small room was pleasing.

"My thanks."

"So you've said." Her voice was gentle now, for the first time. It had all happened so swiftly. His accosting her on the street, his urgently whispered entreaty, her curt instructions that he follow as she secured her cart and led him here.

"Sorry to repeat myself," he said. "I can't seem to properly express my appreciation."

"We'll take your gratitude for granted."

He gazed back at her amber-colored eyes, lingering there a moment. He laid a hand on the clothes she'd brought in.

"Yes. Change into those. I'll get rid of what you're wearing now."

His hand went to his pocket. He pulled out the money, all the notes in a wad. He hoped to keep some of this, needing money to survive; but he had to give this woman something, to balance at least a little of the enormous debt he owed her for her kindness.

"Once you've changed," she went on, even as she glanced down at the money in his hand, "we'll get you safely out of here."

"Before I go, though . . ." Did she want it all? He would give it, if she said.

She looked up. "That'll help when we get you settled."

It wasn't making sense. "We?" He gestured vaguely toward the front of the small house. "Ondak, you mean?"

"Ondak. Others. Change now." She exited, pulling shut the door.

From his coat he took his coins and the falsified travel pass that might still allow him to leave the city. How much did the Felk know about him? Would the soldiers be waiting for a minstrel trying to pass the city limits? And *who* had betrayed him, and *how?*

It was maddening to think about. He had been so very cautious, had moved so secretively. And yet soldiers had come for him, and he had been forced to kill one of their number.

There was no time to regret the act, no time to feel the dismay he imagined anyone must feel upon taking a human life for the first time. He could see the soldier's lifeless face. Could even smell his blood, there in that foul alley.

Yet . . . how many dead had been left at U'delph? Did the Felk soldiers who'd butchered his wife and children feel regrets for their deeds? Did it matter if they did?

When Quentis returned, Bryck had changed into the clothes. Again she nodded approval. Outside, he heard the rain returning, pattering the roof. Quentis was wearing a cloak.

"Come along," she said. "It's time to go."

Since he had placed himself in her hands, he went.

THE WAREHOUSE HAD fallen into recent disuse, as had happened to those facilities in Callah from which the Felk had thoroughly conscripted goods and horses. This one had been a freight service, Quentis told him as they stood in shadows. Her voice was soft, low, calm. Animal scents on the air, but no beasts in the stalls. One shattered wheel leaned on a wall, but there were no wagons.

Bryck's new clothing included a thigh-length coat and a brimmed cap that hid his greying hair and made his newly shaven face appear even younger. It was a worthy effort at disguise, but he hoped not to have to test it against the eye-sight of soldiers armed with a good description of him.

The Felk patrols were in the streets, not on established routes and not at normal times. Armor rattled, voices barked. It looked like the full strength of the garrison that had turned out. Presumably the murder Bryck had committed had touched off this activity.

With Quentis and Ondak he had traveled here street by street, stealing along, taking cover when necessary. They had entered this building by the cargo dock, where there were loose boards. Quentis had lit the stub of a candle that guttered atop an empty cask.

A figure now emerged into the circle of pale light. He wasn't alone, but his companions stayed in the shadows.

"Tyber!" Ondak said with some relish.

A mask of freakishly unhealthy skin floated into the candlelight, a face immediately cut by a strangely winning smile, despite the man's horrid teeth. The creature named Tyber opened his arms away from a plump body, and Ondak—rather rounded himself—moved into the embrace. The two aging men slapped palms against backs, cackling with satisfaction.

Ondak turned with an arm still around Tyber's broad shoulders. "That one's Quentis, my younger cousin. The other . . . a minstrel."

Eyes widened in Tyber's blemished face. "The minstrel with the news from Windal?"

Murmuring voices rose in the shadows. It sounded to Bryck like a dozen or more. Why, exactly, had Quentis brought him here? There had been no time to ask.

"The same," said Ondak.

"The uprising," Tyber said solemnly.

"The uprising."

And behind, in the shadows, the voices took up the words.

Tyber nodded at Bryck, turned and waved those shadows forward into the candlelight.

They looked to be typical Callahans—most past the age of conscription, a few younger. They carried weapons, of an improvised sort. Kitchen cleavers, an axe, a mallet. Tyber tossed open a flap of his coat, revealing the jeweled pommel of a short sword that looked both ostentatious enough for a royal honor guard and durable enough to serve in battle.

An adolescent, scratching at filthy hair with scabby fingers, studied Bryck somberly. In fact, they were all staring at him, seeming to want something from him.

"The minstrel," Ondak announced, "killed a Felk soldier today."

Gasps met this news. Ondak had said it with grave pride.

"That's why the whippers have stepped up their patrols," Tyber said, nodding. "Well . . . that's the first godsdamned Felk to die here since the buggers invaded us. Well done!"

Bryck didn't like this attention, didn't like so many eyes on him. He had presumed Quentis was taking him someplace to hide, at least temporarily, until he could arrange to escape the city. Did she mean to put him up here, in this abandoned warehouse?

More importantly, who *were* these people that knew he was a murderer?

Bryck's deed had obviously impressed them; he decided to play on that. "I have indeed killed a soldier," he declared. His audience hushed immediately. "I require sanctuary. Will you provide it?"

They stared mutely a moment. Then Tyber rumbled a chuckle deep in his chest. "The honor is ours, naturally," he said. "Most of us here have heard you before. Your songs, your news of Windal."

"The rest have heard the word passed from others," said Quentis.

"Your news gives us the only hope we've had since . . ."

"The only hope—"

"—hope . . ."

They were all speaking up now. Bryck retreated a step. When he lifted a hand, they quieted. They were being deferential to him, he realized. He was important here. A celebrity, almost. As things had been in his playwright days. So long ago.

Well, he could certainly use this strange situation to his advantage.

"Very well," he said. "I should like to know whose hospitality I am enjoying."

It was Quentis who turned, a frown creasing between her amber eyes.

"Why," she said, sweeping a hand over the small band with their makeshift armaments, "this is the Broken Circle. We mean to rise up against the Felk."

Bryck slowly blinked. But they remained there. Not a dream, not the insubstantial creations that were the characters in his plays. Not even the fictional players who, in the new stories he'd been weaving, had risen up against the Felk in the city-state of Windal. These were the Broken Circle, the rebels of Callah. He had only written the roles. They were to make the parts real.

Finally Bryck pulled consciously at those unused facial muscles that allowed something like a smile to surface on his freshly shaven face. "It's a pleasure to meet you all," he said.

DARDAS
(5)

IT WAS ALL falling into place, like any good battle plan.

Dardas finally ordered a plate of the special rations he'd had sent in from Windal, by portal. The meat was the best he had eaten since Felk, where he had dined with Lord Matokin, and Abraxis, and some of those other chief magicians, on the eve of leading the army southward against Callah.

Matokin had been very expansive that evening. Glasses were lifted in toast after toast. There was excitement in the air, but also unease. Of all those wizard/politicians at that table, only Matokin had seemed truly confident that the Felk military, led by a resurrected Northland war commander inhabiting a nobleman's body, would succeed.

But Dardas had indeed succeeded in the feeble challenges he had so far faced. Callah, Windal, U'delph, Sook. Sook had surrendered, for gods' sakes, without an arrow being shot, or a blade raised. What soft stuff these Isthmusers were made of! In Dardas's heyday, he had faced real opponents, people who had at least put up a decent struggle before he trampled over them.

He let out a small sigh.

"Is the meal unsatisfactory, General?"

Dardas looked up. He was at his table. His aide, who had been rotated into the post just a watch earlier, was packing Dardas's gear. The camp was on alert, ready to be struck at any moment.

"The food is fine . . . Fergon, isn't it?"

"Yes, sir," said the aide. His face was splashed with freckles.

"I'd say it was the tastiest supper I've had in some while," Dardas went on. "Did you get a plate for yourself?"

"Yes, General. Thank you. And I agree. It was a welcome treat."

Dardas wiped his mouth with a cloth napkin, the sort of amenity he'd never known in his previous life. But one had to keep up appearances when one was wearing a noble's body.

"Tell me," Dardas said, "did the troops appreciate it as well, do you think?"

"Most certainly, General," Fergon said. "I think you'll find your praises being sung all over camp at the moment."

"Even among the wizards?"

Fergon paused as he was loading up a trunk. "It's . . . difficult to tell sometimes what those people think. But they have stomachs, too, and they've been eating the same standard rations as everybody else. Yourself included, General."

Dardas waved that magnanimously away. He was pleased his little campaign of eating regular rations had paid off so well. He was pleased also about this latest ploy, the special meats from Windal. Binding his troops to himself was crucial. As Dardas the Conqueror, he had known fierce loyalty from his warriors. As the Felk General Weisel, he wanted the same.

He wanted these men and women to believe they were following *him*, not Matokin.

The real trick, of course, would be convincing the mages.

"Sir?"

Dardas thought for a moment that he had let out another sigh. But, no. Fergon, having finished the packing, was timidly trying to get his attention.

"What is it?"

"I hope this isn't inappropriate, General," Fergon said, "but I wanted to express my personal appreciation."

"For what?" asked Dardas.

Fergon looked genuinely surprised. "Why, for the successes we, as an army, have enjoyed under your command. Your genius for military tactics has become apparent to everyone."

Dardas favored his aide with a droll smile. "Or is it that everyone had low expectations? It's all right, Fergon. Speak freely. You broached the subject. Tell me."

The freckled officer looked at the ground.

"Well, sir . . . I think there might have been *some* reservations, at the start."

Dardas allowed himself a chuckle. "I think I understand, Fergon. That will be all."

"Um, sir?"

Dardas checked the flash of annoyance he felt. Most of his aides knew enough not to infringe on too much of his time. "What now?"

"My father sends his greetings."

"Your father?" Dardas blinked.

"Yes. The Far Speak mages have relayed a few personal messages for the officers. You authorized it a quarter-lune ago. Very accommodating of you, sir."

Dardas nodded. He recalled now permitting the indulgence. It was another ploy, of course. Give his troops and his officers a favor now and then, and they would grow devoted to him. Using those communication mages to pass private messages all the way from Felk was quite a luxury.

"And how is your father, Fergon?" Best to go along with this for the moment, though naturally he had no idea who the man's father might be. Weisel would know, of course. But the Felk noble's personality had evidently been squeezed into nothingness by Dardas's dominant character.

"He says the red grass is knee-high," Fergon said, as if conveying something profound, "and the dogs are running free." The officer couldn't completely suppress the expectant smile that pulled at the corners of his mouth.

Obviously, this was supposed to mean something, Dardas thought a little desperately. Some familiar code between Weisel and this man's father, maybe referring to a joke they had once shared. Whatever it was, a response to it was expected. Godsdamnit, why had he let this fawning, freckle-faced twerp say anything more?   .

"Well . . ." Dardas said, careful to appear unruffled. "That's as it should be, then."

Fergon's budding smile turned to a puzzled frown. "Uh . . . of course, General Weisel."

It was the wrong answer, Dardas thought darkly.

"Enough, Fergon. Leave me."

The aide scuttled out of the tent.

He would have to be replaced, Dardas thought. Maybe *more* than replaced. He'd had no trouble killing that Far Movement mage with his poisoned knife. He was more than willing to commit such a deed again. To be honest, he had enjoyed it.

What he had learned from that mage was certainly valuable. He was basing this upcoming campaign against the city-state of Trael on the knowledge he had gathered about the true nature of Far Movement magic.

One of his great talents in battle, one that had served him so well in his last lifetime, was an ability to adapt whatever resources were at hand to further his position in the field. This was something ingrained in his nature. Once, as a child, when a much larger boy had assaulted him, young Dardas had snatched up a tiny twig from the ground and jammed it brutally into the bigger boy's eye. The twig was just a twig, not obviously useful as a weapon. But wielded correctly and without any mercy or hesitation, it had won him the fight.

Far Movement was powerful magic. The portals, so the mage had said before dying, opened into another reality, the reality *beyond* life.

Dardas had been dead once. He had no clear memories of what that had been like, but obviously his being had survived in some form, or Matokin wouldn't have been able to retrieve him.

His plan was to open several portals around the city of Trael. But . . . no exit portals would be opened. Those holes into the next reality would simply stand wide.

Whatever dwelt in that other world would be free to come into *this* one. And those inhabitants, freed from that milky limbo, would find Trael in their path.

Dardas wanted war. Perpetual war. He felt excitement tingle through him. Who knew what would come out of those portals. Monsters? The walking dead? Whatever, it could only complicate this war, thus extending it until he could consolidate his own position of power.

Someday maybe he would even be in the position to turn the army back northward, to conquer the city of Felk itself and unseat Emperor Matokin.

He laughed aloud, savoring the thoughts, as he had savored every sensation since returning to life.

At the moment he was waiting on Raven's return. How thrilled the girl had been when he named her his liaison officer to the army's magic-using forces. At first, he had thought to use the granting of the title as just another means of tying her tighter to him. But he had quickly realized the immense value of having such an officer at his side.

The rift between his regular troops and his army's magical units had been obvious from the start. That rupture had to be mended. Matokin had given him wizards, the best he had to offer, and told him to make use of them. So be it. Weapons had been turned on their masters before.

In the meantime though, it was crucial that those scouting parties he'd sent ahead to Trael obeyed their new, unorthodox orders. Dardas had figured there would be resistance, especially from the Far Movement mages. Whatever else, this was no doubt a dangerous gambit.

So he had sent Raven, who had a foot in both societies, so to speak. Magical and nonmagical. She wasn't an official wizard, but she didn't fear magic, and her loyalty to the empire was impressive. Dardas had worked to turn that loyalty more directly upon himself, by taking her into his confidence, showering her with attention. He felt his scheme had succeeded.

However, Raven was overdue from her mission. Dardas frowned and stepped out of his tent. He surveyed the camp, seeing that the troops were indeed prepared to move out whenever the word came. Dardas didn't know what exactly would happen when those portals were locked open, but he wanted his army ready to move, in any direction.

He drew in the air. Even this was still exciting, the simple act of breathing. He *had* to stay alive. He needed someone like that wizard Kumbat on hand, at his personal beck and call, for whenever death tried to reclaim him. Matokin's greatest hold over him was the unspoken threat of withholding those rejuvenation spells that prolonged the resurrection magic that had brought him back to life.

It was a complex game, but his plans were falling into place, neatly.

They had bivouacked in a shallow valley. Spotters and pickets guarded the ridges. Nothing was going to sneak up on his army.

Finally, he saw Raven striding across the grounds toward his pavilion. She moved with a greater confidence these days, he noted. It was appealing. Perhaps he would find the time to bed her one of these days.

She saluted when she reached him. "General Weisel."

"Raven," he nodded. They should probably go inside for her report, but he was enjoying the feel of the waning day's breeze on his face too much. "What is the word?"

The girl looked somewhat troubled, he saw. "I contacted three of the four scouting parties, sir," she said. "The Far Movement mages will all comply with your orders when they receive the signal."

"And the fourth party?" he asked.

Raven shook her head. "None of the Far Speak mages was able to make contact. The Far Speak wizard assigned to the fourth squad simply did not respond. Without him to correlate the location, there was simply no way to transport there." She looked rather pale.

Dardas considered. "Well, scouting parties get lost. It is all a part of warfare." Any number of mishaps might have befallen the squad.

"Yes, General."

He peered closely at her. "But there's something further disturbing you, Raven. Am I right?"

"It's . . . nothing, sir."

"I think not. By now, girl, you surely realize that I value you. I've made you an officer. I've entrusted you with important secrets." He moved a step nearer to her. "You must be able to confide in me." He spoke this last in a tone that was like a purr. It was better to charm her than to order her to divulge.

Raven bit her lip, then said, "I encountered some difficulty while I was being Far Moved."

"Difficulty?"

"Yes, General." She explained. It was a strange little tale about hearing voices, a whole host of them, closing in around her while she was in transit through the milky, limbo world of the portals.

"Interesting," he said, genuinely intrigued.

Voices. No doubt the voices of that reality's inhabitants—presuming that Raven hadn't imagined the whole thing. He doubted that, though. She was made of cooler stuff.

"Fergon!" Dardas called.

The aide appeared at once, waiting attentively for Dardas's orders. But there was a lingering uneasiness on the young officer's face. Yes, thought Dardas. Something would definitely have to be done about this one. It could wait though.

"Assemble the senior staff. And get me a Far Speak mage who can communicate with our scouts."

"Yes, General Weisel." Fergon was gone.

"In a few moments, I'll give the signal." Dardas turned once more to Raven. "Exciting, isn't it?"

"Yes, General, it is." Color was returning to her full cheeks. Her breasts were rising and falling as her breath quickened.

This one understood how arousing a good war could be, Dardas thought with a silent cackle. On impulse, he reached out a hand and brushed his fingertips across her cheek. Her flesh was smooth, young.

Raven froze, then flushed heavily.

The senior staff was gathering around the front of Dardas's tent. He dropped his hand. A mage in dark robes came forward.

Now it was time to bring forth onto this Isthmus a whole new breed of warfare, thought Dardas.

I don't think I want to be remembered as the madman who allowed the dead to roam free into this world.

A huge shock went through him. This was Weisel's voice in his head. Impossible!

More impossibly, Dardas suddenly felt resistance when he tried to move his limbs. It was like someone was pulling them in another direction.

I think you have abused my hospitality long enough.

With that, Dardas felt an overwhelming mental force

closing in around his consciousness, strangling him, suffo-
cating him.

It's time you gave me back what you've borrowed.

With a last surge of .effort, Dardas forced open his
mouth to give the order to the mage. Whatever else happened, his plan would go ahead.

AQUINT

(5)

THE GARRISON WANTED blood.

Aquint knew that Colonel Jesile was basically a reasonable man, a fair governor of Callah. But one of his own men had been murdered, clubbed brutally to death, apparently by one of the very people that Aquint had been sent here to investigate.

There *was* unrest in Callah, and that murder indicated that there were rebels.

Like it or not, Aquint had to act like an Internal Security Corps agent. But since that job wasn't too well defined he'd been relying on his instincts, his baser ones. In Sook, he had solved the mystery of the disappearing goods from the quartermaster warehouse simply by seeing the operation from the eyes of the pilferers.

It was something else to try to think like a rebel. But again he'd had some success.

Colonel Jesile had put him on to finding whoever was responsible for the counterfeiting scheme that had been uncovered. Aquint had personally made a few inquiries among old acquaintances and vendors in the marketplaces, people who would never have talked to anybody but a fellow Callahan, though it took some persuading to convince a few that he *was* still a Callahan, despite his front of being a wounded soldier on leave. Just about everyone who had a reason to know considered Slydis the best copyist in the city.

Aquint paid the dwarf scribe a visit, finding on the premises of his workshop the ingenious stamps he'd made for duplicating the Felk scrip. Simple, right?

Not quite. Slydis, under questioning, confessed readily to an accomplice. Aquint had his doubts. One way to take heat off yourself was to direct it toward somebody else, even if that somebody didn't actually exist. Slydis, however, provided a good physical description of the man, and even the location of his lodgings. It seemed the dwarf copyist had had the man followed home after one of his visits to the workshop. Probably he'd done so to ensure that if he was ever caught, he would not be solely blamed for the counterfeiting operation.

Slydis had confessed to printing unbelievable amounts of fake money. Gods knew how much he and the other man he'd implicated had put into circulation. That money made all the scrip in Callah essentially worthless. Issuing it in the first place had been a dubious experiment, Aquint thought. Then again, it wasn't his problem, it was Jesile's.

Slydis had admitted to no other criminal activities, with one exception. He had also manufactured a civilian travel pass for his partner.

The Felk governor was understandably furious. He sent soldiers to arrest this other man, but he had fled the scene, eluding capture and murdering a soldier in the process. Now he was at large somewhere in Callah. They had no name for this man, only Slydis's description. In his room they had found only one unusual possession, a musical instrument, a vox-mellifluous.

Another matter had arisen during all this turmoil.

Somebody in the Governor's Office had finally noticed the pattern of vandalism in the reports that Aquint had first requested upon arrival in the city.

They were the brands on the walls and doors that Cat had seen. A circle with a slash through it. Jesile called Aquint in to ask him if it meant anything to Internal Security.

Aquint had wanted to save this ploy until later, when he might find a way to profit from it. But this, at least, would firm up his authority here. Jesile was deferring to him by calling him in on this matter. It was time to capitalize.

"Governor," Aquint had said, solemnly, "that is the mark of the rebel underground that I am investigating."

The Felk governor's hard face was etched with lines of anger. "And why did you keep this fact to yourself?" he spat.

Aquint met the man head-on, not flinching. "Because I do not answer to this office, Governor. Your domain is Callah. My jurisdiction extends throughout the empire, and my immediate superior is none other than Lord Abraxis himself!"

He was proud of the display, prouder still that it seemed to work. Jesile backed off.

The very next watch, however, the governor had ordered a citywide removal of all those brands that had mysteriously appeared during Lacfoddalmendowl. It was no doubt an indicator of frustration on the governor's part more than anything. The garrison soldiers had removed doors and chopped down wood posts where necessary to carry out the Governor's orders. Also, Jesile had ordered stricter enforcement of the occupation laws, including public floggings for offenders.

Then the murder had happened, and everything went crazy.

The garrison hit the streets in force, when the word had spread. The soldiers entered homes, seized people. There wasn't much rhyme or reason to it. They were searching

for the killer of one of their own, and they weren't gentle
or methodical about it. Jesile eventually reined the patrols
in, but not until after a number of serious injuries had been
inflicted on hapless citizens.

Since that episode, a few days ago now, the Felk had instead conducted systematic searches, without undue bru-
tality. Callah's perimeter security was tighter than ever. No
fugitive was going to get out of town unless he got himself
transported by a Far Movement wizard, and that wasn't
likely. All civilian travel passes had been declared worthless. Slydis had no doubt manufactured a very convincing
one for his accomplice.

"Are you sorry now?" Cat asked one day, apropos of
nothing.

"About what?" Aquint wasn't particularly in the mood
for the boy's habitual criticisms.

"About wishing for this."

"I never wished—" Aquint started, then caught himself.

Of course Cat was right. He *had* wanted something like
this. He had even thanked the gods for sending a trouble-
maker to Callah, so that Aquint's job as an Internal Security agent would stay secure.

"Shut up, boy," he grumbled.

The problem was, this might be too difficult of a problem to handle, despite the fact that Aquint didn't really
know for sure if there were rebels here. According to the
evidence, they only knew that the copyist had gotten the
idea and the funding for a counterfeiting operation from a
second, unnamed individual. That second man had murdered a Felk soldier during his attempted arrest.

But that killing might have just happened in the heat of
the moment. Maybe the man was so desperate to avoid
capture that he had been driven to commit the murder.

So, all they had for sure was a counterfeiting setup, with
two operators. That didn't necessarily entail an uprising
against the Felk. That meant two greedy, inventive men

had dummied up batches of fake money. Frankly, Aquint admired the scheme.

As for those slashed circles, they could be anything. Maybe it *was* simple vandalism and nothing more.

Aquint and Cat returned to their rooms. It had been a long day of fruitless investigations. Aquint was too tired to even enjoy the luxuries of this apartment.

"Tell me, Cat," he said, putting his feet up, "if our mystery man has a forged civilian travel pass, does that mean he's originally from Callah, and meant to escape the city if things got too hot . . . or he came here, after the occupation by the Felk?"

"Why would he do that?" Cat asked from the soft chair where he had curled up.

"Well, we came back to Callah."

"Right. But we're loyal, upstanding members of the Felk Empire," the boy said archly. "I don't know who this fellow is, but he's not Felk."

Aquint nodded tiredly. This was too much like hard work.

Then a thought occurred to him. "Who, exactly, would have a civilian travel pass? I mean legitimately."

Cat was frowning. "That's a good question. I guess people from the conquered city-states who are collaborating with the Felk. Maybe former government officials who now want to lend their expertise to the new regime. Maybe experts on farming or other civic industries. They might be allowed to travel relatively freely in Felk-occupied territory."

Aquint turned to regard his young friend. "You talk smart when you want to."

"And only when I want to."

Aquint considered. "No. I can't see this man being some consultant or . . ."

"What?" asked Cat, when Aquint trailed off.

Aquint slapped his hands together. "That stringbox!"

"How's that?"

"They found it in his room. A stringbox. By the madness of the gods, how did we miss it?" Aquint grinned. "He's a troubadour!"

"You're that sure?" Cat said.

"It fits. Name me any other category of person who has traditionally had such freedom of movement, even *during wartime,* as a wandering minstrel. Around these parts it's considered bad luck to turn one away. You'll get warts if you do." Aquint laughed.

"Do you really think the Felk would honor that tradition?" Cat asked.

"Why not? We've been around enough of them. They're not all monsters. This man and his 'box probably passed right through a city border checkpoint."

Cat frowned again. "Meaning he already had a travel pass, right?"

"Right. But they confiscate those at the Registry whenever somebody arrives with one," Aquint said. "Then they issue a temporary resident permit."

"How do you know that?"

Taking a haughty tone, Aquint said, "Because, my youthful associate, I've read up on the procedures."

Cat gave him a grudging grin. "Good for you."

Aquint got to his feet, his fatigue forgotten. "So, it's a minstrel we're looking for."

Cat stood as well. "Do we tell the governor?"

"What's Jesile done for us lately? When I make my next report to Abraxis, I'd like to be able to say that we trapped this prey all by ourselves, beating the entire garrison of Callah to him. Maybe Abraxis might put me up for a promotion. Or, better yet, an increase in pay."

AQUINT HAD MADE a couple reports already to Lord Abraxis since arriving in Callah. He spoke through a Far Speak mage attached to the garrison, updating the chief of Internal Security about events in the city.

Abraxis reasserted his claim that all he wanted were results. Aquint could have all the leeway he wanted as far as methods of operation were concerned.

"It's time to contact Tyber," Aquint pronounced.

Cat nodded, and the two of them split up to locate Aquint's former illegitimate business partner. Aquint still hadn't visited his old warehouse, leery of the sorry sight of the place boarded up and defunct.

Vahnka, Tyber's Sook merchant cousin, had been another dependable partner in crime during Aquint's short stay there. Tyber himself had been a valuable asset in unloading smuggled black market items. Aquint had simply never understood why he should hand over good money for licenses and tariffs just because he wanted to move some merchandise.

In the streets of Callah, the Felk were still conducting their searches. Jesile appeared to have called in more troops. One could taste the fear of the people on the cooling air. But Aquint, as he made his way unmolested, sensed something more.

Discontent. Resentment. Anger. These conquered people of Callah had, for the most part, submitted peacefully to this occupation. Now, because of one act of violent rebellion, the Felk were coming down on their heads, in a way that they hadn't since the city's conquest.

It was ironic that Jesile's effort to find one supposed rebel was probably fostering rebellious attitudes in hundreds if not thousands more of Callah's citizens.

Aquint doubted if this would end well.

Shortly before curfew, he heard someone softly whistling for his attention from an alleyway. Aquint had been making inquiries at a slew of taverns, looking for anybody who'd seen a minstrel. No one had.

He squinted at the alley in the gathering twilight. It was possible he'd had one too many drinks while trying to blend in with the patrons.

Cat let himself be seen at the mouth of the alley. "Found him," the boy said.

"Tyber?"

"Who else?" Cat sniffed the air, as if smelling the alcohol on Aquint's breath. As usual, the boy grimaced his disapproval. "You up to paying him a visit?"

Aquint drew himself up with great dignity. "When I can't do this job, I'll let you know."

Off they went. Aquint was still wearing the sling on his left arm. It was annoying him now. On impulse, he tore it off.

"What about your disguise?" Cat asked as they moved through the backstreets.

"I won't need one with Tyber," he said.

"Why not, because he'll still be loyal to you from the old days?" Cat sounded skeptical.

Aquint shook his head. "Because that disguise wouldn't fool that ugly bleeder for a moment."

They came around a corner. Aquint halted sharply. "We're not going *there*?" he said, aghast.

Cat shrugged. "That's where I've heard Tyber is holed up these days."

Aquint had been avoiding it, and now here it was. His old warehouse. It was indeed sorry-looking. The place was nailed up like a poor man's coffin, with loose, careless boards.

"We can get in through the dock," Cat pointed.

But Aquint didn't move. "Why is Tyber here?"

"I heard he tried to bribe one of the garrison officers into letting him set up a contraband operation."

Aquint blinked. "I never read that in any of the Felk incident reports."

"Jesile probably didn't want it in the record. From what I heard, the officer was going to go along with it, for a cut, of course. Then *he* got caught and tried to turn in Tyber. Since then, Tyber's gone to ground."

Aquint nodded. Tyber, like himself, just wasn't cut out

for a legitimate business life. Felk or no Felk, men like Tyber and him had to pursue their own destinies, had to find an angle to work, had to cheat the system. They *had* to.

"Let's go," Aquint said, and he and Cat crept toward the warehouse.

They were nearly at the cargo dock, when Cat's fingers suddenly seized Aquint's shoulder.

"Wait," the boy whispered urgently, a dire look on his young face. He bounded onto a barrel and vaulted toward a window sill far overhead, catching it and pulling himself up and into the shadows.

Aquint faded back to the far side of the street. Peering intently at the loose boards over the dock, he saw now, in the gathering dark, the flicker of candlelight within the warehouse. Something else must have tipped off the boy to some potential danger, though.

He waited, growing worried. Cat could move with great stealth, but even real cats blundered sometimes. In the distance, he heard criers announcing the curfew.

Finally, the boy emerged from the same high window into which he had disappeared. He flitted over to Aquint.

"What *was* it?" Aquint asked the lad.

Cat shrugged. "Don't know. It just felt unsafe."

Aquint ruffled his hair, relieved. "Well, what did you find inside?"

The boy grinned. "Tyber. And some friends."

"Friends?"

"A motley little group. Plus, I'm pretty sure one of them is the fellow who murdered the Felk soldier. He fits the description, minus the beard."

Aquint's eyes widened. "Our minstrel? What's he doing mixed up with Tyber?" Whatever else, that minstrel was dangerous, and his actions had caused harm to the people of Callah.

Cat said, "They've got some pathetic little weapons, and I heard them making plans."

Aquint felt uneasy. "What kind of plans?"

"To overthrow the Felk and retake Callah," Cat said blandly.

Rebels, Aquint thought, dismayed. *Actual rebels.*

"I could go fetch a Felk patrol," Cat offered. "You would have to share the credit for the capture. But there's more than a dozen in there, and I don't think you want to take them by yourself."

Capture the rebels, Aquint thought. *Abraxis would be pleased. But . . . then what?*

"Then what?" he said, voicing the question out loud to Cat.

Cat looked confused. "What do you mean?"

"We turn them in, and then what happens to us? Abraxis reassigns us somewhere else. Are you in any hurry to leave Callah?"

The boy slowly shook his head. Callah, even under Felk rule, was still home to him and Cat. Neither of them wanted to be anywhere else, in the end.

"What do you want to do then?" said Cat.

Aquint's mind was working fast, cutting through the haze of the drinks he'd had.

"You said there's about a dozen of them, with not much in the way of weapons?"

"Old men and women, a couple kids, maybe one real sword among them," Cat said.

Aquint chuckled quietly. "Then, how much trouble can they cause?"

"How's that?"

"As long as there are rebels in Callah, we stay in Callah. As long as we make progress in tracking them down, Abraxis stays happy. Don't you see, lad? We can nab one of these pretend revolutionaries whenever we need to make ourselves look good. And the thing is, these people will think they actually *are* rebels. They'll probably confess to it."

Cat was thinking it over. "You're probably right. That's awfully sneaky, though, even for you."

Aquint looked gravely at his young friend. "Lad, I didn't ask to be snatched away from here by the Felk. I didn't even ask to be made an officer, let alone an Internal Security agent. I was happy with how things were before this godsdamned war."

"So was I," muttered Cat.

Aquint gazed across the street at the warehouse. "I presume you got a decent look at everybody in there."

"Naturally."

"Then we know who our *rebels* are. And we know where they congregate." Tyber must have picked the warehouse as a secret meeting place. Odd that the old black-marketeer had turned into a revolutionary, but war did strange things to people. Aquint knew.

He smiled. The game was entering a new phase here. These would-be rebels would help him sustain the fiction that an uprising was brewing in Callah.

"And the first one we hand over to the Felk," Aquint said as he led Cat away, "is going to be that minstrel."

PRAULTH
(5)

"WELL? WHAT'S YOUR answer?"

"I . . . need time."

"There's none to spare."

"If Praulth says she needs time," Xink said pointedly, "you will give it to her." It was at once a show of assertiveness toward the Petgradite, and subservience directed toward her.

Praulth found, somewhat to her surprise, that she still cared for Xink deeply. They remained lovers. But love, she was learning, was a balance of power. Once, those scales had tipped completely in his favor and she had been absolutely helpless in her feelings toward him, lost in a kind of demented devotion that only the freshly deflowered could truly know.

That unequal balance had since transposed.

The messenger from Petgrad was much older than either her or Xink, and he seemed to radiate contempt for the University. His flesh was leathery, his limbs wiry. He looked built for fast travel. His name was Merse.

"You prefer to stay here?" Merse asked, ignoring Xink. "Looking at word-scratchings and arguing about horseshit that happened a hundredwinter ago? Fine. I'll leave you to it."

Praulth blinked, startled by the man's insolence. He was here at Premier Cultat's behest, he'd said, to fetch her to Petgrad, where her talents were desperately needed. With Honnis gone, the Far Speak link between the University at Febretree and Petgrad had been severed.

Xink bounded to his feet, but Merse was faster, coming fearlessly toe-to-toe with the younger, taller man. Merse's ready stance, the fists at his sides, and the combative glint in his eyes all demonstrated that he was more than willing to brawl. Xink, realizing this, wobbled back a step.

"You won't speak to her in that manner," he said nonetheless, voice impressively steady.

Merse's wind-worn face showed a glimmer of teeth.

"Sit," Praulth said, "both of you."

They were in her and Xink's quarters, in the Blue Annex. Praulth, these last few days, hadn't left these confines. Honnis was gone. Her work as a military strategist—she'd thought—was done. But she didn't know what she was supposed to do with herself now. Somehow it seemed impossible that she could simply resume her studies as a fourth-phase pupil. Too much had happened.

She couldn't go back, but how was she to go forward— *as* what?

Now, here was Merse, telling her she was still needed, still important. It was curious that his manners didn't suit the entreaty he was conveying from Cultat.

"I think your skills as a diplomat require some honing, Merse," she said, trying out a droll tone. Sarcasm and other subtleties of speech were still new to her.

"Diplomat? Petgrad's got no *diplomats*." He had returned to his chair, as had Xink.

Praulth lifted an eyebrow. "Then how does your premier propose to assemble his alliance?"

"He's sent out his family," said Merse.

She absorbed that. "That seems risky."

A sneer pulled at Merse's lip. "It is, young lady. We're all taking risks. Don't you know what's at stake?"

"I do," Praulth pronounced somewhat icily.

"Then why the hesitating? Let's go. We can be back to Petgrad by the middle of tomorrow."

It still felt overwhelming. *Leave* the University? She had never considered such a course, not even as an eventuality, after her primary studies were through. She had meant to stay on here as . . . as . . .

Did she still have academic aspirations? Did she imagine she would one day inherit Honnis's post as head of the war studies council? That seemed as unreal now as leaving.

"Why can't Cultat send one of those—those Far Speak magicians?" She heard the slight quiver in her voice. She was delaying. "It could be as it was with Master Honnis."

Before he passed into final unconsciousness, Master Honnis had used that remarkable form of magical communication to report—rather ghoulishly—his imminent demise to his wizardly contact in Petgrad. Praulth had sat alongside the cot and watched, amazed by the proceedings.

Merse was shaking his head. "You'll be safer in Petgrad."

"Safer?" Xink asked.

Merse didn't look his way but responded anyway. "The Felk are on the verge of invading the southern half of the Isthmus. They didn't have much trouble capturing the north part. If they come raging this way, do you think this—what do you call it?—*campus* will stand? Petgrad is the most powerful free city. We've got defenses. If the Felk win the Isthmus in the end, I promise you, we'll be the last to fall."

Praulth felt fear's cold fingers under her flesh. But she felt something more. Excitement. Perhaps even relief that this war wasn't going to pass her by after all.

She stood.

"Xink, did you wish to accompany me," she asked, "or remain behind?" She heard nothing in her voice to indicate which she preferred. He still had a career in academics ahead here at the University, under Mistress Cestrello.

Xink looked back at her with his gold-flecked blue eyes.

PRAULTH LOOKED DOWN at the marker in the tall grass. It was just a temporary one, a plank of wood jammed upright into the ground. Honnis's name was inscribed with a few crude slashes. Here a grander, more thoughtful stone testimonial would stand one day.

Jumper-pine was the variety of timber; the fact summoned itself from her memories of Dral Blidst, the lumber town of her childhood.

She was uncertain whether her mentor would prefer anything more than this simple hunk of wood. Honnis had practiced irascibility as if it were a faith. He hated false sentimentality. If he could be here, alive, he would probably spit scorn at the idea of a monument to his life. He would slap away the tears of mourners. He would do these things without a thought for anyone's feelings.

Praulth missed him.

The marker had been put down in the overgrown foliage that ringed the faculty housing at the center of campus. The trees here were in the grip of autumn, sobbing away their brittle leaves. It was a bathetic setting for Master Honnis's grave, more so since the circular window of his quarters was visible from here, high above, the pebbled glass throwing back the midday's cloud-muted light.

"Idlers," Merse was grumbling a few steps behind her.

Those quarters had been emptied. Honnis's belongings were like most personal effects—junk to the eye that didn't know how and where they fit into the convolutions of a life. Honnis had lived an enormous span of years. He had little in the way of belongings. What he'd been rich in was paper. Parchments. Scrolls. Documents, treatises, scholarly texts that ranged the length of the Isthmus. It was an immensely valuable private collection, and he had bequeathed all of it to the University's Archive.

"Layabouts," Merse continued.

Praulth turned, seeing that he wasn't referring to her and Xink. Instead, Merse's hard gaze was toward the students that walked the campus paths, a veritable army of robed figures going to and from their various studies.

That, of course, was the essence of Merse's objections. "You think they should all be going to war, don't you?" Praulth said. She and Xink were both wearing traveling clothes. It felt strange being without her robe.

Merse had only grudgingly agreed to halt here. His horse was waiting with hers at the edge of campus. They would have to stop at the stables to procure another mount for Xink.

"Young bodies," he said. "Strong hearts. They could learn to carry swords in their hands as well as they carry dusty words in their heads. It's a waste."

Xink made to step forward once more, his earlier lesson perhaps already forgotten. But a small wave of Praulth's hand—what *power* she wielded over him—stopped his move. She looked levelly at Merse's coarse face. A smile that had nothing to do with happiness tugged at her lips. There were emotions available to her now that she had never had use for before. Disdain. Self-righteousness. She had earned them.

"The only way to fight a war is to hack bodies then?" She tried, with some success, to duplicate Merse's sneer from earlier.

"You've already got a witty rejoinder picked out," Merse said flatly, "or else you wouldn't poke at the subject."

Verbal sparring, only a lune ago, would have been unthinkable for her. Now she struck back. "I would guess

you're a fast man, Merse. Fast on a horse. That's why they
sent you here. If I asked you why *you* weren't off joining
up with Cultat's alliance, you would tell me you'd had no
choice in the matter. You serve the war the best you can.
Well, I serve—"

Her brows, beneath her bland, brown hair, drew together.

While she spoke, Merse had removed an old scratched
bracelet from his coat, gripping it tightly in one hand. He
murmured words she couldn't make out.

When his face cleared, he said tonelessly, "Sorry. I
missed most of that. You'll have to repeat it for me someday. Shall we go now?"

Xink didn't understand; she did. She had seen Master
Honnis work the spell on his deathbed. She stared at
Merse.

"I just told Petgrad we're on our way," he said.

"You're a wizard," Praulth breathed.

"As much as we have in the way of wizards here in the
south. There's a house in Petgrad, a particular noble blood-
line. A large family. The premiers have kept us, down
through the years. Supported us. Made sure we kept in
practice. Just in case there was need for our kind one day."

"You're from a *noble* house?" Xink intruded.

To Merse, he was now invisible and mute. "We can
work the Far Speak," the Petgradite said. "Not much else.
But we're the ones who have been scouting this war from
the start."

"Your . . . family has been—" Once more she didn't
finish. Honnis had received reports from the field of the
Felk advancement, faster than any news could travel by
messenger.

"See," Merse said, "Cultat's not the only one who's got
family at risk. I've got cousins, brothers, sisters . . . sons,
and daughters."

His tone had softened finally. There was feeling in his
weathered face. Praulth nodded solemnly. Then she spoke

a good-bye to Honnis—aloud, the words tight and emotional in her throat, disregarding what her mentor might
think of such a display—and they went to collect the
horses.

"Do you know how the premier's plans are progress-
ing?" she asked moments later, as she faced the challenge
of climbing into a saddle for the first time in years. "Is he
anywhere near assembling his alliance?"

Merse vaulted onto his mount, as if clambering onto a
comfortable chair. "He finally secured the people's mandate and approval of the Noble Ministry to fully activate
Petgrad's army."

Praulth was surprised. "I would have thought Petgrad's
military would already be mobilized. What about the
rest?"

"The first missions to the neighboring cities have come
back successful. Seems people aren't as stupid or stubborn
as some expected."

Behind her Xink was having as much difficulty getting
himself aboard his horse as she was mounting hers. "What
did *you* expect?"

Merse gave his reins a lazy flick; it looked like a shrug.
"I tried not to expect anything. Petgrad has accumulated a
good number of—well, *enemies* isn't the word. But other
cities envy us. Our prosperity. Our stability. I didn't know
how quick anyone would be to fall into an alliance with
us."

"I suppose," Praulth said, "we're all facing the same
enemy now."

Merse grunted. "Figured that out, have you? Thank
gods Cultat knows how to pick his military experts."

An angry flush went through her, but she found herself
without a ready retort. Well, she was still learning such
things. She wanted to know if the premier had gathered
enough troops to reenact the Battle of Torran Flats, as she
had suggested, but she didn't want another barb from
Merse just yet.

Whatever the current state of the war, she was going to be a part of it. Premier Cultat needed her. She was crucial. She was going off to face Dardas, and that thought was so utterly astounding, it made her giddy.

At last she was fixed into the saddle. She and Xink had packed some supplies, but belongings were useless. Besides, what could she bring away from the University—this place of learning and self-fulfilling academic advancement—that could help in what she was going to do?

Xink had settled matters with the head of the student body council. To her surprise, the man had said that their quarters in the Blue Annex would wait for their return. Unusual, considering the widespread need for student housing on campus. Perhaps Xink's status as Attaché had leveraged it.

Praulth let a soft laugh drift past her lips. The horse moved under her, following Merse's.

If status had anything to do with it, surely it was *hers*. Perhaps word of her accomplishments had spread among the faculty.

They left the campus, then picked their way quickly through the township of Febretree. When they reached the road north, Merse set the pace. It was a fast one, and Praulth didn't know if she was up to handling an animal at such speed for any length of time. But she held on. Xink did the same, at her side.

She looked at him, suddenly wanting to speak. His dark hair whipped very becomingly behind him. His face was as handsome as ever—high cheekbones, soft lips. Praulth felt herself surge, reflexively. The excitement was emotional and physical. She didn't begrudge the sensations.

Xink had deceived her. Yes. As Honnis had deceived her. But Xink had also volunteered to accompany her on this journey. He was leaving behind an even higher academic ranking than she was. He had a future with Mistress Cestrello and the sociology council. Yet, he had not hesitated. Praulth was going to Petgrad, so he was, too.

She smiled, watching him sidelong, as they bounced and bounded atop their steeds. She smiled until he noticed and tentatively returned it. Then she looked ahead, watching the road unfold toward a destiny that awaited her in a city she had never seen.

RADSTAC
(5)

HER FINGERS DRUMMED the pommel of her combat sword, which she had refused to swap for an inferior Felk-issued one. She also didn't think much of their uniforms. She'd retained her bracers and the leather armor that protected her upper body. Such minor variations in gear were common to soldiers in any military, however, and shouldn't draw undue notice.

They had infiltrated the vast Felk encampment by means of magic that Radstac hadn't known existed a lune ago.

Deo wore his borrowed Felk garb with perfect naturalness, the crossbow he'd commandeered from one of the scouts slung casually at his side. He was a dead shot with one, he claimed. Whatever else, he was no braggart.

Radstac knew who he intended to kill with the weapon. Finding that individual in this sea of personnel and equipment might well undo those intentions.

They were walking away from the place where the second mage had opened the corresponding portal, linking her

and Deo's bizarre journey from that small scout camp.
Radstac had stayed focused during that jaunt, narrowing
her honed, *mansìd*-stimulated senses so that she concerned
herself only with the forward step she took and the one
which was to follow. Ignore the white chaos all around. Go
forward. Step-by-step. Pay no heed to those unsettling
sounds in the depthless distance. Reach the far end. It was
a simple matter.

Those brief moments had, nonetheless, constituted one
of the most disturbing experiences of her life. But her
stride and face now gave no signs.

She was listening, waiting for the alarm to be raised behind them. She suspected that Deo, by her side, was doing
the same. Those two wizards in the scouting party had
arranged for this transport. The one that communicated
over distances—the female of the two—had coordinated
the opening of the portals with her counterpart here at this
camp. Then the wizard who worked the actual portal
magic—the male—conjured a . . . *breach*, which Radstac
and Deo had entered. To emerge here, which evidently was
quite some distance from where they'd started. Yet they
had walked no more than ten steps. Amazing.

Radstac didn't know, however, if that Far Speak wizard
had passed a warning along as well. She might have, even
with the sword edge that the bandit chief Anzal had help-
fully held to her throat while she performed the communicating magic. Who knew what these Felk magicians were
capable of? They were quite unlike the cloistered healers
that existed on the Southern Continent.

That bandit gang had at last received their payment for
services rendered. Or at least the promissory note that
could be redeemed in Petgrad. Deo had put his signature to
the document. The bandits were doubtlessly pleased that
they hadn't had to personally deliver Deo to the Felk after
all. This shortcut had facilitated things.

But it did bring up another point, Radstac mused. What
was *she* still doing here?

They heard no alarm. Around them the camp buzzed and bustled, apparently in readiness to move out. It was a staggering number of troops, filling this shallow valley, a larger army than any Radstac had ever seen. She had already known that this war was not a typically petty Isthmus conflict, but seeing the evidence spread so impressively about drove the fact home.

How, she wondered, was all this going to end? Deo's uncle had hopes of raising an army to meet this one . . . but it might well be too late for such measures. *Look* at these numbers. And these Felk had magic—remarkably sophisticated magic—on their side.

If they did indeed capture the entire Isthmus, would they be content with that? Something cold rippled through Radstac's innards at the thought. It was a possibility she had not considered before. But it was an eventuality that her cold-blooded mercenary's mind had to acknowledge.

What if the Felk, having conquered this land, decided to invade the Southsoil?

She stayed alert, as she and Deo picked their way along. No one accosted them, which was fortunate.

They had left the Felk scouts in the hands of those bandits. Deo hadn't given any last orders about their disposition, which likely meant that Anzal's band had simply done the sensible thing and dispatched the whole group. Radstac couldn't imagine what else they would do.

And why exactly wasn't *she* doing the smart thing? Accompanying Deo on this final leg of his self-appointed objective to assassinate the commander of this huge army was not a wise decision on her part. Then again, it wasn't her decision. Not really. She was still in Deo's employ . . . although she suspected that if she asked to be released, he would grant the request. But she couldn't bring herself to go.

Do the smart thing first. Next, the most economical, the safest, the most self-fulfilling, and the thing that will most confuse your enemies. When all that is done, do the stupid thing.

Evidently Radstac had reached this last point in her personal itinerary of behavior.

Deo's elbow nudged her leather-padded ribs.

"The high ground," he said softly.

She nodded.

He was really going to try it. Find a vantage, find his target. Put a crossbow bolt into the war commander who had led this army to capture half of the Isthmus. Radstac imagined she knew what would immediately follow that assassination—or its attempt. The Felk would seize them, and their deaths would likely be appropriately grandiose, if they were taken alive. Radstac assured herself that this last wouldn't come to pass. Nor would she let Deo be captured.

They climbed the mild grade. There were still a few tents erected on the ridge.

She wondered why this army had halted. This wasn't a mere rest period; they had bivouacked. She wondered further if they were indeed headed for Trael. Too late in that case for the diplomatic errand Cultat had sent Deo on— and which Deo had abandoned. That alliance the premier had in mind would have to do without Trael. Once the Felk reached the city, its fate would be sealed.

A sergeant, standing on the ridge, frowned their way.

Radstac's hand was still on her sword's pommel. With a pivot of her hips and a fast smooth draw, she could decapitate the sergeant before he uttered a sound. What she would do after that, however, was unclear.

Deo saluted. His manner remained easy. They kept moving. Radstac felt the sergeant's gaze on her facial scars. She stared back with colorless eyes, until he shrugged and turned away.

Deo let out a breath. "I think soldiers are supposed to salute their superiors," he said quietly.

"I'm not a soldier. I'm a mercenary."

They moved along the ridge. Deo was scanning the

camp below, blue eyes picking through the tangle. Radstac considered the odds of spotting this army's leader, a lone individual who might not even be wearing identifying insignias, who might not be out in the open, who might not—

Deo stopped. Radstac tried to follow where he was now peering so intently.

"I see officers, a number of them, gathering . . . there." He pointed furtively with his chin.

Radstac gazed, eyes narrowed. It was hopeless, just a jumble of troops and horses and wagons and gear. Deo must have keen eyesight, indeed. Then she did see. Distant bodies in the uniforms of officers. They were converging on a tent. She focused there. She saw.

"He's the one," Deo said, voice low and hard, eyes suddenly filled with wonder. He had never expected to get this far, Radstac reminded herself.

She could see the figure, standing out in front of the tent. Emblems of rank on his uniform, his very stance commanding. Someone at his side. Female. Stout. The site was some distance off. It would be quite a shot, if Deo could manage it.

His arm was rising. Radstac caught it, held it. She felt how tensely he gripped the crossbow.

"What," she gritted, "you're just going to shoot from here, right out in the open?"

Deo blinked back at her.

Don't do this. She nearly said it aloud, though it wasn't her place.

"Take some cover at least," she said instead.

A tent was nearby, its flap open and stirring in the breeze that was picking up. Deo nodded, slipped inside. She followed.

There were a few crates inside, a cot, nothing more. Deo crouched behind one of the crates, cranking the crossbow vigorously, the string tightening, tightening, quivering with the desire to let fly the bolt that he laid in the firing groove. Radstac had never been good with projectile weapons. She liked her blades, liked her hooks. Liked the immediacy that went with them. But those who could handle bows were impressive in their own rights. She hadn't forgotten the notch that bandit archer had taken out of her left ear.

Deo rested on one knee, planting elbows firmly on the top of the crate. He put his eye to the weapon's sights.

Gods, Radstac thought. He was really going to do it. Up until now this entire episode had somehow remained unreal, like the swirly narrative of even the most vivid dream. Surely something would cause Deo to forsake this ill-advised venture. Surely they would turn back while they still could.

She stepped aside, away from the open flap. The ebbing sunlight was at their backs. The tent's interior was in shadow. This was, she admitted, a good vantage point. It offered a clear shot at the target, though that shot was going to have to be uncannily accurate.

Deo's lips were working silently as he steadied and aimed. Concentrating. Droplets of sweat stood out quite suddenly on his forehead. His shoulders were bunched. Crow's-feet etched around his squinting eye.

Radstac quietly drew her sword. The next moments promised to be lively ones.

She saw Deo's finger squeeze the instrument's trigger. There was still enough *mansìd* in her that she could actually see the bolt as it launched. The flanges of feathers— purple and white—shivered as the hand-length metal bolt shot out through the tent's flap. *Twang* went the bow string. Deo let out a sharp gasp, not unlike the sounds he made during lovemaking, Radstac noted.

At that moment it occurred to Radstac what they should now do.

She tugged the flap shut. Deo was rising from behind the crate. "I have to see if I got him!" he cried breathlessly.

She thought she heard voices rising outside. She sheathed her sword.

"Take off the tunic." She wrested the crossbow from his grip, broke the stock cleanly over her knee and jammed the pieces into one of the crates.

Deo had never gotten his rightful chance to be Petgrad's premier. He was instead merely Cultat's nephew, a publicly adored philanthropist, a hero of the people without having done anything, really, to have earned that regard. If he had just now succeeded in killing the Felk war commander, all that would change. He would rewrite his place in Petgrad's—and even the Isthmus's—history.

Whether he had just succeeded or not wasn't important to Radstac at the moment.

Deo shed the tunic. He was confused. He looked like he was actually going into shock, paling, lips moving wordlessly once more. The enormity of what he'd done was overtaking him, Radstac judged.

Her right hand clapped over his mouth, clutching his jaw. Her left moved sharply, snapping the twin prongs from their sheaths in her glove. Fist swinging, a weight of leather and metal. Her hooks caught flesh.

She wrestled Deo onto the cot. He went almost bonelessly. Outside, a commotion was now definitely rising.

Deo kept his jaw clamped when she released it. She was straddling his body. She put pressure on the wound with both hands. The cut was shallow and precisely made.

It was entirely possible, Radstac had realized in a flash of insight, that no one would see exactly where the shot was fired from. A guess could be made from the angle, wherever the bolt landed, but the two of them might actually be relatively safe here. Fleeing the scene would draw attention; and just how were they supposed to escape this camp now anyway?

But *this* might just work.

In a few fierce whispers she explained it to Deo. He listened, teeth gritted.

"We're scouts. We met bandits. You got wounded. We've just returned to camp."

Deo's grimace verged toward a grin. "I play the wounded man, right?"

She resisted the urge to grin back. Now wasn't the time to enjoy Deo's charms. "This won't even mark you as bad as your dueling scars," she said, keeping up the pressure on the wound she'd opened across his chest. Warm blood seeped out over her fingers, dribbled onto the canvas cot, but the flow was already slowing.

She mopped up the blood with her sleeve, then removed the small aid kit from a pouch beneath her armor. She always brought this north with her. She'd mended any number of her own wounds on Isthmus battlefields. She now deftly threaded a needle and started sewing up Deo's gash.

"Can you handle the pain?" she asked, not pausing.

He nodded, once, a short jerk. The alarm outside was growing louder, closer.

They might live through this. They might. It was a good ruse. Those Felk would be looking for an enemy, for an assassin, a sniper. They would find in this tent two soldiers. One hurt, one tending to her colleague.

That was just how Radstac and Deo were discovered a few moments later.

RAVEN
(5)

IT WAS IRONIC. General Weisel was treating her more like a daughter than Lord Matokin, who was her actual flesh and blood. Weisel went out of his way to include her in things. He was interested in her. He trusted her.

Matokin trusted her, too, though, didn't he? After all, he had given her this assignment of spying on Weisel.

But there was something more. Raven was barely willing to admit to it. Weisel made her feel . . . desired. He had gotten her these new clothes, which flattered her body in a way she had never experienced before. Men now *looked* at her. She knew what they wanted to do to her and the thought frightened and excited her all at once. She had never known any kind of love in her life, though twice before she had experienced quick, grunting, unsatisfying sex, once in her home village with a boy as outcast and homely as she, and once at the Academy.

The disturbing thing was, she lately found herself desiring Weisel. He was a handsome man, and he radiated power. Raven felt herself longing for him. It was an effort to contain these feelings, which of course she could never share them with the general.

What was perhaps most odd, however, was that she thought she sensed the same feelings from him. Well, maybe not the very same, but there seemed to be a lascivious look in his eyes sometimes. Raven was still very new to reading these sorts of signals, and no doubt her own desires were interfering with her perceptions. But she couldn't completely shake the notion.

She had returned from her mission. She was proud that she had overcome her fears after that first incident with the portals. That had been unnerving. If she concentrated, she could still hear those eerie voices. And, according to the wizards she had met when she came out the far side, hers wasn't a unique experience; others had heard the voices while in transit between portals.

But Raven had completed her assignment, her first as this army's liaison officer. She had visited the scout parties, all but the one whose Far Speak wizard had not responded. The other three squads were by now in proper position around the outskirts of Trael. Weisel's plan awaited only his signal.

She had enjoyed exerting her authority. Those Far Movement mages had been reluctant to go along with the general's plan, though none had outright refused to obey. Raven was satisfied that her visit had convinced them to follow orders when the time came.

She was glad to be back. She headed for her tent to freshen up and eat a meal, figuring General Weisel would summon her when he wanted her. The wizards in her unit were sitting around the campfire, and conversation ceased as she approached; then, recognizing a fellow magic-user, they resumed.

Raven paused, listening. She had made no general announcement about her new status as liaison officer.

"I tell you, it was murder!"

"Despite what the physicians said?"

"They didn't let a proper healer look at the body," said one of the wizards, who was himself a healer.

Raven's curiosity was piqued. She took a step closer to the fire. "What's happened?" she asked.

The mages drew her into the circle, speaking in hushed voices. "A Far Movement mage died—" one started to explain.

"—was murdered," interrupted another.

"—*died* last night," finished the first. "We don't know anything else for certain. He died in his tent, and the army surgeons say it was a paroxysm of some sort. That's all we know."

"It is not," the healer said. "I've heard the tent where he was found was slit down the side, like a knife had cut it."

Raven frowned, not understanding.

"So that someone else could get inside the tent," the healer went on, "and commit murder."

"That's outlandish speculation," one of the more moderate wizards said. "We're getting carried away here . . ."

"What?" one of the Far Speak mages countered. "You think the so-called regular troops don't resent us, aren't afraid of us? You think there aren't some among them who'd like to see us all cut to ribbons?"

"Some," the healer said, sighing. "Not all."

"Something like this only takes one. Somebody to slip inside a tent and—"

"What, exactly? How do you induce a lethal fit like that?"

"Well, he, that is, I . . ."

The argument went on. Raven excused herself, taking a plate of food into her tent. She hadn't heard about the death, and wondered if it was even true. Plainly the wizards had been sitting there hashing out the subject for some time, no doubt embellishing it with secondhand rumor and vague conjecture made up on the spot.

She shook her head sadly. Whether or not the death had

been murder, it was a stark example of the rift that existed between the two factions in this army.

A mage had died, and the first thing everybody thought of was he had been killed by someone from the regular troops. Those prejudices had to be eliminated. It was her job to see that this military became successfully integrated.

Perhaps Matokin had been too hasty in inducting mages into the ranks of the Felk army. A slower course might have been wiser.

Raven bit her lip, setting aside her plate, no longer hungry. What was this? She was questioning Lord Matokin, the Emperor himself.

She remembered what Weisel had told her, his personal theory about Matokin's true plans for this war—a war that would never end, that would keep him in supreme power safely back there in Felk.

It couldn't be true. It *couldn't*.

With a great effort, Raven shoved the entire matter out of her mind. She looked down, seeing a big, black bug crawling across the canvas floor of her tent. She stared hard at it, concentrating. A moment later it burst into a little ball of fire.

SOON ENOUGH, GENERAL Weisel did call for her. She approached him where he stood outside his tent and made her report. He didn't seem too bothered by the missing scout party.

When he asked if something else was troubling her, Raven opted from among her choices to tell him about the incident with the portals. Weisel listened, patiently.

Yet all the while Raven felt a budding excitement. She tried to repress it, but being so near the general was inflaming. She felt her breath quickening. What would it be like, she wondered, to *touch* him?

Then something truly astonishing happened. After General Weisel ordered his aide to assemble the senior staff officers, he lifted a hand and brushed her cheek. It felt as if sparks followed the path his fingertips had traced. Raven's face heated, flushing. She felt faint.

Luckily, she regained herself as the officers gathered, along with a Far Speak wizard, one who hadn't been at the campfire earlier. Weisel was about to give the order that would be relayed to the scouts. The portals were going to be opened. Weisel had told Raven what might follow: it would surely be spectacular.

A new stage of this war was set to begin but all Raven could think of was the thrill, very strong now, of being in the general's presence.

Then, something was wrong.

Raven peered, frowning, at Weisel. The general suddenly looked like he was . . . struggling. She couldn't explain it, but she knew in a flash that something had happened to him.

Weisel was trying to move his lips. None of the other officers was yet aware that something was wrong. Raven felt a surge of protectiveness. Whatever was happening to the General, she had to help.

She lunged toward him. As she did, she saw a small, fast movement out of the corner of her eye, something passing overhead and falling earthward. Still reaching out toward the general, she was suddenly shoved very hard. She landed face first, the impact knocking the air out of her lungs.

Who had done this? But she ignored the thought. It wasn't important. She had to reach Weisel. She scrambled back onto her feet. Only, she couldn't manage it. Her legs kicked uselessly behind her. Her hands dug at the ground, trying to leverage her weight, but it was no good. Her limbs weren't doing what they should. She could barely move her right arm at all.

Something was very wrong indeed.

Time appeared to be slowing, in some impossible way. She could feel her heart beating, but it was an eternity between the beats. She watched a boot step near her outstretched hand. The dusty leather crinkled as the boot's owner put weight onto it.

Godsdamnit! Raven tried again to stand, her fingers clawing at the dirt now. The place where she had been shoved was at the base of her neck, just above her right shoulder. When she tried to flex that shoulder it wouldn't move right. There was no pain, but she was beginning to think there ought to be. It felt like something was lodged there.

In the distance, voices were rising in an agitated clamor. She saw more booted feet going by, but no one stopped for her. Everything remained eerily slow. She had heard that time could warp itself like this in moments of mortal jeopardy.

Where was General Weisel?

The commotion grew but Raven realized it wasn't in the distance at all. It was going on all around her. She felt cold suddenly, very cold. The light seemed to be fading, as if dusk had come all at once. She strained to make out individual voices from the babble around her.

"Crossbow bolt!"

"An assassin!"

Her struggling limbs were even weaker now than they'd been just an instant ago. She could barely lift her head to keep her face out of the dirt.

"The girl, the young magician—she stepped in front of it!"

"She saved the general!"

Her dimming thoughts were becoming a jumble, and she knew she was ebbing toward something that might be unconsciousness, or might be something more drastic. Even so, she heard and understood that last shouted comment, and it provided the last warmth she would probably ever know.

She found, in the strange stretching of time, that she had the time to reflect on her life. She saw herself as a frightened and awkward child, a disappointment to her mother. She saw herself at the Academy, determined to become the best wizard she could be.

It had all led to this. She liked herself much more as she was now, an adult, with important responsibilities.

She had saved the general. She had stepped in front of the bolt of a crossbow, fired either by accident or intentionally. He would continue to expand the boundaries of the Felk Empire, until all the Isthmus was under one rule. It was an admirable cause. It was the grand vision of Lord Matokin, her father. She wondered if he had ever suspected, for even an instant, that she was his daughter. Maybe her mother would get word to him some day. Maybe he would know, and be proud of her sacrifice.

She had saved Weisel, who had helped to make her own life worthwhile. That made her sacrifice truly meaningful.

Still, she wondered why someone didn't help her. Why didn't . . . why didn't Weisel pick her up from the ground, hold her, comfort her? She was so cold now.

She found the time for one last coherent thought. Raven wondered if Weisel had given the signal to open the portals and let the dead loose into this world.

The few. The proud. The stupid. The inept.
They do more damage before 9 a.m.
than most people do all day...
And they're mankind's last hope.

ROBERT ASPRIN
PHULE'S COMPANY
SERIES

Phule's Company   0-441-66251-X

Phule's Paradise   0-441-66253-6

by Robert Asprin and Peter J. Heck
A Phule and His Money   0-441-00658-2

Phule Me Twice   0-441-00791-0

No Phule Like an Old Phule   0-441-01152-7

Available wherever books are sold or at
www.penguin.com

B018